A Mary MacIntosh Novel

PANDEMIC PREDATOR

Maureen Anne Meehan

www.maureenannemeehan.com
info@maureenannemeehan.com

Table of Contents

Chapter 1 1
Chapter 2 14
Chapter 3 19
Chapter 4 30
Chapter 5 39
Chapter 6 47
Chapter 7 59
Chapter 8 66
Chapter 9 71
Chapter 10 79
Chapter 11 86
Chapter 12 93
Chapter 13 100
Chapter 14 104
Chapter 15 109
Chapter 16 113
Chapter 17 117
Chapter 18 120
Chapter 19 123
Chapter 20 127
Chapter 21 131
Chapter 22 133
Chapter 23 136
Chapter 24 140
Chapter 25 144
Chapter 26 148
Chapter 27 152
Chapter 28 155
Chapter 29 157

Chapter 30 160
Chapter 31 163
Chapter 32 166
Chapter 33 169
Chapter 34 173
Chapter 35 176
Chapter 36 180
Chapter 37 183
Chapter 38 187
Chapter 39 191
Chapter 40 196
Chapter 41 200
Chapter 42 204
Chapter 43 209
Chapter 44 211
Chapter 45 214
Chapter 46 219
Chapter 47 222
Chapter 48 225
Chapter 49 229
Chapter 50 232
Chapter 51 236
Chapter 52 238
Chapter 53 240
Chapter 54 243
Chapter 55 245
Chapter 56 249
Chapter 57 251
Chapter 58 254
Chapter 59 256
Chapter 60 259
Epilogue 263
Books by Maureen Anne Meehan 265
About The Author 266

Chapter 1

Her twenty-year-old body lay twisted in the center of the Medicine Wheel–a circular alignment of rocks on the western peak of Medicine Mountain in Northern Wyoming. Her long, thick, dark hair was matted to her scalp, caked with coagulated blood and other bodily fluids. It appeared that she had been raped and tortured for days before being set free from torment. Her lips, which had once been luscious and full, were grimy and speckled–as if she'd been forced to drink a cocktail of ground coffee and mud. Her face and neck were covered in odd-shaped, purple bruises, giving the impression that her ruptured blood vessels were desperately trying to escape the horror. Even her skin looked like it had attempted to detach itself from the bone. Yet, she was still breathing.

Two rangers from the United States Forest Service found her ravaged body sprawled on the twenty-eighth stone spoke of the Medicine Wheel. At first glance, they assumed that she was dead. As they approached, they noticed her chest cavity propelling out and heaving in, like a fish suffocating on air. The rangers felt for a pulse, but her veins collapsed and formed bruises the moment they applied pressure. They tried to perform CPR on her, but as they compressed her chest, thick, black mucus spewed from her mouth. They rushed her down the mountain to the nearest hospital in Sheridan, and hurled her onto the first gurney they could find in the emergency room. Nurses and doctors scrambled to find a vein strong enough to accept an IV, but their attempts were futile. The victim's veins wiggled and collapsed like overcooked spaghetti. Blood was seeping from every orifice of her body. Without an IV, she would soon die, but no vein would hold steady. She coughed a few times–a choking, gagging cough like that of an asthmatic–and when the chunk of a clot oozed its way from her mouth, she appeared to have a reprieve. But the relief only lasted a few seconds before the gagging started again.

Her pupils were dilated and her eyes, although still open, were vacant. She coughed viciously again when the doctors attempted chest compressions. She felt the rough hands of the doctor pushing hard on her sternum, but his efforts did not help her capture any air. Instead, she felt like she was swimming in a sea of mud and that someone was holding her under. She felt the cold blade of scissors cutting her clothes away from her body and heard a woman's voice.

"We're losing her, doctor. BP's down to sixty."

"We need to get an IV in this girl," the doctor shouted. "Now!"

The girl heard metal clanging on an instrument tray and felt another cold sting, this time in her foot.

"The vein held," a nurse shouted, triumphantly. "Start running a—"

"Holy shit!" the nurse yelled. "The vein . . . disintegrated. She's losing blood, doctor. BP's down to fifty. Forty. Hold on, sweetie. Hold on. We need to . . . "

The girl could not hear the nurse anymore. Noises faded out, but a light shown in. The girl felt an overwhelming sense of warmth and calmness, and felt herself moving closer to the light. Her legs felt like they'd grown wings—butterfly wings—a beautiful shade of lapis. The light filled her up entirely. She did not hear the high-pitched beep.

"We lost her," the doctor said, deflated. "She's gone." He turned away, his head bowed, and without looking at her face, tore off his surgical mask. His oldest daughter was about the same age as this girl, and she also had long, dark hair and large, green eyes. It was harrowing. He took a deep breath, trying not to imagine what had happened to this lifeless young woman. Within fifteen minutes of arrival, she laid dead, parts of her intestines disgorged on the ground beneath the gurney. Behind a plastic curtain in the emergency room of a hospital in a small, quiet, western town, other medical personnel shook their heads and wiped their eyes, for they didn't fail many young people. And this young woman didn't stand a chance. All the medical training in the world could not have saved her, yet they all felt like they had done nothing to help her. They couldn't. Her body was not capable of accepting aid.

The attending physician was Dr. Jonathan Rowe, a thin, forty-seven-year-old man with a deeply receding hairline and thick, frameless glasses. Dr. Rowe, who looked as capable of holding your confidence as well as saving a life, called the sheriff and explained that he had a mysterious death on his hands. The sheriff responded immediately. Mysterious deaths were uncommon in his small town. Sheridan, nestled at the base of the Big Horn Mountains in northeastern Wyoming, is quintessential Old West with a contemporary veneer and an entire downtown area declared a National Historic District. Cowboy fights and drunken brawls were common occurrences on any given Friday night, but the cause of such skirmishes was usually too much alcohol or a cheating lover. The sheriff wasn't accustomed to the term, "mysterious death."

The pathologist met Dr. Rowe and the sheriff in the emergency room. Dr. Rowe suggested awkwardly that the girl might have been raped, based on the bruising and blood between her legs. But the pathologist quickly concluded that he would be unable to determine cause of death without performing an autopsy. It was agreed that an autopsy would be ordered, but the sheriff wanted to notify next of kin first. *Who was this girl?* No one at the hospital could identify her. Whatever trauma had caused her death distorted her looks beyond recognition.

As the pathologist made notes, the sheriff, a medium-sized man in his mid-fifties with a pot belly, handlebar mustache, and ruddy cheeks, looked over his shoulder anxiously. The sheriff, who had attended to many car accident victims in his day, disliked being stared at by the dead. He reached over and lowered her eyelids.

"Please don't touch her," the pathologist said in a curt tone.

"Sorry. I just hate looking into dead eyes." The sheriff rubbed his own tired eyes before noticing that he had some of the girl's blood on his hand. He groaned in a low tone and excused himself to go to the restroom to wash his hands. When he returned, Dr. Rowe and the pathologist were discussing possible causes of death in a hushed tone. The sheriff paced the floor, waiting for the doctors to include him in on the conversation.

Dr. Rowe kept his back turned from the sheriff, hoping that he'd take the clue and allow them a private conversation.

"Why don't you go talk to the guys who brought her in? Maybe they could shed some light on this," Dr. Rowe finally suggested. The sheriff nodded imperceptibly, as if he was already on his way to conduct the interview before the suggestion was made. The doctor reached into his blood- spattered lab coat and retrieved a few white tablets. He popped them into his mouth, thrust his head back, and swallowed without water.

While efforts were being made to identify the victim and to clean up the bloody mess in the ER, the sheriff interviewed the two Forest Service Rangers that found her. "What were you two doin' up there at Medicine Wheel?" he asked, suspiciously. The two men, both in their late twenties with stubby beards and unkempt long hair, stumbled for an explanation. The elder of the two rangers, a tall Native American with a round face and broad shoulders named Ronnie One Feather, spoke first, explaining how there had been reports of vandalism at Medicine Wheel and they'd gone there to check it out. The sheriff took notes as the ranger nervously explained how they'd found her body draped across the twenty-eighth spoke that radiates from the rock pile hub in the center of the wheel. The sheriff cleared his throat. "Ain't never been to Medicine Wheel," the sheriff said flatly. "Maybe you should explain what this place looks like."

Ronnie explained how the wheel is a grouping of flat white stones, arranged in a circle about seventy-five feet in diameter, at the top of Medicine Mountain. "There are twenty-eight spokes that radiate from the rock pile hub in the center. We Native Americans believe that it was built by our ancestors thousands of years ago, either as a place of spiritual worship, or maybe an astronomical calendar, or maybe even a burial ground. We believe that our people -"

"Let's focus on the girl. How do you suppose she got there? See any folks around when you found her? A car? Footprints?"

Ronnie looked at his ranger buddy, David Thrift, and shrugged his shoulders. "I didn't see anyone else around. Like I said, we went there to investigate a report of a disturbance. A man called the ranger station and said that someone had set the worship fence on fire. When we got to Medicine Wheel, there was no fire that we could see. So we walked around and that's when we found her."

The sheriff watched closely as Ronnie answered. Ronnie kept looking at David Thrift while answering the questions, as if he was trying to get his story straight. The sheriff was pretty sure that they were not telling him the whole story. After twenty years of serving the community in the sheriff's department, he'd learned to read people pretty squarely. He asked the two young men to stay put for a few minutes while he made some phone calls. After talking with the county attorney and a local judge, the sheriff asked that both men volunteer DNA samples. David Thrift agreed. Ronnie, who was suspicious of the government in general and believed that Indians were treated unfairly in the judicial process, declined, explaining that he first wanted to talk to a lawyer about his rights. This, of course, made the sheriff all the more suspicious.

* * *

Perched at her desk in downtown Sheridan at the law offices of Harrison and MacIntosh, attorney Mary MacIntosh stared blankly at a foot- high stack of pleadings in front of her. It was late October, and she was feeling a sense of change. The fall had been unseasonably warm, and the trees still had plenty of golden-brown leaves clinging to their branches, which was unusual. Perhaps a winter storm was on its way. She took a sip of strong, black coffee and set her mug back down on the coaster at the edge of her desk, near the phone. Normally, she was a morning person, but today, she was not quite awake. She had a bad dream in the middle of the night, and couldn't get back to sleep. She dreamed that she was on a trip to the Galapagos Islands and was staying overnight in Ecuador before boarding the cruise ship. In her dream, she was visiting a bird and butterfly aviary. Near closing time, she didn't hear the announcement that the gates to the aviary were being locked for the day. She was trapped inside the aviary, and couldn't get out. Birds were unsettled by her prolonged presence, squawking loudly and flapping their wings wildly over her head, before dive-bombing at her. She tried to fight them off, but there were too many birds. She awoke from her dream in a panic. Her pajama top was soaking wet with perspiration. She weaved herself in a sinuous curve around her sleeping cat and tried to drift back to sleep, but it was hopeless.

She recounted her dream as she took another long gulp of coffee, wondering what the dream meant. A few scenarios came to mind, but she decided that she had too much work to do and shouldn't spend her morning nitpicking her psyche. She drew in a deep breath, ready to tackle her jam- packed day of meetings and court appearances.

Mac, as her law partner called her, wore a dark gray suit with a cream blouse, and black heels that at the moment lay askew under her desk next to her bare feet. She had long, wavy, auburn hair, and large doe-like brown eyes. She was tall, with a slender, athletic build, and she idly twirled her hair as she read, a nervous habit dating back to her teenage years. She told her secretary, Megan, a perky, young blond, to hold all calls so that she could finish her dictation before she went to court. Megan poked her head in Mac's office and said that a hysterical client was on the phone, insisting on speaking to Mac immediately. "She says it's an emergency," Megan said unhesitantly. Mac rolled her eyes and nodded. Of course, Mac thought. It's always an emergency, according to the client. She picked up the phone and punched the third blinking light.

"Ms. MacIntosh, this is Jacqueline Bontierre. You remember me from the Powder River Basin trial? Something horrible has happened and I need your help. I am the one–"

"Hello, Jacqueline. Of course I remember. What can I do for you?" Mac asked. She had represented Jacqueline Bontierre, along with forty-nine other plaintiffs, in a class-action lawsuit against methane gas developers in the Powder River Basin of north-central Wyoming. They won a large verdict against the developers. Mac remembered Jacqueline as a beautiful French woman who was strongly opinionated and sure of herself. Jacqueline and her husband owned a sizable ranch on Spotted Horse Creek and were cattle ranchers by trade.

The Bontierres were unable to have children of their own and they found adoption in America to be problematical. They searched abroad and were happy to find three beautiful little girls in a Bucharest orphanage. Ana, the eldest of the three, had been sold into child prostitution at age six.

Her younger adoptive sisters had been spared sexual abuse. The Bontierres knew of Ana's experiences and were willing to take her in and help her learn how to trust and love.

"It's Ana. She's missing," Jacqueline stated. She spoke so hastily that it was difficult to understand her.

"Ana? Isn't she living in Colorado?" Mac asked.

"Ana moved back to Sheridan six weeks ago so that she could attend community college. Her roommate called yesterday morning to say that she hadn't come back to the dormitory after class. I reported it to the police, but they haven't done a damn thing to find her. They say she's probably run off with a boyfriend, making snide remarks about her past juvenile record. Well, I know my daughter and after everything she's been through over the past few years, including a six-month rehab program in Colorado, she would *never* be so stupid to run off with some boy. I know that in my heart. Something has happened to her."

"I'm so sorry, Jacqueline. I can understand why you are concerned," Mac said. She wondered why Jacqueline was calling her, however. She was afraid to ask what Jacqueline wanted her to do about Ana's disappearance, but she asked, nevertheless. "How can I help you?"

"I want you to call the sheriff and tell him that this is a serious matter and that if he doesn't take it seriously and treat Ana like he would any other citizen of this county that we're going to sue him for discrimination."

Mac thought about Jacqueline's request before responding. Ana had a troubled past and it wouldn't be unfair for the sheriff to give it a day or two to see if she showed up. "Jacqueline, I understand that you are very upset and you have a right to be, but making threats to the sheriff probably won't help your cause. Why don't we focus our energy on finding Ana? Have you contacted the clinic in Colorado where she went through rehab? Maybe someone from there has heard from her, or perhaps an old boyfriend–"

"Miss MacIntosh, I thought we had a better working relationship than this!" Jacqueline said thickly. "I know my daughter and something has happened to her. I thought you were different from the other people in this small-minded town, but you're not. You're just like the rest of them—assuming that my daughter has found her way back into trouble. Well, I guess I know where I stand with you. You get a nice chunk of change off my methane gas verdict and now you could care less about me and my family. Forget that I called." The line went dead.

Mac set the phone back in its cradle and tilted back in her chair. Had she been too cavalier? Should she have offered to call the sheriff and try to convince him to take the matter more seriously? As her guilt rose up like a sprouting weed, she quickly grabbed the phone and punched the familiar number.

"Sheriff's office, Mandy speaking." Mac knew Mandy well from the methane gas trial. She quickly explained the nature of her call and asked if she could speak to the sheriff. "The sheriff is at the hospital investigating a mysterious death. You can leave him a message on voicemail if you like."

The words "mysterious death" rolled around in Mac's head, thinking about Ana's disappearance, trying not to put the two together. "What kind of mysterious death?" Mac ventured. Normally, she wouldn't pry into police business, but her concern for Ana was overriding.

"Don't know yet. Sheriff didn't have time to explain much. Said that he'd be out of the office for the rest of the day probably. Like I said, you can leave a message. He'll likely check back later."

Mac left a brief message mentioning Ana Bontierre, and asked that the sheriff call back. Mac was unsure of her opinion of the sheriff. When she first moved to Sheridan from Jackson Hole a year prior, Mac called on the sheriff to investigate death threats she'd received as a result of taking on the methane gas industry in the class action lawsuit. The sheriff was not overly sympathetic or responsive, initially, and his casual attitude bothered her. She understood how Jacqueline might feel if the sheriff was showing her the same lack of concern, but also had grown to understand that the sheriff had a method to his investigations. He was calm and fairly methodical, and it seemed that he usually got to the right answer in his own way, on his own time. The members of the community held him in high regard. It was just that certain things bothered the sheriff, and methamphetamines were one of them. Since Ana had dabbled in meth, a decision that bought her a trip to rehab, perhaps the sheriff was less inclined to call out the troops to help find her.

After Mac left the message for the sheriff, she called Jacqueline Bontierre to apologize and let her know that she would follow up with the sheriff. Jacqueline's answering machine picked up, so Mac left a message in a repentant tone. Mac had lived in Sheridan for only a few years and was working hard to build up a healthy client base for her law practice. She did not want to burn any bridges—especially with former clients who were well respected in the community.

After leaving the voicemail messages, Mac gathered some paperwork on her desk and shoved it into an accordion file. She then went to Sheridan National Bank for a quick meeting before she had her first court appearance for the day. Mac had recently landed the bank as a new client, and had agreed to help the real estate department rid itself of unwanted assets. The bank was hot to unload one asset in particular, an old farmhouse, primarily because the property was strapped with a number of federal and state tax liens. The old farmhouse was located in a nearby community called Big Horn, at the base of the Big Horn National Forest. The farmhouse was dilapidated, and the accompanying barn and stockyard were junk heaps, but the buyer didn't seem to mind. In fact, the buyer had agreed to purchase the place subject to the liens and satisfy the past-due debts to the government. The vice president of the bank, confused and surprised by the generous yet imprudent offer, asked Mac to review the terms of the purchase contract and sit in on the final meeting with the buyer to make sure that he wasn't trying to pull a fast one. The offer seemed too good to be true. The property had been vacant for years, and many local residents of Big Horn claimed that it had been used as a methamphetamine lab. Others claimed that it was haunted. Why would a young guy from South America want to buy the farm and pay off all the liens to the government? The bank hired Mac to find out.

After meeting with the bank officers, Mac put on her black, wool jacket and walked two blocks up Main Street to the courthouse. The old courthouse building was capped with a beautiful dome which shone brightly in the morning sun. A new wing to the old courthouse had been added some years back, and housed the county recorder's office and a number of other public services. Mac pulled open the glass door to the recorder's office. Standing at the counter was a handsome man whom Mac estimated to be in his late thirties or early forties. Mac told the clerk behind the counter why she was there. The clerk nodded at the gentleman at the counter, and told Mac that he was the buyer of the farmhouse.

When Mac met Gilbert Bonita for the first time, she was struck by his physical beauty–and she sensed that he knew it. He stood six feet four inches tall and sported an athletic build. He had almost black hair with a radiant sheen and large, dark eyes. He walked right up to her and introduced himself with the boldest confidence. "I'm Gilbert Bonita and I'm here to buy the old Walton place from the bank. And, if you're lucky, I'll take you to dinner once the deal is done." He was certain of his terms, both in buying the foreclosed farm and that Mac would agree to dine with him. He was well- spoken and cultivated, and she detected an unidentifiable foreign accent in his voice.

After Mac spoke with Gilbert Bonita and perused the file, she made a recommendation to the vice president of the bank. The vice president went along with Mac's recommendation and accepted Bonita's offer, relieved to get rid of the dumpy, decrepit house and the unkempt property. Mac, on the other hand, wasn't sure of his offer for a dinner date. He was devastatingly striking and well-built, but she was still working through a recent break up with her former boyfriend, Greg. She was adjusting to the single life again and was starting to make new friends. She was happily independent and didn't want to complicate her life. A dinner date with a bank client sounded awkward.

When escrow closed on the farm that afternoon, Mac was prepared to decline Gil's invitation to dinner that night. However, when Gil told her that he was taking the bank president to dinner as well, Mac knew that she was stuck. The bank was her newest and largest client, and declining the celebration dinner would be in poor taste.

As they dined on a lovely sage chicken that Gil ordered, Mac admired Gil's size. His hands were very large and his shoulders broad. Not only was he large in size, but also in bravado. He'd traveled the world extensively and knew how to maneuver in style. His ego seemed insurmountable, yet his charm was almost boyish. "I grew up a peasant in Peru," Gilbert said, taking a sip from his vodka. "My mother was from Romania, and she was sold to a Peruvian businessman. The businessman discarded her after a few years and she was back on the streets doing what desperate women do. She discarded me, as I was a burden to her. I never asked who my father was, but I believe it to have been the Peruvian man."

"How did you survive?" Mac asked, horrified by this man's nonchalant description of his childhood. The sorrow of Gil's life invaded Mac, like a terrible drug, but he seemed impervious to his woes. He spoke flatly, as if he was reading from a script.

"An American family stationed in Peru allowed me to work on their property in exchange for room, board and education. They paid for me to attend a private school, for which I am grateful. I have remained in contact with this American family, and today they live part of their time in Florida and part of their time here in Wyoming. That is why I chose to stay here for some time." He explained how he'd left Peru as a young man and traveled the world, vagabond fashion, until he wound up in Moscow. He'd worked his way up the ladder in a Russian pharmaceutical company, and was now a part- owner. "We focus most of our research on antiviral drugs," Gil told them.

"But enough about business. Let's talk about a place I will take you when you accompany me to Eastern Europe." Gil talked directly to Mac, as if the bank president were invisible. "I'll take you on a cruise from Moscow to St. Petersburg on the Waterways of the Czars, and show you the Yusupov Palace and Petrovdorets, Peter the Great's Grand Palace. We can venture to Voronet in Romania, or what we call the 'Sistine Chapel of the East.' It is a beautifully painted monastery from the fifteenth century. Northeastern Romania was under threat of invasion from the Turks at that time, and the fortified monasteries were covered with biblical scenes to educate the illiterate Orthodox Christians. Your eyes will glow when you see the lapis blue dome. I will show you all the treasures of the land that my ancestors called home."

Mac heard the hedging of conflicting voices in her head: one told her to run like hell from this guy–far and fast and never look back. The other voice told her to give him a chance. She was not as worldly as Gil, and perhaps foreigners were more forward than Americans. Maybe he was of a giving nature–anxious to share his love of the world's riches. She wanted to be positive, but he was like a scratchy wool sweater–uncomfortably handsome. As Mac got to know him over dinner, and learn of his hardships growing up an orphan in Peru, his struggles to find work in post Cold-War Russia, and his desires to return to his native land, her trusting heart vetoed her scrutinizing head. She decided to give him a chance.

* * *

As Gil walked Mac to her car after dinner, she asked if he needed to fix up the farmhouse before he moved in. "Oh, Bella, you Americans have too many rules, I'm afraid. I've been living there for the past two weeks, preparing it for my needs. It requires a good deal more cosmetic repair, but I have accomplished what I must for now." Mac was shocked by his presumptuous nature, but careful not admonish him. The deed was recorded now and her client had its money. Besides, what harm did the bank suffer from the prospective purchaser squatting on the property for a few weeks before the deal closed? It was unlawful and unscrupulous, but she didn't feel compelled to tattle. Still, she couldn't quite rationalize his excuse. Did his orphan nature make him feel entitled to take what he wanted? Questions snowballed in her mind, yet she didn't feel comfortable asking him.

His large, rough hand touched her elbow as he gently guided her to her car. He smelled of vanilla, she thought, or was it heather? A sweet scent, for sure. He held her car door open and allowed her to slip past him into the driver's seat. He kissed his first two fingers and placed them on her cheek. "You are so lovely. Tall. Elegant. Smart. Confident. I will see you again tomorrow for dinner. What time shall I pick you up?" Mac didn't know how to respond, and as she fumbled for words, he spoke. "Six o'clock. I will pick you up at your office. I know the way."

With that, he turned and walked away, down Main Street and around the corner, disappearing from sight. She felt a cold chill run down her spine–a warning signal? Or is that what she felt when she first met Greg? She thought back to that moment on the courthouse steps in Jackson Hole. She remembered that meeting Greg for the first time caused a flutter in her tummy and a warm flush across her face. Not a chill down her spine. But, it was fall here in Sheridan, and the evening air was carrying a coolness about it–warning the birds that it was about time to migrate south for the winter.

* * *

When the telephone rang at eleven thirty at night, Jacqueline Bontierre was certain that Ana had come to her senses and was calling home to be bailed out of another bad choice. She glanced at the digital clock as she quickly grabbed the receiver, afraid that the phone would wake and anger her husband. Then she remembered that Mr. Bontierre was out in the barn, tending to a sheep that had been caught up and nearly strangled in a barbed- wire fence. The wool around his neck had been ripped to the jugular, and Mr. Bontierre was not sure whether the ewe would make it through the night.

"Is this Mrs. Bontierre?"

"Yes. Who's calling?"

"Mrs. Bontierre, this is the sheriff. You called me yesterday to–"

"I know who you are. Are you calling to apologize? It is a little late, don't you think?" Jacqueline then realized that he might be calling with word about Ana. She quickly adjusted her tone of voice. "Have you found her?"

There was a long pause. "I'm not sure. I need you to come to the hospital."

"Is she hurt? Oh God! I knew it. Did she overdose?" Before the sheriff could answer, Jacqueline said, "I'm on my way."

Chapter 2

Jacqueline Bontierre was surprised at how unnerved she felt. She had received many calls like this before: Ana was in a car accident. Ana was in jail for drug dealing. Ana violated probation by crossing the state line. Jacqueline was accustomed to driving to the police station, rehearsing her speech along the thirty-minute drive. For some reason, her hands were shaking this time. She didn't bother telling her husband that she was leaving. He would insist on coming, be angrier than a bull when he saw his drugged- out daughter, and the ewe he was desperately trying to save would die—which would be Ana's fault for luring him away with her outrageous behavior. Jacqueline left him a note on his nightstand and drove down the driveway with the headlights off. When she got to the main highway, she flipped on the headlights and accelerated.

Half-way through the drive, anxiety set in, and she needed to tell someone that Ana was in trouble. Her husband would not hear the phone out in the barn, and it was too late to call her sister who lived on the east coast. She decided to call Mac, her lawyer.

As Mac pulled away from the curb after her date with Gil, her cell phone rang. She pulled it out of her purse and answered. It was Jacqueline Bontierre. At first, Mac could barely make out what she was saying. Cell service in Wyoming was notoriously bad, and Jacqueline's voice kept breaking up. From what she could decipher, Ana was at the hospital and Jacqueline wanted Mac to meet her there, in case the sheriff was questioning her without reading Ana her Miranda rights or following proper police procedure. Mac normally would say no to any late-night requests, but something pleading in Jacqueline's voice made her agree.

Mac arrived at the hospital before Jacqueline. She sat in the ER waiting room and picked up an old copy of *People* magazine, not really paying attention to the articles, but trying to busy herself and squelch her desire to search for the sheriff. She'd seen his car in the parking lot and figured that he was behind one of the ER curtains, questioning Ana. She bent down, pretending like she was picking something up off the ground, and looked underneath the curtains that were within view, but all she could see were feet sheathed in surgical booties and legs in scrub pants. If the sheriff was around, she couldn't tell. She listened to noises, but didn't hear anything except the groans of patients and the wheels of gurneys on their way to and from radiology.

Jacqueline arrived about ten minutes later wearing a crumpled pajama top, jeans and a ring of mascara under her eyes. Despite her disheveled appearance, she looked beautifully French—with her dark yet graying hair pulled tightly back into a messy chignon and her olive skin clean of make-up. She charged up to the nurse's station and demanded to see her daughter.

"Her name?" the station nurse asked.

"Ana Bontierre."

The nurse looked surprised for a moment, and then quickly referenced a list on her desk. "Let me find where they've taken her."

Jacqueline tapped her fingers on the nurse station desk like a drummer tolling on his drum. The nurse nodded into the phone and spoke quietly, and when she hung up, she looked forlornly at Jacqueline. "The sheriff is on his way to take you to her. You can have a seat over there."

Jacqueline was not about to have a seat anywhere. She waited, and tapped, as the station nurse tried not to be annoyed, until the sheriff turned the corner. Wearing his standard-issue tan uniform, the sheriff looked pale and distressed. He greeted Jacqueline cautiously, and then gently led her to a chair next to Mac. "Please, Mrs. Bontierre," he said, nervously caressing his thick mustache. "Have a seat."

"I am fine standing, thank you. Where is Ana?"

"I'm sorry, Mrs. Bontierre, uh, Jacqueline," he began, as the words slowly crept out of his mouth. "I'm sorry, but I think we have found your daughter."

Not understanding, Jacqueline said, "Is she okay? What happened? Is she in trouble?"

The sheriff chewed on his lower lip, fighting back a tear. "I'm sorry . . ." he said again, shaking his head despondently. Mac jumped from her seat and tried to steady Jacqueline.

Jacqueline crumpled into the chair next to Mac, her legs surrendering like a white flag. "The doctors did everything they could to save her, but I'm afraid that she didn't make it." The words spilled out of his mouth in one long breath. He refilled his lungs with a snorting breath, and then he shoved his hands into his pockets, jangling his keys. He looked at her disconsolate face and continued. "I'm going to need you to come downstairs with me to the morgue and identify her."

Identify her? Words crashed together in Jacqueline's mind and she burst into loud sobs. In the past few years, Jacqueline had prepared herself for this moment, imagining what it would be like to hear that her daughter would no longer share their meals or be kissed goodnight or join them at the breakfast table. She had pictured the casket and the flowers and the funeral service. But after Ana successfully completed rehab, she seemed different–convincing in her desire to clean up her act. Jacqueline had let her guard down, and had begun to picture flowers for a wedding–not a funeral, and now she was paying a heavy price for it. Mac grabbed her by the hand, then the elbow, trying to slowly reel her into an embrace, but Jacqueline stiffened. "What happened to her?" Jacqueline asked, in a terse voice.

The sheriff sucked in air, letting out a loud sigh. "Cause of death is still in question. I'm sorry that I can't be more specific. We will have to wait for an autopsy report."

Jacqueline's shoulders slumped, allowing Mac to pull her in for a brief hug. She pulled away abruptly and narrowed her glare. "Drug overdose?"

"I can't tell you for sure. I'm sorry." The sheriff tugged on the right side of his handlebar mustache, looking like he wanted to say something more.

"Did someone hurt her?"

The sheriff looked sideways for a split second before he answered. "It is possible. She appears to have suffered some trauma."

"I hope you are going to prosecute with an even hand, sheriff. I hope–," she said, and then broke into a wrenching sob.

* * *

The basement of Sheridan Memorial Hospital smelled sterile and was free of the noises and bustle of the ER directly above. The sheriff motioned Mac and Jacqueline through steel-framed double doors and beyond into a cold, barren hallway. The walls were painted an infertile green, and had been left undecorated. No hospital "Mission Statement" or motivational scenery was framed to aid the injured or ill. Only painted cement. The sheriff led them to a room with a sign overhead that read "Medical Examiner–No Entry Without Permission."

"We're supposed to wear these," the sheriff said, pointing to masks, caps, gloves, and slippers.

When they entered, the pathologist was busy at work performing an autopsy on Ana. He looked shocked to see them approach. He quickly slid the white sheet up over the girl's body, only exposing her face. Jacqueline took a step forward, examining her daughter. She reached out to touch her cheek–to feel the life of her daughter. The pathologist gasped under his mask, prepared to admonish her for touching his specimen. Somehow, he caught himself, and remained silent.

Ana looked like she'd been beaten. Her eyes were swollen and purple. Her lips were puffy and red, traces of dried blood pooled at the edges of her mouth. A trail of blood led from her left tear duct, down her cheek, and around her jaw line, disappearing, like a river that had run dry.

"May I?" Jacqueline asked, gently lifting the sheet that covered her daughter's body.

"No, well, I am in the middle of my . . . procedure. I don't think it is a good idea–"

It was too late. Jacqueline had peeled back the thin slip of cotton that had shielded her from the horror of Ana's death. Jacqueline screamed out and then quickly covered Ana's body.

Mac saw Ana, purplish and unzipped, like a discarded ragdoll that had been left to rot in the rain. Mac had seen autopsy reports and photos before, when her legal secretary was murdered in Jackson Hole. Yet, in person, it was even more shocking. The Y-shaped incision over Ana's chest cavity revealed a mess of bloody, mushy organs, none of which were identifiable. Ana's skin was bluish-purple and bruised in dozens of places.

"Mrs. Bontierre," the sheriff said, softy, only out of procedure. "Is this your daughter?" He hated asking. Salt in the wound.

Without a word, Jacqueline burst into a screaming-sob, like that of a lamb caught in the snares of a hunter's metal trap, and ran out of the pathologist's lab. Mac followed after her, finding her halfway down the hall, crumpled into a lifeless ball, wretching.

Mac threw her arms around Jacqueline and held her tight. After a few minutes of hysterical crying, Jacqueline collected herself. The hysteria turned to sorrow—invading her like a terrible drug. And minutes later—the sorrow turned to anger. She pulled back from Mac's embrace and with native contempt said, "Find out who did this to my daughter, Mac. You do whatever it takes, spend whatever you need. I don't give a damn what it costs. Use all the money from the methane gas if you have to. I want you to find who did this to my baby and I want this monster to pay. Do you understand?"

Chapter 3

After Mr. Bontierre drove away from the hospital with Jacqueline sedated and asleep in the back, Mac drove to her apartment. She was exhausted and shaken, and felt a tearfully heavy storm gathering within her. Fully dressed, she collapsed on her bed and closed her eyes for a moment. *Who could have done this to Ana? Did Ana get herself mixed up with the wrong kind of people again? What could have been done to help this poor girl?* She wandered the back pathways of her mind, thinking of how her mother must have felt when Mac's father was killed. Mac remembered the uncontrollable sobbing and that her mother's bedroom door was closed for days on end. Mac was only four years old, but she had the anchor of those memories planted firmly in her mind. She had never spoken to her mother about it, but could only imagine Jacqueline's pain to be as deep.

Mac looked out her window at the sliver of a moon which barely pierced the shelter of the grayish clouds, trying to rid her mind of the mental image of Ana on the gurney. She thought of Gilbert Bonita. She compared him to the moon, which was subtle, yet alluring. Her mind quickly drifted back to the Bontierres. She fell asleep with her hands folded on her chest–holding on to her heart to keep the hope from escaping it.

* * *

Mac awoke to a light flurry of snow–the first snow of the year. It was late October, and the whirls of wind were taking the colorful leaves from the trees and tossing them amongst the snowflakes, making the sky look like a giant blender. She strapped on her running shoes and hit the trail, picking up speed as she ran toward the mountains. The sun was just cresting in the east, shining gorgeous rays westward toward the majestic mountains, illuminating the newly snow-dusted purple mountains in a magical, Christmas-like way. The air was cool and sharp, like the blade of a knife, and Mac had to breathe through her nose so that she wouldn't get a sore throat. The searing of her lungs made her feel alive and worthy. For Mac, running was her refuge—her antidote to stress and loneliness. She prayed and meditated during her runs, grateful for the day, contemplative of yesterday and tomorrow. Today, she prayed for the Bontierre family.

After her run, she headed to the office. After brewing a fresh pot of coffee, she placed a call to Jacqueline Bontierre's cell phone. No answer. She called the ranch, but again, no answer. She called the sheriff's office, but Mandy said that there was no further information that she could report. "You should starting choking down the Vitamin C though, because when I was at The Coffee House this morning, everyone was talking about the flu. So, get your flu shot early this year. That's my advice for the day."

Mac had never had a flu shot before, and she remembered that Greg had warned her that there were so many strains to the flu that it was unwise to get a shot for one type because it could make you susceptible to another, more viral strain. Greg traveled into the dense jungles of Africa and South America with his job and was well-read on outbreaks of viruses and diseases. He'd been immunized for just about everything known to man and was cautious when it came to the flu. Mac decided to pop an extra vitamin or two and forego the shot for now.

It was a good decision, as it turns out.

* * *

The pathologist expedited his report the next morning, based on Dr. Rowe's urging. His medical opinion was vague, claiming that an unknown virus had invaded Ana Bontierre's body like a predator—devouring all organs vital to her existence, and leaving behind useless tissue. Her flesh had liquefied at the same time that her blood had coagulated, throwing blood clots that lodged in every organ necessary to sustain life. He could not confirm rape conclusively, due to the swollen nature of her labia. He was certain that she'd been physically abused, but he could not determine, with medical certainty, whether a blunt object had been used to beat her. He admitted in his report that he had never seen anything like Ana's tissue samples, and could not conclusively determine a cause of death. Further tissue analysis would be required.

Jacqueline Bontierre was seated in Mary MacIntosh's office when the autopsy report churned across her fax machine. Mac allowed Jacqueline to read it first, in private, before she viewed the report. Distraught, angry and agitated from the mood stabilizer she took that morning, Jacqueline insisted on calling the pathologist at home. She wanted to know whether he thought Ana had suffered in death. Mac discouraged the phone call, but as Jacqueline's agitation grew, Mac decided that it was worth the effort to place the call.

In a small town such as Sheridan, most resident's home numbers were listed in the phone book. Mac dialed and to his credit, the doctor answered the phone, despite the fact that he'd just finished working the graveyard shift.

Of course, the pathologist could not tell Jacqueline, with medical certainty, what Ana had known or felt. Nevertheless, in his matter-of-fact way, he explained that Ana's muscle tissue had died while the blood clots were being displaced, and that, in all likelihood, the blood clots found lodged in her brain cut off her central nervous system in a way that kept her from feeling the sensation of pain or the necessity for breath. This information, clinical in nature, was meant to soothe Jacqueline, yet it only made her wince in horror at the thought of her daughter's vibrant young body rotting internally. Jacqueline accused the doctor of having a terrible bedside manner and even told him, flat out, that she thought that he was covering up something. In Jacqueline's mind, Ana had been deliberately killed.

Mac took the phone away from Jacqueline and continued the conversation with the pathologist in the conference room of her office. Mac apologized to the doctor. "She's in shock. She doesn't mean to attack you. She's angry and devastated and frustrated."

The pathologist was empathetic toward Jacqueline, yet quite unnerved by Ana's bizarre death. He explained to Mac how he believed the virus had attacked Ana's body and how it had viciously devoured her, like a hungry lion. This was no ordinary virus and he knew it.

Dr. Rowe was equally distressed by the autopsy report. There was protocol to abide by, and Dr. Rowe knew that his job would be on the line if he didn't follow it. He called the CDC and spoke with the chief virologist about the case and she suggested that he send samples of Ana's tissues to her attention. So, he asked the pathologist to carefully package samples of every kind of tissue that he could identify from Ana's body and ship them to Atlanta to the attention of the Center for Disease Control and Prevention. He also asked the pathologist to send samples to the National Institute of Allergy and Infectious Diseases. The remaining samples would be properly stored for analysis by the other agencies that would become involved if the virus turned out to be some sort of virulent contaminant.

Dr. Jocelyn Sharp, Chief Virologist of the Special Pathogens Branch of the Center for Disease Control, told Dr. Rowe how to handle the samples and where to ship them, and then instructed him to quarantine the hospital and sterilize it thoroughly to prevent viral proliferation. All hospital personnel that aided Ana Bontierre were to volunteer a blood sample for analysis, and were to be restricted from work for at least five days to ensure that the virus had not spread. But it was too late.

* * *

Ronnie One Feather returned to the emergency room two days later, complaining of a severe headache, cough and fever. His symptoms worsened rapidly, and he soon had trouble breathing. Dr. Rowe recognized him immediately as the ranger who'd found Ana Bontierre at Medicine Wheel. Trying not to overreact, Dr. Rowe administered a flood of antibiotics and secured him to a ventilator. Double gloves and masks were required for all hospital personnel assisting Ronnie. As his breathing grew raspy, Dr. Rowe inserted a laryngoscope to clear the passageway, but this only exacerbated Ronnie's breathing difficulties. He started coughing up large blood clots and thick, tar-like mucus. Within a day of being quarantined in what Dr. Rowe hoped was a sterile medical unit, Ronnie spewed blood from every orifice and was dead.

Still, Ronnie's death looked like it might be a coincidence, so Dr. Rowe decided not to risk creating hysteria until he received the results back from the CDC regarding Ana's death. This seemed rational until Carrie Wynne, a nurse who had been administering to Ana, was wheeled into the ER with what her husband believed to be congestive heart failure. Her family had a history of strokes and heart attacks, and although Carrie was only in her fifties, it appeared that her heart was giving out. She had been a smoker for twenty years, after all, and with her family health history, it would be natural to assume that Carrie was reaping what she'd sown. She was rushed to the operating room and opened up, but like Ana, her tissues were detached, as if they had seceded from her heart in some type of revolution. A bypass or any other life-saving type of operation was futile. Dr. Rowe cleaned out as much disconnected tissue as he could and closed her up as quickly as possible. She was dead within the half hour.

Dr. Rowe had a problem on his hands and it wasn't clear to him how to deal with it. He'd read in medical journals about contagious flesh eating diseases and how such a disease affected the central nervous system. If he was dealing with a similar disease, a complex quarantine would be necessary to stop the spread.

Dr. Rowe informed the CDC of the deaths of Ronnie One Feather and Carrie Wynne. He agreed with the CDC's instruction that anyone who had been exposed to Ana Bontierre after her body was discovered at Medicine Wheel would be quarantined until further notice. This meant that all attending medical personnel, along with the pathologist and the sheriff, would have to be isolated until the CDC was finished conducting its analysis of Ana's tissues. The hospital emergency room would be declared a "hot zone."

Unfortunately, in small-towns hysteria spreads as quickly as a wild fire, and the buzz of the hospital serving as a "hot zone" had everyone in the gossip chain frantic. Authorities overlooked the fact that David Thrift, the other ranger on duty with Ronnie One Feather, was wantonly roaming the mountain region. The Forest Service had been notified of Ronnie's death, and had been asked to contact David Thrift and direct him to the quarantine unit in Sheridan. However, David was a loner, and on his days off from work, he typically strapped a sixty-pound pack on his back and wandered into the wilderness. He rarely told anyone where he was going or when he would return. Despite the fact that his behavior was in violation of Forest Service protocol, he was a very self-sufficient naturalist and could survive in nature for long periods of time. This fact would prove to be fatal in a few days–for David, and the creatures who dined on his rotting corpse.

* * *

When Dr. Rowe took the call from CDC virologist Dr. Jocelyn Sharp, he was not feeling one hundred percent. He'd been working around the clock in the quarantine unit, and perhaps was suffering from a lack of sleep. At first, he thought he was hallucinating when he heard her urgent tone and strict instructions. "Let me be perfectly clear here, Dr. Rowe. We are dealing with H5N1, which is commonly known as the avian flu or bird flu. This particular strain of the flu is referred to as a Highly Pathogenic Avian Influence, or as we call it, HPAI. The virus spreads through the bloodstream to infect every tissue and organ. Death is generally by hemorrhage or suffocation. It is thought to be spread by migratory birds and we have seen it mostly in Asia in the poultry population. What we have not seen from this extremely deadly virus is high human-to-human transfer. However, in light of the fact that two other people in your community exposed to the virus have died, we are considering this as a possible explosive chain of lethal transmission. We are in the preliminary stages of electron microscopic analysis. Amplification is highly suspect at this time. Do you understand the gravity and seriousness of what I'm telling you? We are sending virologists your way as we speak and they will be setting up a 'hot suite' in your hospital."

Dr. Rowe felt like she was talking gibberish to him. *H5N1? Explosive chain? Hot Suite? Amplification?* "Dr. Sharp, I'm not sure I understand–"

"I'm sending a Biosafety Level 4 laboratory your way to help your community deal with what could amount to be an HPAI outbreak of gargantuan proportions. It could wipe out every living person in the community of Sheridan. Fifteen thousand people could be dead in a few weeks if you don't follow my directions. I'm not exaggerating or overreacting, Dr. Rowe. We haven't seen a hot agent like this in the United States since 1918, when the Spanish flu wiped out some one hundred million people world-wide. Some speculate that it started in Kansas, but spread to nearly every part of the world. The local is always global. Those are my words of wisdom for the day. I need to run. Call my assistant, Dr. Amir Fahrid, with any questions."

The local is always global. Like an echo, the words kept repeating themselves.

* * *

"My daughter did not consume duck!" Jacqueline Bontierre shouted. "She was a strict vegetarian, Dr. Kokinda. This . . . this accusation that my daughter ate rotten duck and it somehow poisoned her furthers my belief that you don't know what you are talking about! This is some kind of government conspiracy against my daughter. She got in trouble with the law a few times and this is your way of getting back at her. I want her body released immediately from that hospital and I want a proper burial." Jacqueline Bontierre had not showered for days. Her long, black hair fell free from its usual French twist, and the oils at the roots shone brightly in the autumn sun. Her clothes were soiled and she had dark circles encasing her eyes.

Dr. Karen Kokinda, a tall, thin scientist and director of the National Institute of Allergy and Infectious Diseases was trying to placate Jacqueline, explaining that the contents of Ana's stomach showed signs of ingestion of duck prior to death. Dr. Kokinda was an expert in duck and other waterfowl migration—not because she was a naturalist, but because she was an authority on the correlation of bird migration and the flu.

At the end of every summer, millions of ducks and geese gather in Siberian and Canadian lakes for their annual migration. As they congregate, the flu viruses that have been naturally replicating in the intestinal tracts of the birds begin to develop and ripen. As the ducks set sail to the skies, the flu viruses that are in their intestines are excreted into waterways along the migration path, creating what Dr. Kokinda refers to as "viral soup."

Other birds and species along the migration path ingest the "viral soup," which increases the likelihood of the spread of infection globally. What has always fascinated Dr. Kokinda is that by the end of the winter season, duck influenza diminishes to almost nil and doesn't generally return until the next fall migration season. The duck population remains virtually unscathed by this rampant spread of viral toxin, yet humans can suffer greatly from it. The degree of the harm depends on a number of factors, such as weather patterns and the particular type of virus the ducks generate during the migration.

It is no secret among the scientific community that flu viruses come from the wild birds of the world. Understanding how a flu virus invades a human is a bit more difficult. Normally, for an avian flu and a human flu to merge, they have to infect the same animal, such as a pig. Cells in the respiratory systems of pigs have the necessary receptors for both avian and human hemagglutinin. A pig could catch avian flu while drinking from a pond on a farm where a duck excreted the virus. At the same time, the pig could be exposed to a farmer with the human flu. The two viruses could then regroup, creating a crossbreed virus, which could then infect human cells once again. This new hybrid flu would be new to the human immune system and highly virulent. Dr. Kokinda had published many papers on hybrid flu, but her most recent studies had focused on the H5N1 strain of avian flu, and how it could spread to the human population without the necessity for the "pig factor," as she called it. She was certain, and quite worried, that hemagglutinin mutations, much like what happened in the 1918 pandemic of Spanish flu, would eventually cause a pathogenic H5N1 outbreak among waterfowl and wild birds, and the mutated avian flu would then spread like AIDS, but faster, and there would be no cure.

Dr. Kokinda tried to explain to Jacqueline Bontierre that there was a direct link between duck and her daughter's death, but there was no way that Jacqueline was going to accept such a suggestion. She was so offended and disturbed by the remarks that she insisted that the mayor hold a town meeting that night to discuss the ridiculous rumors that were spreading. When the mayor's personal assistant informed Jacqueline that the mayor was out of the office, offering condolences to the sheriff's family, Jacqueline eased off. Apparently, when the sheriff closed Ana's bloody eyes after she died at the hospital, he was directly exposed to the avian flu virus. The sheriff had been in quarantine after Ronnie One Feather and Carrie Wynne died, but by that time the virus had already invaded his body and there was no way to stop it.

When Jacqueline heard how the sheriff contracted the virus, she realized that perhaps she was being unreasonable. Maybe Dr. Kokinda knew what she was talking about.

* * *

When Dr. Amir Fahrid took over the quarantine of Sheridan Memorial Hospital the next day, he had his crew buzzing around like a swarm of bees, sealing off quadrants of the hospital with specialized equipment and issuing orders like a drill sergeant. A native of India with short, dark hair, dark skin and thick glasses, he'd worked directly under the command of Dr. Jocelyn Sharp for ten years. In his soft, yet direct voice, spoken through a microphone inside his biosafety suit, he instructed his pathologist to perform an autopsy on the sheriff, and then insisted that Ana Bontierre receive a proper CDC autopsy. During his rounds, he had a long conversation with Dr. Rowe, whose flu-like symptoms were beginning to show. Dr. Rowe, who remained in quarantine, explained what happened to Ana Bontierre, and how he and his staff had tried to help her. Dr. Fahrid listened patiently with one ear, while continuing to issue orders to his staff. He knew that Dr. Rowe did his best, but this virus was lethal and unstoppable without proper antivirals administered early and often. As Dr. Rowe spoke, Dr. Fahrid watched the transformation, as Dr. Rowe's eyes grew vacant and droplets of blood seeped from his nostrils. He ordered another dosage of antiviral medication into Dr. Rowe's IV, and then quickly went to the decon room and sprayed himself with a pump sprayer filled with a bleach compound.

The morgue had been transformed into a Level 4 lab, completely sealed off from the rest of the hospital. Inside, Dr. Fahrid carefully reviewed Ana Bontierre's autopsy results and examined her body with great specificity. He noticed a stone-like structure drawn with permanent ink on the inside of her right thigh. The roughly etched stone structure looked like an old house that had fallen apart–or perhaps the drawing was incomplete? It looked like a pictograph. He double-checked the autopsy report to see if the mark was noted, but it was not. *Who drew this on her? What did it mean? Why wasn't it noted on the autopsy?*

* * *

When word about the H5N1 avian flu outbreak reached the media that day, the residents of Sheridan didn't know what had hit them. The community was a mixture of ranchers, miners, professionals and government employees–most of who had never heard of this strain of flu. Some were aware of the SARS outbreak a few years prior in Asia, but most did not follow it closely. They had no idea that the media would descend upon them like the plague in hopes of capturing a "bleed out" for the evening news. Cheap motels flashed their "No Vacancy" sign for the first time since summer's rodeo. The highways were clogged with locals who'd packed up their families and their pets and as many animals as could fit in their horse trailers and headed out of town. Of those remaining, the most commonly uttered words were: flu, outbreak, hot zone, and Stiflu.

Stiflu, a powerful bird flu antiviral medication, had been on the market for years, but had not been stockpiled in the United States. For years, leaders in the World Health Organization and flu experts had been begging governments around the world to stockpile Stiflu in case there was ever another pandemic flu outbreak similar to what happened in 1918 with the Spanish flu. Globally, most countries had not stockpiled the drug. Flu vaccines such as Stiflu are disliked by drug companies because they are both difficult and costly to produce. They also become obsolete after a certain period of time. If the virus mutates, the drug becomes ineffective. Reich, a Swiss corporation, is one of the few pharmaceutical companies that manufactures Stiflu. If there was an epidemic, Reich would be flooded with orders and would be unable to meet global demand for the drug. The United States had remained woefully shy in its stockpile, despite repeated requests from researchers. John Kerry made the lack of a stockpile a big issue in his campaign against President Bush, raising the practical question of who would be entitled to the stockpiled medicine.

Hospital staff, serving the needs of patients whom are already infected? The patients themselves? Government officials? This quandary has not presented itself in America in a long time. Yet, in a small town in Wyoming, a local pharmacist was placing repeated telephone calls, emails and faxes to the CDC, World Health Organization, and Reich itself, trying to get some of the medication in his hands so that he could meet the increasing demands of his community.

Mac, who had learned that Ana allegedly died from the avian flu, was one of the first people to approach the local pharmacist to ask if she could get a dose of Stiflu for herself and her staff, and also for Jacqueline Bontierre. The pharmacist did not have Stiflu, and had been told that the CDC was only going to administer Stiflu to those persons in quarantine. The stockpile shortages were so severe that the mere mention of the outbreak had government officials in every major city in America scrambling for the drug. He could only offer Mac a substitute, which was not going to help anyone already exposed to the deadly strain.

When Mac informed Jacqueline about the Stiflu shortages, her response was, "I don't know why you are wasting your time looking for an anecdote to some mystery virus! You should be looking for the perpetrator of the crime! Have you spoken to any eye witnesses? Have you interviewed Ana's college roommate? Have you spoken to the bartender where she was last seen?" Before Mac could answer any of Jacqueline's questions, she continued. "Well, despite the fact that I am paying *you* to track down my daughter's murderer, I have doing *your* job. Do you care to know the answers to these questions?"

Chapter 4

Mac drove south of town on cottonwood-lined U.S. 87, through rolling ranchland, surrounded by pointed mountainous peaks in the background, to an outskirt community of Big Horn. Instead of having dinner in town with Gilbert Bonita, Mac had agreed to drive out to his new farmhouse to see what he had done with the place. It had been an abandoned dump for years, and despite the fact that he'd been squatting there for a few weeks prior to the close of escrow, she couldn't imagine that he could have turned the place into an *Architectural Digest* feature in just a month's time. Mac had a stack of notarized paperwork and a recorded deed from the bank to deliver to Gilbert, and used the documents as an excuse to visit him. Something about this man intrigued her. She was not interested in getting involved in a relationship with him, but she admitted to herself that he was attractive and mysterious.

The aspen and cottonwoods enlightened Gil's property with dusts of gold, amber, crimson and auburn, making the white farmhouse stand out like a cloud in heaven. Mac arrived at the gate, got out of her SUV, slid the padlocked chain over the post, and drove over the cattle guard onto his property. With taped-over windows and a sheet of graffitied plywood covering the glass plates of the front door, Mac wondered why Gil paid good money for the place. It looked like a drug dealer's hangout.

Gil was proudly waiting for Mac on the enclosed screen porch with a glass of red wine in his hand. He looked handsome, wearing a denim button- down shirt and faded blue jeans. His dark hair was slicked back and his smile was wide. He offered her the glass as she climbed the three wooden plank steps onto the porch, allowing the screen door to slam behind her with a bang.

"I see you haven't fixed the screen door yet," Mac joked, accepting the wine with her right hand and handing him the documents with her left. He smiled wide, admitting that he had far bigger projects to worry about than a loud screen door. He thumbed through the documents, hardly giving them a second glance.

"You look lovely," he said. Mac was comfortably dressed in a turquoise sweater and Levi jeans. Her long, auburn hair was pulled back off her face, but flowed freely over her shoulders. Gil escorted her through the entrance, showing her into the main entryway, which consisted of a white stairway leading to the second floor and a hallway leading toward the back end of the house. The walls looked like they'd served time in a war—scarred with marks and dents and holes. Mac followed Gil to the kitchen, which smelled like garlic and other home-cooked aromas. The appliances were old, but the kitchen was clean, and iron-cast pots steamed from the stovetop. He had set a rectangular table in the center of the kitchen, with a single yellow tulip in a white vase in the center. Gil opened the lid to a large pot and stirred once with a wooden spoon.

"I hope you can join me for dinner," Gil said. Mac had not planned on staying long, but it appeared that he'd gone to a lot of trouble to make a nice meal.

"Oh, s-s-sure. I wasn't expecting to be here long. Looks like you are a good cook."

Gil smiled. I had to learn early in life how to fend for myself. After surviving on tortillas and beans for years I decided that I'd better learn some other recipes." He put the lid back on the pot and then motioned for her to follow him on a tour of the rest of the house.

The dining room contained an old, round table with six chairs, but nothing else. No other furniture was on the main floor. The upstairs had only two bedrooms, one of which was furnished with a lumpy-looking double bed.

"The furniture was left behind by the former owners. I haven't had time to buy any yet," Gil said. The bathroom had a leaky faucet and an ancient bathtub which rested on clawed feet. The toilet was rust-stained and remitted a constant sound of flowing water.

She followed him back down the staircase and around toward the kitchen. There was a door in the hallway under the staircase.

"Do you have a basement?" Mac asked, as she reached for the handle. He quickly grabbed her hand.

"There is no electricity down there and I'm afraid it is infested. Water flooded the basement last year during the spring run-off, and I think it sat there for months before it dried out. It is not safe. Please, follow me. Dinner is ready."

Mac sipped on her wine while Gil danced around the kitchen, pulling pots and pans out of the oven. He had his back to her, but continued to converse. His shoulders were wide and muscular, his forearms lean and strong. His dark hair was combed back off his face, sleek with gel and shiny. His hands moved masterfully, adding a spice here and a garnish there. All the while Mac told Gil that she'd spent most of her day dealing with the flu epidemic and that she hadn't accomplished much. He acted surprised, as if he hadn't heard of the outbreak. It was possible, she supposed, to have not heard the news of the avian flu outbreak if he hadn't left the seclusion of the farmhouse in a few days, as he stated. She filled him in on Ana Bontierre, and the sheriff, and the medical staff that had died from the virus. "I heard that Dr. Rowe died yesterday. He was such a nice man, and he had this adorable wife and three kids. It makes me so sad to think that they will have to grow up without their father."

Gil seemed genuinely interested and somewhat surprised. "I remember something similar when I lived for a time in China. It was terrible. People were very sick and some died, and the government killed most of the chickens. People were very upset about the chickens," Gil said, as he set Mac's plate in front of her. Her eyes widened. "I lived for a short time in Italy, in a place called Monterchi, by the Tiber River. That is where I finally learned the ways of cooking. This is one of my favorites, called Anatra in Porchetta. You shall enjoy."

Mac stared at roast duck, string beans, mashed potatoes, and red beets. "What is wrong?" Gil asked, watching Mac gape at her food. "You look ill. Are you alright?"

"Yes. I mean, no. It's noth-nothing," Mac choked. "I'm so sorry. I guess I forgot to tell you that I am a vegetarian," she lied. "It looks wonderful, and I will enjoy the rest of the meal with you. I can only imagine how much effort you've put into this. The presentation is beautiful."

She didn't have the heart to tell him about a conversation she'd had earlier in the day with Jacqueline Bontierre regarding Dr. Kokinda, and Dr. Kokinda's research about ducks spreading the avian flu virus.

"I was unaware that you are a vegetarian. You should have told me." Gil looked hurt. He hastily scraped the duck off her plate and dumped it back into the roaster where it landed with a splash. Drippings cascaded down the wall behind the stove and trickled out of sight. The burden of his silence weighed heavy on her as he dropped the plate of vegetables in front of her.

Gil picked up his fork and knife and sliced into the duck's carcass, withdrawing a thick slick of brown meat and placing it on his tongue. He chewed, swallowed and then sipped his wine. "This virus. You say it has killed five people already?" Gil asked. Mac nodded, relieved that the uncomfortable silence had lifted. She spoke nervously, filling him in on the quarantine and the mass media pouring into town like hungry wolves. "This is very exciting for a small town, no?"

Mac sensed a certain glee in his eye, as if the circus had come to town. "I don't know if I'd call it 'exciting.' It is scary and horrific, for sure."

"Delicious," he said, as he bit into his second slice of roast duck.

* * *

When Mac got home from dinner with Gil, she fed Ted, her yellow tabby cat, and then flipped on the news. Four different stations were broadcasting on the avian flu. Channel seven's anchorwoman was interviewing an official spokesperson from the World Health Organization.

"In late January 2004, WHO activated its influenza pandemic preparedness plan in response to confirmation in Vietnam and Thailand of severe disease caused by an H5N1 strain of avian influenza. The strain of flu was directly linked to the poultry populations of these two regions."

The broadcast showed photographs of dead chickens at a farm somewhere in Asia. "The disease has no vaccine and no specific treatment once illness becomes severe. Like any flu, if caught in time and treated, a victim can be spared."

Mac flipped to channel four. On the screen, there was a picture of white mice in a cage, with a caption reading, "Did these mice cause the Wyoming outbreak?" The anchorman reported on the story. "Three mice infected with H5N1 avian influenza virus apparently disappeared from a laboratory in Russia about two weeks ago. Although health officials said there was scant public risk, authorities quickly launched a search. The mice were unaccounted-for at the Siberian Health Research Institute, which conducts bioterrorism research for the Russian government. The mice were injected as part of an inoculation and vaccination experiment, investigators said."

Mac changed the channel again, and the news headline read, "What Comes First? The Chicken or the Egg?" The reporter explained how flu vaccines are traditionally grown in millions of fertilized eggs, a process that takes months. The lengthy production cycle makes it difficult for drug makers to keep up with mutating flu strains and limits the quantity of vaccines that can be produced.

Mac channel surfed again. More reports on flu outbreaks. She turned off her television and crawled into bed, but was unable to sleep after watching the news. She tossed and turned and flipped her pillow, trying to settle into sleep, but her mind was still churning. She thought of Gil. He had gone to painstaking efforts to make her a lovely meal, yet she had behaved like an idiot. She wasn't a vegetarian and he knew it. She had chicken with him the first night they went out, after escrow had closed on the farmhouse. He didn't call her on it, perhaps because he was being a gentleman, but his feelings had to be hurt when she declined to eat the roast duck. On the other hand, he seemed so nonchalant about the viral outbreak and the deaths, as if it were common, everyday occurrences in his life. But perhaps they were. He'd lived in many poor regions of the world and had probably seen more than Mac would ever know. To Gil, a viral outbreak might be the equivalent of the chicken pox. He'd lived in places where medicine wasn't readily available and people died of epidemics all of the time. She was almost relieved that he was leaving the country for a week on business.

Her mind then wandered to her old boyfriend, Greg. She wondered whether he was working on an assignment with *National Geographic* somewhere fascinating. She missed him. Eventually, she fell asleep, but not without intense dreams. She dreamed that she was walking on a cliff, high above a gathering of people whom she knew well. They were there to see her, or to pay their last respects to her. Was this her funeral? She was not in a casket. They were not looking down upon her–she was floating over them. She saw her father, who'd died when Mac was age four. He was smiling up at her like a proud father might do. She saw her mother, who looked profusely sad. Then there was Harry, Mac's law partner, who was as much a father- figure to her as he was her mentor and one-time boss. Harry looked disappointed, as though Mac had made some error in judgment. And then she saw Greg, who looked the saddest of all, like he'd been trying to find her and when he finally did, it was too late. She was floating too high for him to reach her. She felt Greg grab for her, grazing her ankle with his reach, which startled her awake. Then she realized that it was only her cat, who'd settled in to sleep next to her right leg.

She looked over at her digital alarm clock on the nightstand, and when she realized that it was three in the morning, she tried to go back to sleep but it was no use. Her mind was clicking away, and she had an upset stomach. *Was it the avian flu? Didn't it start with a fever and stomach problems?* Trying not to be a hypochondriac, she decided to get up and check her emails, hoping that it would cause her to think of something other than the avian flu. Since the media coverage had hit the national news, she had received sixty-two emails within the last twenty-four hours, mostly from friends and family making sure that she was okay. She typed one generic response and pasted it into each reply email, letting friends know that she was safe so far, and that the outbreak, if indeed it was an outbreak, was localized, or so they thought.

The one email that didn't get the generic response was from Greg. He'd contacted her for the first time in months, wondering whether she was okay and letting her know that he was in Indonesia doing a story for *National Geographic* on terrorism. His email was long, detailing that he'd spent a good portion of his summer researching and reporting on the avian flu, particularly its affects in Asia. He mentioned that he contributed to the piece featured in the October issue, and suggested that Mac read it. Based on his knowledge of migratory birds and overall health standards in the community, Greg was surprised that an H5N1 outbreak could happen in Wyoming, but admitted that past outbreaks, dating back to the previous century, were often a mystery, and that she should take all precautions necessary for her safety. At the end of the email, he offered his condolences for the death of Ana.

She dug through her stack of mail, pulled out the *National Geographic* and read the article Greg recommended, which was informative and well-researched, but also a little frightening. The section that resonated deeply with Mac was the mystery of how people get infected with the virus. "Right now, we believe most cases are related to people somehow being exposed to sick or dying or dead poultry," said the contributor. *Well, what does that mean? Does that mean that people touched it? Did they eat it? Did they breathe in dust containing chicken feces?* The fact that no one knows how people contract avian flu made Mac realize that there was little to no sure-fire means of staying clear of the virus. She knew one thing for sure–she was not going to eat or touch any poultry for a long, long time.

* * *

By the end of the week, fourteen more people in Sheridan had died from avian flu. The CDC recommended that hundreds of chickens, ducks and geese be slaughtered and tested, both to determine contamination and to hopefully stop the spread of the virus. Ana Bontierre had been declared the original host, or "patient zero." The sacred ground of Medicine Wheel was officially closed off to the public until the entire area could be analyzed and eventually sterilized.

Ana's whereabouts for the two weeks leading up to her death were a subject of paramount inquiry, but due to her isolated nature, Jacqueline could not account for her daughter. Neither could Ana's college roommate.

At Jacqueline's insistence, Mac acted like a private investigator and looked under every proverbial rock, but she could not find out much about what happened to Ana in the last few days of her life. Ana had literally disappeared for two days before she was found on the mountain and no one had a clue as to where she'd been or with whom. Without such information, the investigators and scientists were speculating wildly about the boundaries of the hot zone.

Not much mention had been made of the mysterious markings found on Ana's inner thigh. Despite her wild and somewhat bohemian nature, Ana had always professed a great dislike of tattoos. Dr. Fahrid described the markings as a picture of a stone hut, partially dilapidated, with mountain peaks in the background. Perhaps it was a clue as to Ana's whereabouts prior to her death. *Had she drawn on herself, trying to communicate where she had been when she contacted the virus?* No one knew for sure.

The inquiry regarding the markings probably would have diminished if not for a report from the Associated Press that another H5N1 outbreak had been confirmed in Hong Kong. A thirty-year-old woman had been admitted to the hospital, diagnosed with acute asphyxiation. She was intubated immediately and suction was administered, retrieving the first of several large blood clots from her esophagus. When the tracheotomy proved unsuccessful, she was rushed to surgery. There, they found that her lung tissue had been completed destroyed. She died on the operating table. Horror spread through the hospital ward, as Hong Kong was no stranger to avian flu. The media quickly focused on the markings that were found on the woman's inner right thigh. Like Ana Bontierre, a pictograph-type sketching of a rock house was etched on her skin with some type of permanent marker.

Photographs of the sketch were circulated across the wires, piquing the interest of Dr. Jeffrey Plattenburg, a tall, thin, decorated officer and scientist with the Federal Bureau of Investigation's Behavioral Science Services, based in Quantico, Virginia. Dr. Plattenburg was a profiler for the Investigative Support Unit of the National Center for Analysis of Violent Crime, and he found it remarkable that two women who mysteriously bled out on gurneys in hospitals half-way around the world from one another were tagged with nearly identical man-made markings. He quickly gathered as much information as was available on both women and logged it onto a VICAP form for entry into the profiler computer database. He would need more data on the victims: the police reports, photographs, information on the area where they were from, medical examiner reports, and a map of each victim's movements before death. Dr. Plattenburg was considered the FBI's "best of the best" when it came to solving violent crime. He was driven by the slightest of details and had a sixth sense and ability to think like a killer. No detail was too small. No piece of evidence was overlooked. He was often hired by private attorneys to testify as an expert in criminal trials throughout the United States.

After comparing the information and evidence on the two women with similar tattoos and similar causes of death, Dr. Plattenburg was sure that he had a serial killer on his hands, which provoked a certain thrill in him.

Chapter 5

Bird watchers from around the world travel to Hong Kong for annual bird festivals. Hong Kong celebrates the migration that occurs each winter to the Mai Po marshes, which are located on the outskirts of the city. Mai Po is an estuary mangrove swamp where freshwater and saltwater intermeshed, forming a diverse habitat for an extraordinary variety of birds. One of Hong Kong's most prized ducks is the falcated teal–a dark-billed, white throated, green-headed beauty, treasured by the Asians for its remarkable exquisiteness. The teals breed in eastern Siberia before their annual fall migration through China and on to the Mai Po marshes. Because they are a treasure, they were spared from death during many avian flu outbreaks. Indeed, some scientists claim that compassion for the falcated teal ducks contributed to the outbreak in Hong Kong and Hanoi in 2003.

The 2003 outbreak began when a doctor from China traveled to Hong Kong for a family event. When he arrived, he complained of flu-like symptoms, and checked into a hotel in downtown Hong Kong. It turned out that the doctor either had SARS or the avian flu. He infected several airline personnel who traveled with him en route from China to Hong Kong, along with at least sixteen guests on his hotel floor. By the time the WHO Global Outbreak Alert and Response team pinpointed the doctor as the "patient zero," nearly four hundred people from five countries world-wide had been infected with his symptoms.

Chinese leaders, more worried about the impact of the SARS epidemic on trade and economic growth than about human health concerns, enforced strict censorship. When *Time* magazine covered the story, it triggered a political tsunami. Chinese officials finally reacted by sealing off villages and quarantining millions of people, but some say that the entire episode was a big cover up to the reality that an influenza pandemic was staring China in the face, and China was far more concerned with global perception than it was with a global cure.

An important distinction between SARS and the avian flu became clear during the 2003 outbreaks. Unlike influenza, SARS needs about five days to incubate, and doesn't become contagious for about a week after the onset of symptoms such as a cough. On the other hand, influenza, especially potent viral strains like H5N1, moves swiftly, and becomes highly contagious days before the onset of symptoms. Moreover, some spreaders of flu never have outward symptoms, making it virtually impossible to quarantine and contain.

The contagious nature of H5N1 would prove to be disastrous over the course of the next few weeks.

* * *

Elena Costea's body lay cold and stiff in the Hong Kong morgue. Her organs had been stripped from her like parts from a stolen car. To the general public, she had no name–she was just known as "H5N1–Hong Kong." But Dr. Jeffrey Plattenburg of the FBI knew virtually everything it was possible to know about Elena Costea. For example, he learned that she was a prostitute in Hong Kong and had lived there for approximately nine years. She lived in the slums of the city and had no family there to speak of. Investigators quickly learned that she lived in what one might consider a "co- op," but it was really a youth hostel for wayward ladies, managed by a group of low-class pimps who understood the value of "time-sharing" the prostitutes. Elena was recruited from a street corner in Bucharest, Romania, where she had turned tricks of her trade since childhood.

In Eastern Europe, child prostitution is a multi-million-dollar business, preying mostly on poor children ranging in age from thirteen to eighteen, many of them Russian, Romanian, Czech, Hungarian, Ukrainian, and Polish. There is a thriving market for young prostitutes, and at checkpoints along the German-Czech border, otherwise known as "kid prostitution alley," teenage girls from Eastern Europe, looking to escape poverty, hop into cabs with long-distance truck drivers. If the girls are lucky, they are sold to pimps in Germany, France or the Netherlands. If they are unlucky, they are shipped to Hong Kong or Bangkok. Elena was unlucky and was sold to a low-bidding Asian pimp. She was a beautiful teenager, with long, thick, brown hair and radiant turquoise eyes, exotic in looks and attitude. The pimp knew that he could get top price for her if he marketed her to high-end clients. But, as the high-end clients visiting Hong Kong from Western Europe and America sought younger and younger girls because of AIDS fears, her rank in his hierarchy diminished. Despite her beauty and poise, she began to earn less and less. The girls that serviced the high-class clientele were allowed to live in a decent apartment with running water and a private bathroom. As Elena's earning power diminished, her pimp forced her to live in the filthy co-op with the rest of the low-earners.

But one evening, Elena's luck changed. Or so she thought. A debonair man approached her on the street and asked her to join him for dinner at a nice restaurant on the top floor of a downtown Hong Kong high-rise. He treated her with respect and kindness during the meal, and even ordered delicacies for them to share. "Try this," he said, offering her a brown liquid drink. It tasted unpleasant to her, but she knew better than to complain. She swallowed the drink and forced a smile, then gulped a glass of fresh water. The other food they tried was enjoyable. Afterwards, as she expected, he took her back to his hotel for the obligatory pay-back. He explained that the hotel used to be an ancient temple, but had been bulldozed in Hong Kong's desire to become a modern city. He ran a hot bubble bath for her in a clean hotel room tub and soaped her radiant hair in conditioning shampoo–a luxury she'd never known. He carefully dried her body and carried her to his bed. He made love to her slowly, and as he kissed her inner thighs, he paused, grabbed an ink pen, and drew on her. She partially sat up and rested on her elbows, watching him carefully as he sketched. She did not ask questions. She knew better.

When he was finished with her, he left. He did not pay her. The next day, she slept in as late as the hotel clerk would allow. She was exhausted. The contrast of sleeping alone in a bed, on clean sheets, after years of sleeping in the same room with dozens of strangers, had been the best experience of her life. She did not want to leave her cocoon. However, the maid had come knocking a dozen times, as had the manager, and it was time to leave. But when Elena finally pulled herself from beneath the covers and started to make her way toward the bathroom, she did not feel well. She had a headache and nausea and, perhaps, a fever. Too much sleep? She wondered. She hadn't been sick since childhood, perhaps because her immune system had been exposed to such a wide variety of germs that she'd built up strong resistance. Why now? She lay back down on the bed for a minute.

When she heard banging on the door again, she tried to get up, but her head felt heavy. She needed to use the bathroom. She crawled on her hands and knees to the commode and slowly hoisted herself up. But the force of hoisting caused her to cough violently, so much so that she coughed up a clot of blood. The sight of the thick, red mucus on the floor of the bathroom made Elena sick to her stomach. She twisted sideways and knelt before the commode, throwing up twice with her eyes closed tight. She again hoisted herself up on the john to urinate, holding her head in her hands. She rested on the toilet for a time, until she heard the key enter the lock on her door. Horror overcame her when she opened her eyes. The toilet was stained with dark pools of blood. Had she started her period? Impossible. She was mid-cycle. Was she pregnant? A miscarriage perhaps? She would never know. She passed out naked on the floor of a hotel in downtown Hong Kong, alone, and would never again regain full consciousness.

* * *

Dr. Jeffrey Plattenburg found Elena Costea's history interesting, but what fascinated him most was the fact that her autopsy revealed that there were strange markings on her inner thigh. As a profiler for the FBI, Dr. Plattenburg looked for patterns. Anyone who knew him well used the same word to describe him: regimented. He followed the same exact routine every day. He got up at five thirty and went for a five mile run in his quaint Virginia neighborhood. He grabbed the morning paper on the way in the house after his run and set it next to the coffee pot. He switched on the automated coffee maker, which he'd prepared the night before with a fresh filter, fresh water and freshly-ground coffee, and then went upstairs to his bathroom for a shave and a shower. He lived alone because his physician- wife left him eight years prior for an intern she met while doing rounds. He missed his wife, but not enough to look for another one. After his shower, he got dressed in a navy or gray suit, a white, pressed shirt, and a muted tie, and went back downstairs for his black coffee, a bowl of oatmeal and the paper. He then drove the winding roads of Quantico to the United States Army Medical Research Institute of Infectious Diseases, also known as "YouSamRid," where he passed through strict security and parked in his unmarked spot. Three flights of stairs later, he gained retinal access to his laboratory, where he began work each day by scanning the profiling computer for new patterns in his open criminal investigations.

Dr. Plattenburg was thorough and methodical in his research. It had paid off with the BTK killer and with Ted Bundy. He typed in a list of research tasks for his assistant, Dr. Laura Weckesser, to complete. The list involved duck migration and specific Romanian genealogy. He would expect a full briefing by seventeen hundred at the latest, before she left work for the day.

Later that day, after he received a full debriefing from Dr. Weckesser, Dr. Plattenburg prepared a report and sent it to his boss, FBI Director Diana Weiss. Diana was a medium-sized woman with short, brown hair and dark eyes, and an intelligence quota comparable to Thomas Jefferson. She was quick-witted in every way, and after receiving Jeffrey's report, called him.

"Jeffrey, I think you are on to something with the pictographs on the inner thighs," Diana said. "I don't want to call alarm to this, in case it is mere coincidence, but for now, I'm putting you in charge of this investigation on behalf of the FBI. You may use whatever resources you deem necessary and appropriate to investigate these two outbreaks."

Jeffrey graciously accepted his assignment. He liked being in charge and had proven himself time and again to Diana. They enjoyed a very good working rapport, and he was not about to let her down. He would leave for Wyoming first, and then travel to Hong Kong.

* * *

Dr. Jocelyn Sharp had worked for the CDC for seventeen years before being promoted to Chief Virologist of the Special Pathogens Branch. She was short, with crew-cut blond hair and a wide smile. Her teeth were bleached white, though rarely visible beneath the mask she wore nearly around the clock. She was a stickler for protocol and nagged everyone in her path to always wear gloves, no matter what they were doing. She even went so far as to suggest that latex gloves should be worn in every kitchen in America during the cooking process, and recommended that families get in the habit of washing their hands and "gloving up" before each meal. Her two children were germophobes like her—they had to be in order to survive her protocol. Her husband, a high school football coach in Atlanta, was not quite so intrigued with germs. He regularly watched his Sunday NFL games with a bowl of chips on the coffee table and his free hand resting comfortably inside his sweatpants. Jocelyn had to leave the room when he reached for the chips.

When not obsessing over germs in her own household, Dr. Sharp was obsessing about global viral pandemics. In conjunction with the Armed Forces Institute and the Mount Sinai School of Medicine, she'd conducted and published research suggesting that a bird-flu pandemic could erupt in more ways than previously thought and could be as lethal, if not more lethal, than the 1918 Spanish flu. Her research concluded that some mutations of the 1918 virus could emerge, creating a viral strain different from the present H5N1 and the 1918 version. She and her team focused their study on pinpointing the particular pieces of the virus that caused it to be so virulent. Ideally, she hoped that their efforts would cause other researchers and drug companies to hone several versions of vaccines, so that if a pandemic occurred, a variety of ready-made formulas for vaccinations could be reproduced as part of a worldwide effort by all vaccine drug manufacturers to meet the needs of a global outbreak.

Dr. Sharp knew that there were risks associated with publishing the results of her tests; namely, that terrorists could get a hold of the blueprint of the virus, re-create it, and spread it. Nevertheless, Dr. Sharp felt that the benefits of deciphering the viral blueprint outweighed the terrorism risk.

Deciphering the codes to the viruses was paramount to her, and she felt strongly that her efforts would help drug manufacturers produce effective vaccinations, as opposed to spending time and money replicating her research. She felt that she was assisting in global R&D. However, many of her colleagues, including physicians from the National Influenza Center in Rotterdam, thought Dr. Sharp was arrogant and short-sighted, and that her approach unnecessarily risked equipping "viral-terrorists" with the recipe for warfare.

"Dr. Sharp's publication raises questions about how to keep the virus from escaping from a laboratory or falling into the hands of bioterrorists," one scientist said at a recent World Health Organization meeting in Geneva. "Not only has the virus now been created in a CDC lab, but its genetic information has been published in a database maintained by the National Institutes of Health. This is the equivalent to Fed-Ex-ing uranium to Osama bin Laden and waiting for the nuclear warhead to strike."

In response, Dr. Sharp told a *Time* magazine reporter that "our goal is to help other researchers and drug manufacturers track flu viruses to determine which mutations are significant and which are inconsequential. So far, we've discovered ten changes in amino acids that distinguish the 1918 virus from current avian flu bugs like H5N1, suggesting that the virus mutated on its own, without mixing with other viruses. We are working with many pharmaceutical companies in America, Asia and Europe, to see if we can produce generic vaccinations for the bid flu. We are also working with a Russian-based drug company named Tarirescu, which tracks wild bird migration in order to pinpoint the genesis of these viral outbreaks at the onset of cold and flu season. We must ensure that Americans have sufficient antiviral medication in case a global pandemic breaks out. Right now, we are not even close to stockpiling sufficient supplies."

The Wyoming outbreak, and the shortage of antiviral medication, illustrated that America was unprepared for an avian flu outbreak." If the outbreak had happened in a more densely populated city, chaos would have been certain. While it was true that the Wyoming outbreak was isolated and seemingly contained expediently and only fourteen people had died, no one knew about Forest Ranger David Thrift, and his rotting corpse on the ridge of Antelope Butte in the Big Horn Mountains of northern Wyoming. The mountain lions and birds of prey feasted on him, spreading contaminated feces to the elk and deer population. Being that it was hunting season, and hundreds of rifle-toting huntsman were ravaging the mountain forests of doe- eyed mammals, it would take only another few weeks for a new outbreak of the avian flu to erupt in Wyoming and Montana.

Chapter 6

Dr. Jeffrey Plattenburg boarded a plane from Ronald Reagan National Airport en route to Sheridan, Wyoming, via a connection in Denver. He missed his morning run, which didn't please him, and found himself seated next to a mother with a two-year-old screaming "lap child." The child wiped his runny nose with his filthy hand, and then managed to smear the snot all over Jeffrey's dress pants. Since he'd hoped to be in Wyoming for two days or less, he didn't pack another pair of dress pants. The child repeatedly knocked Jeffrey's tray table, and even went so far as to deliberately push some of the keys on his laptop. The child's mother acted like she didn't notice her son's naughty behavior, which frustrated him.

Jeffrey never questioned the fact that he didn't have children of his own. His ex-wife had two little rug rats with her new husband, and in all honesty, Jeffrey was relieved that he was not the father of her children. He couldn't wait for the plane to touch down in Denver. The bumpy, twin engine flight to Sheridan was a slice of heaven in comparison.

After Jeffrey arrived at Sheridan Memorial Hospital, a brick, two-story building with a beautiful view of the majestic Big Horn Mountains, he washed his hands fastidiously before putting on nitrile gloves, an impermeable apron, protective shoe covers, safety goggles, a space suit, and a disposable particulate respirator. Entering a biosafety zone wasn't new to him, but he always felt invaded the minute he walked through the door. He met with Dr. Fahrid first, who showed Jeffrey around, and then allowed him to inspect the medical charts of the patients who'd died from the outbreak.

Jeffrey was interested in the outbreak, but he was most interested in learning about Ana Bontierre. He wanted to know who she hung out with, whether she dated, and if she'd left behind any clues. As soon as he'd interviewed everyone in the hospital who knew anything about her, he quickly headed east of town, to the Bontierre's Spotted Horse Ranch.

* * *

Some of the most gorgeous plains country in Wyoming lies east of Sheridan, where old rural roads are lined with ranchland and winter wheat. In the fall, the green valley turns russet and the cottonwoods catch the fire of changing color, illuminating the horizon with shades of auburn, crimson, bronze, and yellow. As Jeffrey drove east, he could see the silhouette of the Rocky Mountains in his rearview mirror, delineated by rays of sunshine spraying through misty clouds. He loved the mountains and wished that he had more time to explore them during his trip. He'd traveled to Montana a few times with his father on trout fishing trips, and he remembered those times fondly. He missed his father. What would his father think of his profiling job? Searching the country for clues to solve murders, rapes, and other crimes. His dad worked in a coal mine in West Virginia, and was a simple man who enjoyed the outdoors.

As Jeffrey slowed through the tiny town of Spotted Horse, he noticed the lineup of pickup trucks with gun racks and cowboy hats parked out in front of the saloon. A beer sounded refreshing, but he was on the clock. Trailer homes stood next to nearly-collapsed farmhouses, and it seemed as if every dwelling sported satellite dishes alongside a pile of junk in the yard. He kept driving, now in a southeasterly direction, where the highway was lined with red scoria rock. He noticed a good deal of methane gas trucks passing by—and a number of huts for gas production along the side of the road. He'd read about the environmental nightmare that the methane gas development had caused in the area.

He saw a large, wooden archway an eighth-of-a-mile up ahead with iron lettering that read, "Spotted Horse Ranch." Two iron-cast statues of horses stood on each side of the archway. He turned right into the driveway and continued driving his rented Ford Expedition down a shale road. When he pulled up to the beautiful log home, three golden Labradors came charging to meet him. Behind the dogs walked a broken man–Mr. Bontierre. Jeffrey showed Mr. Bontierre his FBI credentials and explained the purpose of his visit. After being reassured that Jeffrey was not a reporter, Mr. Bontierre invited him inside and showed him around the house.

"This land has been in my family for over one hundred years. My grandparents were sheep herders and homesteaded this ranch. But this house is new–methane gas money. We get about sixty thousand a month in royalties from them pumps over yonder," he said, pointing to a large, metal warehouse on the horizon. Mr. Bontierre told Jeffrey about Ana, and how they adopted her from a Romanian orphanage, and how her two sisters still lived with him on the ranch. His words were broken with bouts of tears. "I don't know what I'm going to do without her."

After a long discussion about Ana, Jeffrey asked to speak with Jacqueline. "I'm sorry, but she isn't taking visitors. She's heavily sedated still, and I'm afraid she's not up to talking to anyone." Jeffrey asked if there was anyone else that could give him more information regarding Ana and her whereabouts prior to her death. An old boyfriend? College friends? Her sisters? Mr. Bontierre shook his head, claiming that he didn't know of anyone who had information, but recommended that he meet with their lawyer, Mary MacIntosh. Mr. Bontierre handed Jeffrey one of Mac's business cards and showed him to the door.

* * *

Mac had been in court all day arguing about a hotly contested title dispute on behalf of her new bank client. She was exhausted when she returned to her office. She immediately noticed the smell of burned coffee which drifted from the back corner of the break room–a smell that reminded her of childhood. The office was deserted and her assistant had apparently forgotten to turn off the afternoon pot of coffee. Mac begrudgingly cleaned up the break room, checked the mail, looked at her messages, returned a few calls, and planned to head home for an early bedtime. She heard that a snowstorm was on its way and she wanted to get up extra early the next morning for a good run before the storm hit. She had an email message from Gil, informing her that he was back in Russia on business, but hoped that he'd be able to wrap up things within a few weeks and head back to the peaceful serenity of Wyoming.

Mac smiled to herself while booting down her computer, ready to head home, when a tall, lean man in a dark business suit walked into the lobby.

"I'm sorry, but our office is closed for the day. You can call my secretary in the morning to schedule an appointment," Mac said. Jeffrey studied Mac's expression, memorizing everything he could about her face. He noticed her almond-shaped chestnut eyes framed in long lashes, her strong, high cheekbones, her full heart-shaped lips, her long wavy auburn hair, and the intensity of her stare. In his line of duty, it was a requisite to never forget a face. Hers would be easier than most to remember.

When Jeffrey gave Mac his FBI business card and told her the reason for his visit, Mac let out a compulsory sigh and agreed that they could talk, but only after she'd had a chance to go home, feed her cat, change into comfortable clothes, and have a bite for dinner. Since Jeffrey was staying at a nearby hotel, he quickly offered to meet her in the hotel restaurant and buy her dinner. Mac reluctantly agreed.

When she arrived at the Holiday Inn, Jeffrey was nervously waiting in the lobby. He, too, had changed into blue jeans and a soft, white, cotton shirt. He explained that he normally didn't conduct official business in blue jeans, but that a child had wiped his filthy hands on his pants during the flight.

"Dr. Plattenburg, clean blue jeans are considered proper business attire in certain parts of Wyoming," Mac laughed, "and besides, you look more comfortable. I know I am." She smiled and followed him to the café. As they ate, they discussed Ana.

"First of all, you can call me Jeffrey." Mac agreed. "Next, tell me about Medicine Wheel, where Ana's body was originally found." Mac told him about the history of medicine wheels in general, and that although geologists still aren't sure of their use or meaning, they were likely constructed by American Indians for spiritual reasons or for use in keeping track of the days of the month.

"What was Ana doing up there?" he asked. Mac explained that no one knew why she was there or how she got there, and that both of the

Forest Service men who found her were unavailable for interview. "What does 'unavailable' mean?" Jeffrey asked.

"Ronnie One Feather died from this virus. David Thrift disappeared after the sheriff quizzed him a little about Ana. As you can imagine, he is the main suspect, but no one has heard from him. With the sheriff dying, the town in quarantine, and a thousand media folks running around with cameras rolling, I doubt they're going to find him anytime soon. My best advice is that you check with the U.S. Forest Service–at least they can give you a look at his personnel file. I am heading up there in the next day or two for the same reason. Ana's mother, Jacqueline Bontierre, hired me to find out who killed her daughter. So far, I haven't been very successful in finding clues. Ana literally disappeared a few days before her death."

Mac gave him directions to drive up the mountain so that he could examine Medicine Wheel and meet with the Forest Service.

Jeffrey explained that he was an avid runner and wanted to know if there were any good trails in town for an early morning break-out. "I love to run early. Mind if I join you?" Mac asked. A man of structure who never ran with anyone else, Jeffrey reluctantly agreed to meet her in the lobby at five thirty for a crisp, five-mile loop.

* * *

The air was balmy the next morning–almost Chinook-like. This was a sure sign that the forecasted snowstorm was on its way. Mac met Jeffrey in the hotel lobby and she drove him to the trailhead for their run. The sun was cresting in the east, and the sky was cherry-colored at the horizon, and gradually turned to cantaloupe, then peach, then lemon, then a light blue. "It is beautiful," Jeffrey said, admiring the illuminated snow-peaked mountains in front of them and the woman standing beside him.

"And it is so quiet," Mac offered. She loved the peace and tranquility of the morning. The only noise was a flock of geese honking overhead, flying south in a V-formation.

Forty minutes into their run, Jeffrey was gasping for breath. He was used to running at sea level, and was feeling the effects of exercising at three thousand feet elevation. He tried to conceal his effort to breathe, but Mac noticed. She didn't doubt his level of fitness, and was slightly amused at his drive to keep pace with her. He asked her a number of rapid-fire questions, keeping the burden of talking on her shoulders. Mac told him about her law practice and her relationship with Harry, her law partner. She explained that she went to the police academy after college and loved the forensic training, but that she hated weapons training and that was how she decided to go to law school. They talked mostly about careers, and then the conversation turned to Ana's death. Mac told him what she knew about the Bontierre family.

After their run, Jeffrey asked that she wait for a minute in the hotel lobby while he ran up to his room. He came back to the lobby and gave her another business card. This card included his direct line and home phone number. He would be leaving town in a few days, and wanted her to stay in touch, especially if she learned anything more about Ana. As usual, Jeffrey was keenly focused on the case, but for the first time in a very long time, his interest in a certain beautiful woman also had his attention. Normally, he wasn't so forward, but he couldn't seem to help himself around Mac. Her smile was infectious.

"How can you leave town under the quarantine rules?" Mac asked. "Media folks are making a big stink that they have to stay until the quarantine is lifted. Since people aren't dropping dead as quickly this week as they were last week, the media people are bored here. But you can leave?"

"FBI privilege. And now I get to take two Stiflu tablets a day to prevent the onset of symptoms. A job perk—or drawback, depending how you look at it."

Mac studied Jeffrey as he talked. He spoke with confidence, yet he was humble. They talked for another hour before they parted ways, and as Mac walked out of the lobby of his hotel, she smiled peacefully as the snow gently fell on the tips of her eyelashes. Her grandmother once told her, "Your eyes are the window to your soul. Snowflakes that stick to your eyelashes are guardian angels peering in." Mac wondered what her guardian angels were seeing.

* * *

On his way out of town to investigate Medicine Wheel, Jeffrey called Mac at her office. He enjoyed their run together and wondered if she would consider accompanying him up the mountain. He didn't know his way around, and the Rocky Mountains looked daunting to him. He didn't have much time to investigate the Ana Bontierre matter before he needed to be in Hong Kong, and explained to her that she would be doing the government a big favor. Mac had a ton of work to do, but intuition told her that helping Jeffrey was more important, and she needed to make the trip anyway, for Jacqueline's sake. With Jeffrey's FBI privileges, she would be allowed access across the investigatory tape. She agreed to join him, but she needed to go to her apartment first and change into warm clothes.

Jeffrey drove Mac to her apartment and followed her up the zigzagged concrete steps to the second floor of the brick building. He watched as her delicate hand slipped the key into the lock. She was graceful, he noticed, yet determined. Ted met them at the entry, meowing for attention. Mac gave him a pat on the head as she passed. She told Jeffrey to make himself comfortable while she changed clothes. Jeffrey looked around her apartment, noting the vast quantity of photographs displayed. He picked up a few and studied the faces, trying to determine what roles these faces played in her life.

Her living room was painted a pale green color, which offset the tan, leather furniture. One accent chair was covered in a bright chenille pattern of fruit in baskets. The green, red, brown, yellow, and purple shades picked up the various colors of the artwork in the room. *Monet*, he wondered?

The kitchen was a bright, cheery yellow and was clean. A poster of a woman decked out in running clothes with the "Just Do It" slogan framed the wall adjacent to the refrigerator.

"I'll be out in a second," Mac's voice bellowed from the bedroom. Jeffrey ventured toward her voice. Her bedroom door was cracked open, and he could see the crimson red wall that framed her queen-sized bed. The accent wall to the right of the bed was a honey-tone–soft, yet warm, picking up morning light. Large candles lined the window seal and they looked new–unused.

Mac emerged from the master bathroom in jeans and a red turtleneck. A warm jacket was draped over her arm, and she carried a small, black leather bag. "Just in case we get stuck," she said. Jeffrey nodded at her. *If only I could be so lucky,* he thought to himself.

They drove up the mountains, engrossed in constant conversation. Mac watched as he surveyed Medicine Wheel, intrigued by his deliberate mode of investigation. Jeffrey was certain that Ana's body had been left at this spiritual location for a reason—a message from the killer. He told Mac about other serial killer investigations that he'd been involved with and what he'd come to learn from his experiences. His stories fascinated her.

"Why are you convinced that this is a serial killer? Couldn't it just be this mysterious avian flu or some other virus?"

"The 'signatures' on the victims tells me that there is a perp. A virus doesn't leave a sketch. It might leave bruising or splotching, but not artistic- style sketches. There is human involvement."

"You sound convinced."

"I am. I've been doing this for a long time. There is no question in my mind. That's not to say that I've ruled out a virus, but a human is involved."

When Jeffrey dropped Mac at her office late that night, she felt a certain pang of loneliness. She liked him. She didn't feel chills or tingling down her spine. Instead, she felt the warmth, caring and respect of friendship. She vowed to keep in touch.

She logged into her email before going home for the night. She had an email from Gil.

> *My dearest Mac: Continents divide us, but someday soon we will reunite. The smell of your hair is fragrance in my dreams. Love, Gil*

Torn between Gil's poetic prose and Jeffrey's intriguing intelligence, Mac opted not to respond to the email. It was late and she was tired. With the killer flu lurking about, she couldn't afford to let her immunity weaken. She chose an early bedtime with a steaming cup of peppermint tea.

* * *

Dr. Karen Kokinda, a tall, thin woman, hated to travel. Unfortunately for her, it was a necessary part of her job as director of the National Institute of Allergy and Infectious Diseases. It wasn't that she didn't like to go places, because she enjoyed learning the history and culture of different nations. Her problem with travel was the airlines. She hated to fly. She hated to wait in lines at airports with angry travelers, and she hated waiting for an hour to board a flight, and she hated being in a cramped space next to annoying strangers for the duration of the flight, and she hated to see whether her luggage made it on the same flight that she did. The whole process stressed her out. But what she hated most about flying was the high probability of catching the flu during the flight. As a virologist, she knew how germs circulated in an airplane, and she was keenly aware of documented cases of one person with a chronic virus infecting dozens of strangers on an airplane. The ripple effect of a spreading virus often caused her not to sleep the night before she was scheduled to fly.

When she learned of the outbreak in Hong Kong, starting with patient Elena Costea, she knew that soon she would be on a very long flight across the Pacific. As luck would have it, she had to sit next to a woman of middle- eastern descent who was quite obviously ill with some respiratory virus. The coughing bouts started the minute Dr. Kokinda sat down, and they lasted until she waited in line in customs in Hong Kong. The only reprieve from the coughing was when Dr. Kokinda left her seat and hid in the airplane lavatory. She took an extra vitamin C and sprayed her nose with an antiviral mist every chance she could. It was a long flight.

An expert in the correlation between bird migration and flu, Dr. Kokinda was one of the first people called when the CDC learned of Elena Costea's death. Hong Kong had been a SARS and bird flu hot spot for years, and Dr. Kokinda was rather intrigued with how migration caused Hong Kong to constantly be on the aquatic bird influenza radar screen. In 1997, she traveled there with CDC virologists to account for the deadly outbreak. She noted the extreme weather that year—the wettest year in Hong Kong's meteorological record, with massive El Nino conditions which brought typhoons and torrential rain to southern China throughout the latter part of the summer. Migration was altered and poultry excrement was washed away. When the rains diminished in early November 1997, the virus came back, and it seemed to have a stronger punch, as if mutation might have occurred during the El Nino period.

At that point in history, Hong Kong had just been returned to Chinese sovereignty. There was world-wide concern whether the new Chinese government would allow freedom of press. The random nature of the human outbreaks, coupled with the fact that at least twenty percent of the city's chickens had dropped dead, was the focus of media attention. Hong Kong's local government could not make public health decisions for all of China, but it issued local warnings. And then the local officials issued orders for a poultry killing spree.

Dr. Kokinda saw the poultry killing first-hand, and could account for the horrific display of blood and the overwhelming stench of death. One and a half millions birds were destroyed within the city limits, and many thousands outside the city were killed as well. To Dr. Kokinda, an environmentalist at heart, it was sickening.

When Dr. Kokinda got off her flight, she looked back at the sick woman who sat next to her on the flight. How do pandemics spread? Airlines have to be a major contributor. Thousands of people travel internationally every day. If one person is infected with a new strain of H5N1, and he or she flies from Hong Kong to Rome to London to New York, it is mathematically possible that he or she could infect ten thousand people within a twenty-four hour period. If one passenger can infect thousands of people, what about the migratory birds? If a flock of infected geese landed in a busy park in downtown Hong Kong, or Bangkok, or London, or any other major industrial center, what is to stop the spread of virus?

By the time she arrived at the Hong Kong hospital to meet with the medical examiner that had performed the autopsy on Elena, Dr. Kokinda learned that both the hotel maid and desk clerk manager had been admitted with flu-like symptoms. Stiflu was being administered to both of them, but the treating physician didn't seem to think that the medicine was helping. Both victims' conditions were worsening by the hour. Several other medical staff personnel who had been on duty when Elena Costea was treated were also hospitalized with symptoms. The patients were put in quarantine, and a health warning was quickly issued. For the next several days, every cough, sneeze, sore throat and fever was a source of angst for the population at large.

Headlines around the world read: "Fear of Bird Flu Builds in Eastern Europe." "Orders for Bird Flu Drug Soar." "Links Found in Bird Virus and 1918 Killer Flu." "Reich to Discuss Deals to Boost Stiflu Production." "Inside the Race to Find Vaccine for Avian Flu."

Dr. Kokinda read the headlines from her laptop computer in her Hong Kong high rise hotel. She worried that the headlines would cause a worldwide panic. She checked her email, responding to the concerns of her colleagues, defending her hypothesis about duck migration. She eventually made it through her email list, clicking on the final email from Mac.

Dr. Kokinda: It was a pleasure to meet you in Wyoming. I am sorry that our Meeting was under such terrible circumstances. I've been hired by Jacqueline Bontierre to hunt down the killer(s) of Ana. Based on headlines, is it still your position that duck migration is causing the spread of the avian flu? I met Dr. Jeffrey Plattenburg of the FBI, who believes there is a serial killer involved. Do you think it is a possibility?

Sincerely,

Mac

Dr. Kokinda responded to Mac, attaching copies of some of her research and supporting data. Dr. Kokinda was well acquainted with Jeffrey Plattenburg. She didn't respond to Mac's query about his supposition.

Meanwhile, based on the headlines and the growing hysteria proliferated by the media, thousands of people world-wide fled to their local pharmacies, demanding Stiflu. Despite Dr. Kokinda's migration warnings, Hong Kong had not stockpiled enough of the antiviral medication. World health officials were scrambling. Stiflu was introduced in 1999 to treat patients with the common flu. Demand was relatively modest until it was identified as one of the only drugs effective against the bird flu.

Yoshihiro Ito, a short Japanese man who served as Director General of the World Health Organization, met with a spokeswoman for Reich Holding AG, informing her that Reich might be ordered to allow both governments and private companies to produce the antiviral drug Stiflu under licensing agreements, despite the fact that Reich held the exclusive patent on the drug. "Reich is putting its own interests ahead of world health," Ito said. "The World Health Organization has the right under international trade treaties to break patents during health emergencies. This might be one of those times, I'm afraid."

The Reich spokeswoman countered by explaining, "Making Stiflu is a complex process that would take generic drug makers at least two or three years to master. This drug is quite difficult to manufacture. There is a potentially 'explosive' chemical step in the production process. Without giving away the farm, let's just say that this particular drug cannot be produced generically. We are not hiding the ball or being greedy, as some have suggested. We are being straight-forward with the notion that not all medications of a biologic nature can be accurately reproduced cheaply and quickly."

Ito said in response that, "Chinese and Indian drug companies claim that they would be able to manufacture the drug in far less time that Reich said it would take. International drug patent infringement is contentious, as we all know. Many public health advocates are still angry over the slow pace at which AIDS drugs were made available to poor people in underdeveloped parts of the world, and while drug makers are adamant that effective patent protection is essential to the development of new drugs, we are savvy enough to know that there is a fine line between the protection and expense of research and development versus the need to ensure global health standards."

In the midst of the ongoing battles between health organizations and the drug companies, and the finger-pointing that was beginning to happen around the world because of the lack of stockpiling of antiviral avian flu drugs, eight thousand people were confirmed dead within the first week of Elena's demise. The number would have been much higher if not for the fact that Hong Kong officials were experienced in minimizing outbreaks. Bangkok officials were not so well equipped.

Chapter 7

Life in Kanchanaburi province, west of the capital city of Bangkok, Thailand, was rural and quiet in comparison to the city. The very epitome of the modern, sweltering Asian metropolis, Bangkok is to Thailand what Paris is to France. What differentiates Bangkok from Paris is the heat, noise, traffic, and pollution that obliterate a tourist's desire to stay in downtown Bangkok for long. Outside the city, temples, museums and incredible culture attract people from around the world. But downtown Bangkok attracts a different kind of traveler–one looking for an endless variety of good restaurants, discos, heavy metal pubs, and the red light district of hookers comprised primarily of child sex slaves.

Lucretia Sulea was stolen from her mother's womb at Ploiesti Maternity Hospital in Romania. Her mother was told that Lucretia died during child birth, and was handed a death certificate simply recording that "baby Sulea, female, aborted fetus weighing 1000g, deceased, premature birth, dead at birth." Behind its drab concrete walls, something sinister had been going on at Ploiesti. For years, infants were officially registered dead and were supposedly cremated without documentary proof. A decade or more later, many children who were registered "dead at birth" turned up, alive and well, in orphanages and in the sex slave trade. Frantic investigations by the Romanian health minister were undertaken, and arrests were made throughout the country. Hospital staff was questioned for possible culpability about the alleged baby deaths, and witnesses came forward, identifying members of a mammoth enterprise in child trafficking.

Lucretia Sulea was a victim of child trafficking, and was sold to a sex slave trader in Bangkok. The only thing she'd ever known was that she didn't belong in this city of strangers. She didn't know how to read or write and spoke Central Thai dialect. She had never visited the famous temples like the Wat Phra That Lampang Luang, or swam in the Gulf of Thailand. She never knew of a mother or father, and lived all of her seventeen years in a compound with other children, who also were orphan sex slaves. They lived in a gray, windowless, cement barrack. The rectangular barrack had eight caged rooms, each opening into the center compound. There was a hole in the ground in each of the eight rooms where the girls urinated and defecated. Each room had four wire bunk beds with no mattress or pillow. Each night, Joeng, the owner of his girls, would summon a select few from their prison-like world and march them down Triphet Road, and over to the Chao Phraya River, where men gathered in the Pak Khlong Market, shopping for their evening entertainment. Joeng sold his girls for the night and collected the money. Whether he ever saw the girls again was of no concern to him. But they usually came back to the compound for food and shelter.

Lucretia, a five foot ten inch girl with wiry brown hair and brown eyes, was selected that hot, sticky night by Joeng, and she followed silently behind him on their way to the market. She was not a very pretty girl, unlike many of the exotic Thai slaves, so she generally was one of the last girls sold for the night. But this night, she was lucky. A handsome man sought her out and paid top dollar for her. Joeng was pleased. He said that she would get rewarded at the compound. Lucretia went with her man for a long taxi ride to his hotel, a fancy two-story inn which had formerly been some kind of temple or spiritual hall before being converted. She had never been taken to a nice hotel before. She usually had to perform fellatio on men under city bridges, or had the discourtesy of being slammed up against a garbage bin in a back- street alley. Being escorted up a fancy elevator and into a posh room with clean sheets was a first. He allowed her to undress herself, and even pulled back the bed sheets. Lucretia lay down and breathed in deeply, appreciating the clean smell of bleach and the smoothness of the bed. He was a little rough with her when he entered, but not as bad as some of the other men. Afterwards, he allowed her to share some of his food, which she graciously accepted, and devoured like a hungry wolf. Joeng did not feed his girls well. Lucretia had never eaten off china and had never tasted some of the delicious food he offered. She drank some kind of dark liquid from a tall, thin glass, and it made her feel a little queasy. They could not communicate with words, but his gentle nature assured her that he was a kind soul.

After eating, he motioned for her to recline, and as he gently spread her legs, he crafted some form of artwork on her inner thigh. This seemed odd to her, but it wasn't painful, and he seemed so intent on getting it to look a certain way. When he was done, he motioned for her to get dressed, which she did. He walked her to the elevator, escorted her in, and pushed the "L" button, sending her to the lobby.

It took her a long time to find her way back to the compound that night. She'd never been that far away before. She was tired, and had stomach pains. Joeng gave her a few hours rest when she got home early from the rich man. She was grateful to the man who'd paid so much for her, because sleep was all that her body seemed to want. She felt weary and achy and hot.

Several hours later, Joeng summoned her again, hoping that Lucretia's suitor would be at the market again, but he wasn't. Lucretia was the last girl sold—this time to a forty-eight-year-old farmer from the Kanchanaburi province. The farmer came to the city once a month for a "conjugal visit," and he was not picky with whom he spent his time. As usual, he walked his girl down the banks of the river, under the Phra Pokklao Bridge, and first asked for her to perform oral sex on him. When he was satisfied, he then lifted her skirt and penetrated her from behind, and when he was finished, he told the girl to leave. He did not like to look at her face.

When the farmer returned on the train to Kanchanaburi, he felt like he was coming down with a cold. His eyes were watery and his throat felt tight, and by the time he arrived at his depot, he was coughing heavily.

After leaving the farmer, Lucretia walked back to the compound, but this time, it took her much longer than usual. She felt sick to her stomach and vomited in the middle of the market. She fainted once, and a few people came to her aid and helped her to her feet. She continued her walk, falling ill another three times along the way. When she finally got to her cage-like room, she crawled on top of her wire bunk and fell into a deep, fever-induced sleep. She awoke suddenly, vomiting all over the floor of her room. The seven other girls yelled at her, and beckoned to be let out of the smelly cell. Joeng was furious when he saw that she hadn't made it to the excrement hole, and slapped Lucretia hard across the mouth and nose. Her nose shattered, spewing blood all over Joeng, which infuriated him further. He kicked her in the stomach and told her to leave the compound at once.

Lucretia could not move. She tried to gasp for air, but felt like she was suffocating, and fell to the ground, in the middle of her pile of vomit. Joeng grabbed her by her long, dark hair and dragged her across the courtyard as he yelled Thai curse words at the top of his lungs. He kicked her limp body into the street, turned and closed the compound door behind him. She was ugly and too old anyway. At age seventeen. He'd have to contact his friend and buy another seven-year-old.

Lucretia lay in the street for hours until daylight broke in downtown Bangkok. As the hustle of the city of over six million people started to buzz, a woman and her husband saw Lucretia sprawled out in a pool of blood. They called the police. Many people gathered and tried to help her while waiting for the ambulance to arrive. She was taken to Phayathai Hospital where, after several attempts at revival, she died in a blackened pool of blood. She was transferred to the Adventist Hospital, where an autopsy could be performed. When the medical examiner removed her garments, he found a strange tattoo on her inner right thigh and a rolled-up death certificate stitched into her underwear. The doctor was confused to learn that this seventeen-year-old presumed prostitute had been declared dead at birth in Romania. But confusion wouldn't adequately describe what he saw when he opened her up. Inside, her organs looked like beet soup. Her lungs were a liquid mass, as was her liver and heart. He called in every expert in his field in Bangkok to look at her. Not one of them knew what could have caused such a horrific death. Blood samples were sent to the lab.

A short time later, when the medical examiner learned that she was contaminated with the H5N1 flu virus, he called the consulate, who, in turn, called WHO Director General Yoshihiro Ito, who was in the middle of a pandemic planning meeting with world leaders in Geneva, Switzerland.

* * *

When Dr. Kokinda learned that Lucretia Sulea, patient zero in the Bangkok outbreak, had ingested duck within twenty-four hours of death, her fears regarding migration patterns were confirmed. She believed that ducks must be the carriers of the virus this time–not chickens as in the past H5N1 epidemics. The Wyoming outbreak had been minimalized, with only a few dozen deaths confirmed. The quarantine in such a small town had worked, it seemed. The Hong Kong outbreak was bad, but not as bad as Dr. Kokinda feared it might be. Thousands of patients were being treated in the hospital with Stiflu, but supplies were limited.

The Bangkok outbreak appeared to be escalating by the minute. Within ninety-six hours of Lucretia's death, over two hundred people had checked into city hospitals with flu-like symptoms. Within one week of Lucretia's death, seventy percent of the population in the Kanchanaburi province, including the farmer, was dead. With over six million people living in Bangkok, Thailand's Council of Agriculture ordered the mass slaughter of migratory birds within the city limits. The Council also declared that all poultry raised for sale must be tested for the H5N1 virus.

Like Hong Kong, Stiflu was in short supply in Thailand, and government leaders were asking other countries to share some of their vaccine supply. Leaders in Laos, Cambodia, Vietnam, and Malaysia were reluctant to relinquish any of their similarly small supply, in case their country suffered a similar plague.

WHO Director General Yoshihiro Ito, a short, stout, Japanese doctor, called a meeting among top virologists and scientists to determine what course of action should be followed with respect to the outbreaks. In the past, especially in 1997, most of the human deaths were linked to contact with sick birds. But experts now feared the virus had mutated into a form that could be transmitted between humans.

All chickens that had been tested in Wyoming, Hong Kong and Bangkok had shown no signs of H5N1. If the chicken population was healthy and not the source of the virus, then what? That was the question Yoshihiro Ito posed to world leaders in the study of infectious diseases. Dr. Karen Kokinda voiced her opinion regarding ducks. The National Influenza Center didn't have a solution, but they blamed Dr. Jocelyn Sharp of the CDC for the dissemination of information to the public regarding the source of the 1918 Spanish flu pandemic. Dr. Sharp stood straight—her five foot frame stiff, and explained that her research was helping drug companies develop vaccines. "Stiflu isn't working as effectively as anticipated in this case. Or haven't any of you noticed? The world is relying on Stiflu to save us from H5N1, but it is not working here. My opinion is that the virus has mutated already and we are now seeing the consequences of not having a wide variety of vaccines to deal with mutated strains."

"Like I've been saying for years, Stiflu is a seatbelt," Dr. Ito said. "It helps to minimize the impact of the wreck, but it doesn't stop the wreck from happening–"

"I have serious problems with Stiflu," Dr. Sharp interrupted. "First, two doses are required to spark a robust immune reaction. In a pandemic, authorities would rely on emergency ring vaccination, rushing vaccines to people around the site of the outbreak. Anything more than one dose isn't practical–"

"The issue isn't whether Stiflu is effective against every strain," Dr. Brashires said. "I am the president of Cipla Pharmaceuticals, and we have been able to crack the Stiflu code on a generic level. Despite the fact that Reich claims that Stiflu is too difficult for other companies to manufacture due to its 'explosive' chemical step in the production process, we have been able to manufacture the generic drug."

"Even if you have cracked the Stiflu code," Dr. Jocelyn Sharp interrupted again, this time her face flushed crimson, "it does not mean that this is our miracle drug. We need to figure out whether the H5N1 strain has *mutated!* This strain is melting the insides of its victims. Melting them! Their livers and lungs are mush. They suffocate on their own blood! We cannot get bogged down on stockpiling antiviral meds that may or may not work. We need to find out what strain we are dealing with and see if we can very, very quickly, work together as a global scientific community and develop an antiviral medicine for *this strain!*"

Loud discussions broke out in the large conference room overlooking the high-shooting fountain of Lake Geneva. The Swiss Alps framed the lake, making the picture-perfect meeting room seem tranquil. However, the discussions, arguments and compromises taking place among the world leaders in infectious diseases were anything but tranquil. Voices grew louder and louder until finally, a man standing alone in the back of the room smashed two wine glasses together in a loud clatter. Glass shattered, and everyone turned in his direction.

"Good afternoon," he started, nodding at Dr. Sharp. "I am Dr. Jeffrey Plattenburg, with the Federal Bureau of Investigation in Quantico, Virginia. I am a profiler. My specialty is serial killers. I've been tracking them in the United States for years. Right now, I am especially interested in a certain killer whom I believe is using bioterrorism as a murder weapon."

Jeffrey approached Yoshihiro Ito's table and shook his hand. The silence in the conference room was deafening. Every set of eyes was on him as Jeffrey walked to the podium and began talking. "Dr. Ito asked that I join you today to share vital information that might help us solve this problem before a global pandemic strikes." At this point, every scientist was leaning forward, hanging on Jeffrey's word like cats on a rope. "It seems to me that you are focused on birds. I think that your focus is misguided. I believe that we should be focusing on the 'patients zero' in each outbreak. Who are these girls, and what do they have in common? Why are they showing common viral symptoms despite their geographic differences? How is it that three young women can be casualties from the same strain of H5N1 in a ten-day period of time without rational explanation?" Attendees of the meeting exchanged glances, whispering comments among themselves. "If we focus on these women, and determine what, or who, is causing them to become sick, we might be able to stop this before this virus becomes a global threat."

"You are supposing a lot, aren't you doctor?" a voice stated from the back of the room. "Are you completely ruling out autopsy reports that conclusively prove that these victims died of the avian flu?"

"I am not ruling out anything. In fact, I am assuming that the autopsy reports are true. I am simply suggesting that we broaden our scope with respect to the means and manner in which these young women have been infected."

With that, the conference broke into discussion groups. Meanwhile in India, a predator stalked another victim.

Chapter 8

Bombay (Mumbai) was famous as the pulsating commercial hub of Maharashtra, India. But its unique treasure lies in Aurangabad, with temples as ornate and exceptional as the Taj Mahal. The thirty Buddhist temples of Ajanta date from around 200 B.C. to A.D. 650, and are celebrated for their paintings.

A young Buddhist named Jahal took a walk to Ajanta late in the afternoon in early November. He could feel the temperature dropping, and knew that he probably should head back to the monastery, but something compelled him to walk further. His little sister was calling him from the heavens, where she played peacefully with her God. When she needed her brother, she called upon him in her angelic ways. Today, she asked him to meet her in Ajanta, inside the Kailash Temple, a cathedral twice the area of the Parthenon in Athens and nearly twice as tall. Jahal kept walking. When he entered the Kailash Temple, he bowed low and long. He felt the sacredness. He rose, walked forward, and bowed again. As he approached the shrine, he knelt and graced his head to the floor, raising his hands over his head in unison, offering himself to Lan Na.

He thought he heard his sister whisper to him, but the voice was not familiar. He prayed deeper. He heard her again. This time, he realized that the voice was earthly. He looked to his right and saw her, kneeling in front of another monk. The monk's orange hood was raised, and Jahal could not see his face. He watched as the monk motioned for the woman to drink from a chalice that he held in his hand. She drank, and then grimaced. He tenderly wiped her face with a white cloth, then nodded for her to drink again. She complied. Then he gently guided her to the floor, where he lifted her long, black skirt. Jahal was shocked. He'd never seen a woman's leg. He laid his head down on the cold temple floor and watched as his fellow monk spread the woman's legs apart. She moaned slightly as his hands touched her. Jahal was not sure of the monk's intentions. Her moans were soft, yet almost like pleading. When the monk reached inside the woman, she cried out, and when he lifted his robe and thrust himself on top of her, he covered her mouth to cripple her screams. This went on for some time, and eventually the woman stopped fighting. When the monk took an ink pen from beneath his cloak and began his artwork, she winced. Was this sex, Jamal wondered? He did not know. Jahal felt ashamed for watching, but it excited him. He knew he would repent to Lan Na for this.

The masked monk suddenly stood up and walked out of the temple, leaving the woman on the floor. She was whimpering, like a puppy, and she curled up into a partially-naked, round ball.

Jahal was afraid to approach her. He didn't know whether he would be in violation of his vows if he did. But his sister's voice encouraged him toward her, to help her. When Jahal touched her shoulder, she flinched. He did not know what to do with her, yet her eyes pleaded for help. She motioned for him to take her down the mountain, so he did. She walked behind him the first part of the journey, not uttering a sound. They seemed to be communicating without speaking. Apparently, the girl wanted to go to Bombay. Jahal walked her there. Part way, she vomited, and collapsed in the dirt. Jahal picked her up and carried her. She felt hot, feverish, perhaps, and her cough sounded more like a sputtering, guttural, choking noise as they got closer to the city.

When they arrived in the bustling city, the girl kept making a cross with her fingers and motioning to him. Jahal did not understand. She made a gesture for a drink of water, and Jahal nodded. He walked her to a public garden where she could get a drink. She lapped up water like a tiger in the jungle, and when she was done, she waved to him and then walked on. He did not understand whether she wanted him to follow or not, but he knew that he needed to get back to the monastery. Jahal walked back up the hill to the cloistered men with whom he shared silence.

* * *

Gil continued to email Mac on a regular basis. His prose grew in poetic intensity, as did his suggestion that Mac join him in Europe for a vacation. Mac communicated back to Gil, explaining her commitment to help Jacqueline find Ana's killer. She explained that once the case was resolved, she might consider his offer. He reminded her of his promise to show her to Voronet in Romania. *It is a rare gem, much like you,* Gil said.

* * *

"We have another outbreak," Jocelyn Sharp announced to her team. "India this time. Over one thousand people dead in a week, and there is no sign of containment. An entire monastery has been wiped out, along with a ward of medical personnel. Patient zero's name is Florentina Ursa."

* * *

Florentina Ursa was living well in Bombay. She had been hired by an English family to take care of their three children. She had no formal qualifications to be a nanny, but she had helped raise dozens of girls in the orphanage, and the house mother in the orphanage had depended on her for years. When families from London and other cities around the world were relocated to Bombay as part of job transfers, they were desperate to find good childcare. Florentina, an orphan herself, was a very intelligent young girl. A victim of the child sex trade in Eastern Europe, she found herself on the streets in Bombay. When she first arrived at the gates of the orphanage, begging for work, Raima, the house mother, ignored her. Girls knocked on the front door of the orphanage every day begging for a place to stay. But for some reason, Florentina seemed special. Raima could see the intelligence in Florentina's eyes, and knew that she should take in this dark skinned, light- haired beauty. Raima's intuition paid off, as Florentina quickly learned to speak four additional languages from the other orphans and rapidly adapted to reformatory life. At age twelve, Florentina had learned how to cook, clean, and most importantly, read. She read everything she could get her hands on, and read to the other little girls at night, keeping them happy and entertained.

When the well-to-do Walsh family from London accepted a high- paying job transfer to Bombay, Mrs. Walsh's first consideration was her children. She was told that there was a seventeen-year-old girl from an orphanage that could assist her. At first, Mary Walsh refused to even consider the notion that an orphan street girl could take care of her children in a proper English manner, but Mrs. Walsh's ex-pat connection convinced her to give Florentina a try. The Walsh children fell in love with Florentina the minute they met her. She brought books from the orphanage with her, and read to the children in proper English. She even told them a make-believe story about a girl who traveled to India on a special "spice magic carpet." The Walsh family happily adopted Florentina and, with her assistance, adjusted to the changes Bombay offered.

Bombay is the capital of Maharashtra and the economic powerhouse of India. The most affluent and industrialized city in India, it is the stronghold of Indian foreign trade and free enterprise. Pharmaceutical and petrochemical companies flourish here, as well as textile manufacturers and financial corporations. Bombay is an island connected by bridges to the mainland of India, and was once merely a swamp. As it developed as a trading port, its economic significance became clear. Swampland was converted to industrial warehouses. Major companies from around the world recognized the ease in which they could conduct business in this urbanized port, as well as the cost- effective labor market, and established production facilities. Like the Walsh family, thousands of families in similar situations were transferred to India every year, where they enjoyed the benefits of rich culture, good schools and a stable government.

One of Florentina's favorite places to take the Walsh children, ages three, five and nine, was Victoria Gardens. The gardens, north of the city center, contained Bombay's zoo. Florentina and the children loved watching the exotic animals, but she hated the fact that they were confined in cages. The cages made her think back on her horribly impoverished childhood, and her hell as a child sex slave. Not far from the gardens and the zoo was an area called Chor Bazaar. Known to locals as "The Cages," Chor Bazaar was Bombay's red light district. The young women and teenage girls who worked there stood behind metal-barred doors, and it was there, at age nine, that Florentina was indoctrinated into the repulsive and unspeakable life of a child prostitute.

She was grateful for her job with the Walsh family and never took it for granted, knowing what her life might be like if she was ever forced back on the streets. She felt so lucky to live in a nice home, eat good food, and be surrounded by love. Florentina thought about her good fortune often, and it always left a warm smile on her face.

One day, while she was reading in Victoria Gardens, waiting for the children to get out of school, a man approached her, asking for directions to the Taj Mahal Intercontinental Hotel. The man was very polite, and even complimented her accent, claiming that it sounded familiar to him. They spoke for some time, and she found his company to be quite hospitable. He seemed to understand her, and was interested in her past–not passing judgment, but offering words of encouragement for her success in finding a good job. It was the first time that a man had been kind to her, not seeking sexual favors or anything other friendship. He asked her to join him for tea. She hesitated at first, thinking of whether Mrs. Walsh would find it prudent for Florentina to have tea with a strange man. She decided that Mrs. Walsh would not like the idea at all and that she should decline. The man persisted. She hemmed and hawed, proclaiming her need to be on time to pick up the children, and voicing her concern that if Mrs. Walsh found out, she might lose her job.

The gentleman was relentless, even teasing, and told her that this opportunity to have tea with him would be the best hour of her life. Finally, she agreed. They walked together towards his hotel, which was famous for serving a gorgeous spot of tea with crumpets and jam. For the first time in her life, Florentina felt like a princess. She was being treated properly by a man, and it felt wonderful.

Unfortunately, the Walsh family would never again see her alive.

Chapter 9

It had been a long time since a dozen roses had been delivered to Mary MacIntosh. At first, she looked at the bouquet quizzically, assuming that it had been erroneously placed on her desk. Megan, her perky, blonde, twenty-year-old legal secretary regularly received flowers, so, naturally, Mac initially believed that the gorgeous, long-stemmed yellow blossoms belonged to Megan. But as she opened the card, Mac realized that the flowers had been sent by Gilbert Bonita from somewhere in Russia. The card read, "Thank you for your assistance in the purchase of the farmhouse. I am indebted to you. Until we meet again . . . Gil."

Mac was not accustomed to romance. Greg was adventurous and a good communicator, but he was not overly romantic–at least not in a way in which most women associate romance. When they first got together, Greg took her to San Francisco, and they shared a very romantic weekend together with flowers and candlelit dinners and music. But after that, he suggested outings such as hiking or skiing. The outings were fun, but Mac liked to be treated with chivalry on occasion. Mac read Gil's card again and sighed deeply. He wasn't supposed to be back in the States for another three weeks. It wasn't that she wanted or needed a boyfriend, but she couldn't deny the fact that it felt good to have someone thinking of her. She missed the notion of a relationship–and the security of knowing that a special someone would be calling, asking to take her to dinner or a movie or a weekend getaway. Mac didn't assume that Gil would become that person, but it was fun for her to daydream.

Mac was curious about what specifically Gil did for a living. He told her that he worked for a Russian-based pharmaceutical company, and that the company developed vaccines. She'd read about the other outbreaks of the deadly bird flu in Asia and wondered whether his company was affected by the situation. She wondered whether his company made flu vaccines. She had sent him a few emails inquiring about his job, but he hadn't specifically answered her inquiries. He focused on travel and romance, not on business.

The outbreaks in Sheridan had slowed, but the CDC's quarantine was still in place. Mac heard a rumor that there had been a possible outbreak in a small town on the other side of the Big Horn Mountains, but the rumor hadn't been confirmed by a reliable source. The rumor was that a hunter shot a mountain lion that had tried to attack him. When the hunter skinned the mountain lion, he found the cat's intestines liquid-like and rotten. The hunter went to a hospital in Cody, Wyoming the next day complaining of severe flu- like symptoms and died on a gurney within a few hours of admittance. It was a fact that the man died in Cody, but how he died remained a matter of speculation.

The avian flu outbreaks worried Mac. From what she'd read and seen on television, it seemed that the recent outbreaks in Thailand and India had spread much quicker than in Wyoming and had killed thousands of people. It was scary. Every other article in the paper or broadcast on the television mentioned the words "global pandemic." Hopefully, the virus was gone from North America for good and the rumor about the hunter was just that—a rumor. Not that she wanted the rest of the world to suffer, but having it in her small town was terrifying. She hoped it wouldn't spread to Indonesia, where Greg was working.

Greg was well-educated in the science of the avian flu due to his research and article published in *National Geographic*. His last email to Mac hinted that the outbreaks might be a cover-up for some kind of slip up in the scientific community. Greg didn't elaborate, but Mac could read between the lines. Perhaps there was more to this than the general population was aware.

* * *

"The tattoo-like markings weren't found on Ana Bontierre's body until after the CDC showed up," an investigative BBC reporter announced as part of a global broadcast. "We've obtained a copy of the autopsy report, and it clearly states that Ms. Bontierre's body was 'void of any birthmarks or tattoos' when the autopsy was performed. How convenient it is that Dr. Fahrid found the tattoo on her inner thigh after he examined her! This is proof of a massive CDC cover-up. They painstakingly assembled the fragments of the 1918 Spanish flu pandemic and grew the virus. Then they found that the 1918 hemagglutin gene had two mutations that converted it into an infectious powerhouse, so they fiddled with it some more, and altered the polymerase, making it so that it could enter virtually any cell it encounters–meaning the virus could transfer from human to human. They tested it in mice and cultured human tissue. The test results were published, allowing the population at large access to the genetic blueprint of the virus. This whole serial killer business is a diversion tactic to take the focus off of their screw up!"

The BBC reporter interviewed other scientists who concurred. World speculation continued to mount.

* * *

The call came right on time. Vladimir Checovsky was a punctual man–that was for sure. "You are moving too slow. You need to hit a new city every day. The time is right to launch Rescuflu. We need Europe."

"I think we should hit one more city before we launch the drug," Nicolai Petrescu answered. "Not enough death yet. Thailand has killed only a few thousand chickens. China's mass slaughter was good, but we need more. Perhaps Syria first."

"I don't care about the chickens. That is a small percentage of our gains. It is time to enter the market. People are afraid."

"If you launch now, they will think you are involved. If you wait, you will be the savior. Did you not read Dr. Sharp's scathing report on Tarirescu? He's already accused us of a conflict of interest. He already thinks we could infect birds with a mutated strain, and then produce the antivirals. Do not be stupid. Be patient. You are not a patient man, Vladimir. This is the time to find patience."

"Cash flow is tapped out, Nicolai. Reich is cleaning up on the rush to stockpile Stiflu. We need to cut in. Break the consumer confidence on Stiflu. When we offer another, more effective antiviral, we will dominate the marketplace. I need market share now. So, I will launch. You may continue your assignment, as planned. Perhaps you might accelerate it. Get to Europe. And then, blast America. America. I can't wait until we even the score. And remember, you will be greatly rewarded for your crusade. You are doing a fine job. As always. You have never let me down."

Nicolai considered Vladimir's comments and decided to obey his boss. He would heed his own advice and be patient too. For now.

* * *

Rozalia Oana was born in Damascus, Syria, as the daughter of a teenage Romanian prostitute. Her mother had been stolen at age eight and sold as a sex slave to a hedonistic Islamic guerrilla. Rosie's mother, when she was still alive, wore a veil from head to toe, like other Islamic women, and followed her jelabiyyeh-clad husband around the backstreets of this old city. Damascus's history could be traced back for centuries, and claimed the title of the "oldest continuously inhabited city." It started as a watering hole on the Silk Road, and became a vital link between the Mediterranean and China. Rosie's deceased mother shared the label of "wife" with seven others, and so Rosie had somewhere in the vicinity of seventy brothers and sisters. Her mother died while giving birth to her ninth child, leaving Rosie to be raised by the other wives. The problem was that Rosie and her blood siblings were the only non-Syrian bred children in the polygamous tribe, leaving her as the eldest outcast. The other wives treated her as their personal slave, demanding that she wait on them hand over foot, all the while depriving her of any opportunity to be educated or skilled.

On this day, Rosie was ordered to go to the bazaar to buy provisions for the evening meal. This was one of her favorite chores. She liked walking around in the noisy and crowded bazaar, bartering with the souks for their cinnamon, saffron, cumin, coriander, and roasted nuts. Every week, a few of the souks told her that she must caravan to Aleppo, a trading post in Syria, near the border of Turkey. Beneath a stone vault built during the

Ottoman Empire, nearly twenty miles of covered passages are filled with the frenzied bartering of Arabs, Kurds, Iranians, Turks, Armenians and the famous "covered souks of Aleppo." Rosie loved hearing the souks' stories of the golden era when the *Orient Express* terminated in Aleppo, and how Lawrence of Arabia's unpaid hotel bill remains on display in the Baron Hotel. She heard the same stories every week, but never tired of them, as they were an escape from the confines of her contrived life.

While negotiating the price of a side of goat at the bazaar, a gentleman appeared and stood beside her. Rosie could feel his arm lightly touching her arm, which sent chills through her. As always, she was wearing a full veil, covering all but her mysterious and gorgeous green eyes. He did not wear a jelabiyyeh, and he looked like her youngest brother, but more handsome. Her eyes met his briefly, then darted back to the souk. When they agreed on a price and exchanged money for goods, the man offered to help load her wagon. Rosie declined with a nod, and hoisted the back end of the goat onto the flat herself. She tucked her spices in the front end of her wheelbarrow-like wagon and lifted the two handles to wheel the cart back to her master's home. The man followed behind.

When Rosie did not return home, the eldest wife went looking for Rosie in the bazaar. She was furious. That girl was always talking to men! She would be punished for her tardiness. The goat would not be prepared on time, and their master would be livid. They would all pay the price tonight, but Rosie would pay first. But when she found Rosie's cart overturned on the side of the street, with the goat and the spices toppled to the side, she realized that something had happened. Maybe the wench ran off with a souk. Maybe she fell ill and was in the infirmary. The eldest wife did not care in the slightest, except for the fact that she would have to prepare the evening meal herself. She loaded the cart with the toppled goods and headed back to the master's home.

Rosie's lifeless body was found the next day inside the Omayyad Mosque. The mosque is considered one of Islam's greatest architectural monuments and a sacred place of worship. It embraces a delightfully cool marble courtyard, where shoppers escape the heat of the city and enjoy solitude. The mosque was once the site of the Basilica of St. John the Baptist. In fact, his head remains buried in the mosque's sanctuary.

When the priest found Rosie on the cold marble floor, he quickly picked her up and laid her shivering body on a wooden pew. He summoned medical attention for her and chanted in prayer. Word circulated quickly through the backstreets of Damascus, and several souks recognized her simply by the description of her eyes. She was exotic-looking and wonderfully outgoing. Word spread that she'd fallen ill from the goat she'd eaten the day before, and the souk who sold it rushed to the hospital to see her. Many others followed.

Her emerald-green eyes were blood-shot and nearly swollen shut, encased in purple bruising. Her veil had been removed, revealing her perfectly oval face and olive complexion, now blemished by contusions and discolorations. Every time she coughed and sputtered, blood seeped around the tubes coming out of her nose and mouth. When the nurse tried to turn her head to the side, Rosie erupted in a violent gagging fit, dislodging her breathing tube and splattering everything in sight, including the inside curtain of her cubicle, with a dark, mud-like fluid. The souks and other onlookers quickly backed away, unwilling to watch her gasp for her last breath.

Within two days, the courtyard of the Omayyad Mosque was cordoned off and a constant flow of scientists, police, and other investigators hypothesized how Rosie became "patient zero–Syria." Dr. Jeffrey Plattenburg rummaged through Damascus, inquiring about Rosie's whereabouts prior to her death. The eldest wife of Rosie's master claimed to know nothing about the girl, other than the fact that Rosie liked to flirt with the souks at the bazaar. "She got what was coming to her," the old woman hissed.

It wasn't long before dozens of souks and other Damascus residents were suffering violent, flu-like symptoms. The hospital where Rosie died became a hot suite and the entire radius of the mosque was a hot zone. Any person who had been in the hot zone was ordered to quarantine. Unfortunately, some residents did not obey orders causing the virus to spread like a wild fire.

Jeffrey was almost relieved to learn that Rosie had a similar tattoo- like mark on her inner thigh. He wanted this horror to be the work of a serial killer. If so, he knew that eventually he might stand a chance at stopping the lunatic from his killing spree. But he was greatly worried that no other clues had been left behind on any of the victims. No consistent DNA. No fiber. No prints. It was like a ghost descending upon a victim, injecting them with a deadly serum, and then vanishing into the underworld.

Jeffrey thought back on his knowledge of prior serial killers. Was this killer the Ted Bundy-type? Bundy was a necrophiliac who kidnapped, raped, murdered, and mutilated twenty college-aged women. He kept four heads in his apartment and burned another head in his girlfriend's fireplace. He claimed to have been doing the women a favor–sparing them from a life of pain and misery. Jeffrey believed that the necrophiliac's driving force was sexual control and dominance.

Perhaps this man was more of an erotophonophiliac–gaining sexual satisfaction from the brutality of the killing. Even though the killer that Jeffrey was searching for left tattoos behind, he didn't mutilate female genitalia, like that of a perognyniac, nor did he stab his victims as a substitute for sex, like a picquieriac. Perhaps he was more of a hedonistic thrill killer, deriving sadistic pleasure from the process of killing, keeping the victim aware of what's happening. Although unsure of the label, Jeffrey was sure that he was dealing with a freak who would almost certainly strike again.

Jeffrey continued to contact the other doctors with whom he had lectured at the WHO conference in Geneva. He wanted to convince Dr. Karen Kokinda that this outbreak was not the result of avian migration so that all of the government agencies could focus their collective efforts on catching the killer and not killing healthy birds.

Karen was so convinced that she was correct in her supposition that she was unable to see other possible scenarios. She spent considerable hours telling the media that the ducks were spreading the flu this time. Governments were now ordering that ducks be eradicated.

Jeffrey felt strongly that the eradication of chickens and ducks was wrong. He hated the thought of the senseless killing of animals, and he detested the notion that so many people in poor regions of the country would go hungry without poultry as their staple protein. If he could offer Dr. Kokinda proof, perhaps she would stop talking to the media about the birds, which would help him focus on warning the world that a predator was on the loose.

Jeffrey also knew that he needed to convince Dr. Ito of the WHO and Dr. Sharp of the CDC. Dr. Sharp was so worried about defending her H5N1 published research that she was failing in her efforts to coordinate the quarantines around the globe. Dr. Fahrid was working ridiculous hours to make up for Dr. Sharp's shortfall.

Dr. Ito was so focused on dealing with the Stiflu patent issues that he was failing to effectively delegate responsibilities among the various world health organizations.

Despite his steadfast belief that the world was at the mercy of a serial killer, Jeffrey couldn't help wondering if he was wrong? What if there was no serial killer? Was it possible? He didn't think so, but doubt was his enemy. He needed to link the victims together. What did they have in common? They all were either prostitutes of childhood victims, from what his FBI team gathered, but there had to be a commonality. There needed to be an impenetrable thread that linked them together, or linked them individually to one person. His team was hot on the subject, but so far, had been unsuccessful in their research.

Jeffrey called Mac from his overseas investigation to see how her investigation was going. They discussed her progress, or lack thereof and also talked about the other outbreaks. Mac questioned the commonalities among the victims prompting a discussion about the case in more detail than Jeffrey was allowed to disclose. He gave Mac the names of all the victims and information about their background. Although none of the information was technically "top secret," it certainly wasn't Jeffrey's protocol to speak so openly about a pending investigation. Somehow with Mac, he felt confident that she would honor confidentiality.

After he finished his telephone call with Mac, another call came through to his hotel room. When Jeffrey learned of the outbreak in Turkey, he was excited, in a scientific sort of way.

Chapter 10

Istanbul, the former Byzantine capital known as Constantinople, is a modern, bustling, exciting city on the Bosphorus in Turkey, the only country in the world straddling both Europe and Asia. Surrounded by the Black Sea to the north and the Sea of Marmara to the south, the city is literally an isthmus. It is also a key trading route. One of the Byzantium's greatest legacies can be found in Istanbul–the Hagia Sophia, or Church of the Holy Wisdom. The massive dome of the Hagia Sophia, and her four graceful minarets, rise above the city and form an impressive meeting place. In fact, it is one of the largest enclosed spaces in the world.

Maria Monteau loved looking out the window of the hotel where she worked, seeing people roam through the lovely grounds of the former church. She'd read about how the church was converted into a mosque when Constantinople fell to the Ottoman Turks, and how much of the original gold and marble and nearly four acres of mosaics had been plundered at that time. Oh, how she wished that the mosaics had survived. After finishing her shift as a cleaning lady at the Four Seasons, one of her favorite pastimes was roaming the city, studying mosaics, and learning about the Old Testament through the eyes of artists. Maria's faith in God was the cornerstone of her being, and though she'd been stripped of her virginity by horrific men who paid her pimp to have sex with her, she knew that her prayers connected her closely with the Virgin Mary.

Maria was born in Constanta, a port city of Romania, along the coast of the Black Sea. She remembered very little about her childhood, only that her family was very poor and that there was never food to eat. Her mother and father both worked hard, but the money was not enough to feed eight mouths. Maria was the fourth child born in her family, and the fourth girl. She has two younger brothers, but she can't remember their faces. At the age of seven, her father told her to walk with him to the port dock, that he needed help with a shipment of some sort. Dutiful Maria followed along, happy to have a moment alone with her father, who was always too busy working or playing with his sons to pay much attention to her. She chatted with him about her brothers and sisters, careful not to complain about anything. Her father hated it when he heard complaints. "You are lucky to have a roof over your head. Many children live in the streets," he would say. When they got to the end of the dock, there was a small vessel waiting, with two men and three young girls on board. One of the men approached Maria's father and spoke with him in broken sentences. The man looked Maria over once and then handed her father some money. The man grabbed Maria by the arm and forced her onto the boat. She cried and yelled to her father, but he turned and walked back down the dock, never looking back. One less mouth to feed. One less girl in the house.

Her father had sold her into prostitution—something Maria knew nothing about. She cried the entire way to Bulgaria, where the men stopped and picked up two more girls, and continued to cry until she was locked in a dark room with three Ukrainian girls and one Bulgarian girl. For the next six years, she cried each time a new man shoved her down on her back and thrust himself inside of her. The cries became that of anger instead of sorrow. She would never understand how her father could betray her on such a level.

One morning, Castov, her owner, walked into Maria's cave-like room and told her to gather her things and leave. She was free to go. Just like that. He shoved a little money her way and told her about a place where they take in girls like Maria. So she packed what few belongings she had and walked to the half-way house that Castov had mentioned, where she was offered room and board in exchange for work. A nice hotel in town had made a deal with the local Turkish government to hire people in need, like Maria, in exchange for permission to build in areas which had previously been off-limits due to zoning laws. Maria was fortunate to get hired by the Four Seasons Hotel, first in laundry service, ironing the crisp white sheets before they were replaced on the beds. Then, as time proved her proficient and hard-working nature, she worked as a maid.

The half-way house received half of her wages for rent, and Maria was allowed the rest of the money.

On her one day off a week, she attended religious service, and then usually wandered through the city, enjoying the museums, especially those with art. She often basked in the rays of the stained-glass windows of the Mosque of Sultan Suleiman the Magnificent, the largest and most beautiful of all the mosques in Istanbul. It was here that a fellow Romanian approached her, claiming that he was lost, asking for assistance in finding his hotel, the Pera Palas. She knew the location of this exquisite hotel and offered directions. When he seemed confused by her description, she offered to walk him there, since it was on her way home. He was gentlemanly and older, and seemed soft-spoken and kind. He asked her what she was doing so far from home, and Maria started to tell him a lie. But something about him seemed caring and gentle, and before she could stop, the floodgate of tears streamed down her cheeks as she told him the tale of how her father sold her to Castov. The gentleman, who finally introduced himself as Nicolai Petrescu, wiped the tears from her cheeks and assured her that she had done nothing wrong to deserve such horrible treatment. He told her how beautiful she was and how lucky some man would be to take her as his bride. This made Maria cry even harder, as she knew it was untrue. No man would ever want her. She was not a virgin. Nicolai tried to calm her, insisting that she join him for a light meal before he walked her back to the half-way house. Not wanting to be alone, and feeling safe and loved for the first time since childhood, she agreed. She told him of her favorite museum, the Kariye, and Nicolai suggested that he purchase a few provisions at the market and they enjoy a picnic together in the gardens adjacent to the museum. After dining, they could stroll through the mosaics and frescoes depicting biblical scenes from Adam to the life of Christ. She loved the fact that he was also religious.

* * *

When Maria didn't report for work the next morning, the manager of housekeeping services was not pleased. Maria had never missed a day of work, and had always reported early for her shift. He called the half-way house to see if she was ill, so that he would know whether or not he would need to call in a replacement. The Four Seasons was expecting a large convention party later that day and the rooms would need to be immaculate. No one at the half-way house had seen Maria or knew anything about her whereabouts. He would have to call in a replacement, and probably have to pay them extra to work on their day off.

* * *

When the museum curator opened the Kariye the following morning, he was struck by the splendid beauty caused by the light shining through the dome, illuminating the mosaics in a way unseen by the viewing public. He loved this time of day, before the crowds entered and clattered his turret with noise. He enjoyed his morning walk through each room, ensuring that everything was in its proper place. But when he entered the south fresco wing, he was horrified to find a body tucked into the fetal position, lying on the floor below the depiction of the Virgin Mary after giving birth to the Christ child. The woman was moaning softly, and trickles of blood dripped from her lips. Her eyes were wide, yet vacant, and were crisscrossed with a roadmap of broken blood vessels.

The curator gasped and ran to her side, offering what he believed to be CPR, pumping her chest and blowing into her mouth. Although the curator didn't know it, each chest compression turned her lungs into a Jello-like mush, throwing blood clots into her bloodstream. Maria choked and sputtered, and not knowing what else to do, the curator picked her up and carried her to his office, where he called for an ambulance. When the ambulance arrived, the doctors also attempted CPR, further damaging Maria's internal organs, and causing her to vomit black, speckled fluid into the air. They rushed her to the hospital, where she continued to vomit and convulse, and spew fluids from every orifice. By now, most of the world had heard of the mysterious outbreaks in China, Thailand and India, and when two of the emergency nurses saw the blood flowing from her mouth, they refused to treat her. Other staff openly criticized the nurses, demanding that they assist, and an argument emerged in the hospital. Was this another bird flu patient? Who had the right to decide which patients to treat? Doctors yelled at the nurses to assist, reminding them of their duty to care for the sick and the Hippocratic Oath. A shouting match broke out. The nurses walked out of the hospital, refusing to expose themselves and their families to what they believed would be a death sentence.

Other medical staff continued to assist Maria, but with a certain level of trepidation. As was protocol, masks and gloves were worn by all, but there was a noticeable sense of fear in the air.

* * *

Hunting season in Wyoming and Montana was sacred to many of the residents. On any given pre-dawn Saturday in the fall, one could expect to see men dressed in orange and brown camouflage driving a pickup truck through town, heading up into the mountains in hopes of tagging a six-point buck. However, after the hunter who gutted the mountain lion fell dead in the Cody hospital and his autopsy confirmed that he had been infected with the avian flu; many hunters expressed apprehension about shooting his prey. Rumors were flying around the coffee shops of the small, western towns that the deer and elk were diseased with the bird flu. Hunters feared that in gutting their kill, they would become infected with the lethal virus.

Mac understood why hunters were relinquishing their tags for the season, requesting a deferment to hunt next year instead. She even predicted that if the government didn't accept the returned tags and allow the hunters a deferment, that some might initiate litigation over their hunting rights. What Mac didn't predict was a lawsuit filed against David Thrift's estate. The family of the man who died in the Cody hospital filed a lawsuit against David Thrift's estate claiming that the forest ranger knew or should have known that he was infected with a lethal virus and by subjecting the animal population to his dying corpse, he recklessly contaminated animals. David Thrift's family requested that Mac represent them in the lawsuit. She was confident that she could get the case dismissed. David Thrift's whereabouts remained a mystery and there was no evidence that he infected any animals with the virus. It was mere speculation that he was in any way involved in Ana's death. It was tangential at best to allege that he somehow infected the mountain lion too.

Gil called Mac from Russia and explained that he was going to be delayed on his business trip. He explained to her that his boss was being somewhat unreasonable regarding the marketing of a new product, and that he would be required to stay in St. Petersburg a few additional weeks. Mac told Gil about her new lawsuit and how the avian flu had spread to the animal population.

"That is quite fascinating," Gil said. "I am sure that this has put a damper on the hunting season. Think what it must be doing to the food chain."

Mac agreed, filling Gil in on the details.

"Maybe your idea of being a vegetarian isn't so bad after all," Gil joked. Mac laughed at herself, thinking back on the incident at the farmhouse where Gil served her duck. "Tell me more about the virus. What have you learned?"

Mac told Gil as much as she could, careful not to tread into the murky waters of revealing anything confidential that Jeffrey had divulged to her. Gil was very interested, and asked many questions about her investigation. After they ended the international call. Mac got busy drafting a response to the David Thrift lawsuit.

* * *

Dr. Ito stood before the electronic map in the banals of high security of the WHO office in Geneva. Retinal scanning allowed entry into the lobby. Voice and fingerprint scanning was required for further access into the inner sanctuary. The final gate-keeping device was new to the security world. The scanner mapped out the spinal chord, from skull to sacroiliac, and only identical matches were allowed.

Dr. Ito and his team had a map of the H5N1 outbreaks pegged in red electronic tacks. Superimposed on the glass atlas in yellow lights were the areas of concern, where future pandemic outbreak might cause widespread viral death. The map lit up every major city in the world.

Dr. Ito was hoping that there was a pattern to the outbreaks. Did they follow the natural migratory patterns of a certain bird? Dr. Kokinda seemed to think that the falcated teal was the culprit. Dr. Ito had his right-hand man send the electronic information regarding the outbreaks to her, along with a request for migration corroboration. He hoped that she was right. But he didn't have a good feeling about it.

Chapter 11

The pressure was mounting world-wide for the WHO to step in and require Reich to share the Stiflu patent. Dr. Ito did not like to flex his international trade treaty muscle, but with each new outbreak, it looked more likely that his hand would be forced. As Director General of the WHO, he was scheduled to give a lecture to world leaders on this day, including the President of the United States, the Prime Minister of the United Kingdom, and to other leaders of nations from around the world. He reviewed his speech carefully, knowing that every syllable would be under scrutiny. After smoking his last cigarette of the day, he dressed in his customary black suit and red tie, and rehearsed his opening in front of his staff. He turned and looked out the picture frame window, and watched in silence as the first flakes of snow started falling. Soon, the Alps would be dusted with shimmering snow and the trees would be barren of their colorful leaves. He could see the fountain in the middle of Lake Geneva, shooting high into the air. He loved this city. He missed Tokyo sometimes—the food and his extended family. But he had fallen in love with Geneva. To him, Switzerland was one of the greatest countries in the world. He took a deep, appreciative breath before proceeding through the high security doors that protected the room full of world leaders. It was noisier in the banquet room than ever before, he noted. Tempers were high. The last time he remembered feeling this much tension at a WHO meeting was in the 1980's, when the AIDS epidemic became a world plague.

After thanking the attendees for coming, he addressed the health concerns of individual nations, stressing the importance of having a "Pandemic Plan" in place on a national, state and local level within each province or country. He then affixed his reading glasses and began explaining the crisis with respect to pharmaceuticals. He wanted to make sure that all leaders understood the impact of the WHO stepping in and forcing a company, such as Reich, to give up a patent.

"The WHO has never made it a practice to step into the shoes of governments around the world and tell them how they should regulate the manufacture of drugs. In fact, we work with organizations like the CDC, NIC and the United Nations to promote drug company research and development, and strongly encourage all drug companies to keep the poor in mind when manufacturing drugs. Globally, we like to see generics because they are more affordable for the needy. We want to ensure that all human beings on this planet get the medical attention they need. But, by the same token, there is a sense of unfairness in stripping a branded pharmaceutical company, like Reich, of a patent for a drug that they have spent tens of millions of dollars developing.

"Many of you, as world leaders, are asking me to compel Reich not to enforce its Stiflu patent, thereby allowing generics to produce the antiviral drug in this global emergency. I understand your concern that you want and need a certain stockpile amount of the drug to satisfy a growing panic within your borders.

"As you may know, regulatory agencies such as the FDA consider Stiflu to be a drug rather than a biologic. However, Reich has informed the generic companies that Stiflu would be difficult to manufacture on a generic level. They claim that there is a potentially "explosive" chemical step in the production process and that it would take a generic company several years before it could produce a generic Stiflu without safety concerns or efficacy. I don't know if Reich's statements are true, but if so, Stiflu may have the same risks as a biologic.

"As the avian flu continues to spread, it appears that Reich will not be able to keep up with demand for Stiflu. The pressure on Reich to allow Stiflu to be produced by others will increase. Many of my colleagues feel that Reich's warnings about production complexities are no more than a last ditch effort by a giant pharmaceutical company to maintain its monopoly. In some countries, like India and China, where the avian flu has caused the most damage so far, generic companies have claimed that they can safely produce Stiflu.

"You see, Ladies and Gentlemen, my decision is not clear-cut. The majority of you have expressed your opinion that I should simply force Reich to relinquish its patent rights. There could be significant ramifications if I do. I'll give you one scenario that the World Health Organization has shared with the National Influenza Center and the CDC. Scenario number one is that we force Reich's patent rights aside, and allow the generic companies to produce Stiflu. Reich's warnings turn out to be right and oseltamivir, or generic Stiflu, turns out to be is completely ineffective or even worse, unsafe. Who will be to blame?

"We want to do what is right, but we are forced to address these ethical dilemmas. Please bear this in mind. I will now open the floor to discussion. Any questions?" Dr. Ito looked out over his reading glasses and perused the room. Every world leader had their hand in the air. The meeting would run late, as predicted by his staff.

* * *

Margareta Canja knew that she would die at the hands of a strange man. Plucked from childhood at age six by her mother's pimp and repeatedly raped on a daily basis ever since, it was her destiny that an angel from the heavens would rescue her from the miserable life in which she was born. Living on the streets of Bucharest, Romania, was all she'd ever known, in large part because her lazy whore of a mother never cared enough to drop off Margareta at an orphanage. Too many questions would be asked, and Margareta's mother was not one to give answers. Most prostitutes, like Margareta's mother, found a back-street abortion clinic when they wound up pregnant, but Margareta's mother was too lazy to get an abortion. Margareta would have preferred to never have been born.

When a man approached her on the streets one day and offered to take her for a drive in his new car, Margareta readily accepted. She didn't care where they were going or if they would return. Maybe this man was her Prince Charming. She laughed at such a ridiculous notion. There were no Prince Charmings, or any other nice men, in her mind. Just disgusting loafs who couldn't wait to stick themselves inside of her and toss a few coins into her mother's grimy robe. This man was probably just like the rest of them. At least he was clean-shaven and spoke full sentences. He wasn't drunk. He didn't curse. And he had a car that could take her away. That was good enough for Margareta.

They drove for several hours that morning, following the Danube River northeasterly, until they were very close to the Black Sea. Margareta had never set foot out of Bucharest, and was amazed at the beauty of the beaches along the coast. The man, who identified himself as Nicolai Petrescu, stopped at a local market and bought her fresh fruit, bread and a cold soft drink. She ate with him on a bench, and watched him throw bread crumbs to the birds. She marveled at the variety of birds that flocked to get a hand-out. She was used to dirty, pesky city birds, like pigeons, poking their nasty beaks every which way to get food. The birds along the tributary of the Danube were beautiful, white sea birds and they reminded Margareta of angels. The man spoke to the birds and told them that they were his messengers. Margareta did not understand, but she didn't really care to. She was happy watching them soar high and lunge back toward earth, as if in complete control of their destiny. Oh, how she wished she were a bird. She would be able to fly away, high in the sky, and come back to earth only if she needed nutrients. She noticed that the man was watching her marvel at the birds.

Without warning, he grabbed her by the arm and nudged her back toward his car. His mood seemed to change, and he began driving at a much faster rate of speed. For two hours, he did not speak and did not look in Margareta's direction. Had she angered him by paying too much attention to the birds? She decided to ignore him and focus on the beauty of this warm, fall afternoon. The sun was still high, and its rays shone brightly over the peaks of the mountains ahead of them. She had no idea where they were going, but it didn't matter. She'd never seen anything other than the filthy alleyway where her mother took up trade, and she was amazed at the sheer vastness of the world around her. She could see country for miles, and the colors! The green grass carpeting the rolling hills and the blue sky and the pine trees poking their tips up over the horizon moved her spirit to a new place. She found herself smiling again. A smile felt strange on her face.

Suddenly, the man, Nicolai, slammed on the brakes and skidded to a stop. He was angry at something, but she did not know what. He pulled out a map and studied it for a time, all the while nervously raking through his hair with the fingers on his left hand. He uttered a curse word in a strange language. At least she assumed it was one of those kinds of words, since his tone was angry. He shoved the gearshift into reverse, grinding the gears until the car jerked, and backed up a few hundred feet. He looked around, as if he was trying to find a road. He studied the map again, shoved the gearshift into drive, and floored it. The tires let out a screech, which startled Margareta, yet, at the same time, left her exhilarated. She'd never known speed. It was exciting.

After cresting a hill, she could see a village ahead. The sign said, "Suceava." Margareta had not heard of such a place. They stopped briefly to use the restroom, get gas and purchase food. It did not occur to her to try to run away from Nicolai, or to seek help, for she did not feel endangered any more than she did any other day of her life. She would not have cared if she were in danger. Such a fleeting emotion did not register in her world.

After leaving Suceava, they headed west, toward the setting sun. Margareta could see a number of colorfully-painted castles perched high on the rolling hills. She did not know this, but she was witnessing the painted monasteries of Moldavia. They were at the base of Voronet, known by Romanians as the Sistine Chapel of the East.

Nicolai parked the car on a small side road and motioned for her to walk with him. She followed him through the pine trees and up a steep hill. At the top, there was a four-foot high stone wall encircling the monastery. As they walked, Margareta could see that part of the wall had been destroyed. They climbed over the age-old rubble and walked through the well-kept garden. The garden had a number of religious statues, all enshrined with candles and offerings. They came to an immense wood-plank door with wrought iron locks. Nicolai slid the iron clasp to the right and heaved the door open. She followed him inside, where she gasped at the glory of the art on the walls, rising as high as her neck could crane.

The monastery was painted inside and out with sophisticated frescoes depicting biblical scenes. She stared at a particular work of art depicting the story of Jesus' death, and the Stations of the Cross, bordered and embossed in gold. The ceiling was cerulean blue—a mixture between the colors of the sky and sea. She smiled again at the sheer beauty before her. She noticed that Nicolai was smiling back at her. He had brought her all this way to see this lovely place. He was being kind to her, and he offered her a place to sit in a pew. She sat next to him and watched as he unwrapped the food he'd purchased in Suceava. They ate bread, cheese and pate. It tasted delicious. He offered her a drink. She accepted, but when she brought it to her lips, it smelled foul. She put the drink down. He demanded that she drink it. She put it to her lips and swallowed. It was putrid. She spit it out.

Nicolai grew quite angry with her. He grabbed the chalice from her hand and forced it to her lips. She pursed her lips tightly together, refusing to drink. He pulled back on her light brown hair and stuck his thumb in the corner of her mouth, forcing it open a bit. She fought back, kicking him in the knee. This only angered him, and he pulled her close to him and tightened his grip. With her head tilted back and her mouth slightly ajar, he thrust the chalice to her lips and tilted it upward. The reddish-brown fluid seeped into her mouth. He dropped the chalice, sending it clanging to the floor, and held his hand over her nose and mouth, forcing her to swallow. She fought again. This time, he elbowed her in the ribs and then slapped her hard across the face. She did not cry. She knew better. Instead, she bit down hard on his hand, drawing blood.

Fury raged in Nicolai's veins. He had to be in control of her. She would pay dearly for her ungrateful manner. He yanked a handkerchief from his back pant pocket and tightly gagged her with it. He then threw her to the ground and forced his knee into her spine. She let out a loud moan. He ripped off her panties and drove himself into her with such extreme might that his own pain was excruciating, yet titillating. While thrusting himself in from behind, he yanked back on her neck and then rammed her head into the pew. She was uncooperative. Unappreciative. Her end would be relentless. And it was. He left her bloody, half-naked body at the foot of St. George's statue.

Two nuns found Margareta, near death, and drove her to Suceava, where a private tour plane had just landed. Knowing that she would not get the medical attention she needed in the isolated region of Moldavia, the pilot agreed to take her back to Bucharest.

Despite the fact that Margareta's mother was only three miles away in Bucharest, she would never know that her daughter lay dying in a private room in the city's largest hospital. But ten days later, Margareta's mother succumbed to her own death, along with nearly twenty thousand other Romanians who died from the rampant spread of the avian flu.

Chapter 12

In Nanning, China, Jo-Chen Liang took a ten-minute break mid-day, and hastily swallowed his white rice, washing it down with luke-warm, black tea. He did not have time for lunch. He darted back out into his fields, bellowing "To bajiao" to his workers, the Chinese word for a fruit called star anise. Few people knew of this small, eight-pointed, star-shaped fruit, but to Jo-Chen Liang, it was his life. He'd been up since dawn, shouting at his workers to pick, pick, pick. They must pick quickly to fill orders from Bangkok and India. Until a week ago, Jo-Chen Liang could scarcely feed his family. His crops were plentiful, but demand for star anise was low. Star anise was mostly used as a Chinese spice for meat, curries, pickles and liqueurs. It was also used medicinally to help digestion or freshen breath. But when the avian flu spread, and few countries could get Stiflu, some generic drug makers decided to take things into their own hands. The seed pod from star anise forms the genesis for oseltamivir, the generic name for Stiflu. With wholesale prices quadrupling in just a few days' time, Jo-Chen knew that he should double his farming staff and meet the demand as quickly as possible. He was going to take advantage of this crisis. He knew, based on experience, that the demand for star anise would probably never again be this high. He would be rich by the end of the week. This made him a happy man. "To bajiao!" he shouted again.

* * *

Jeffrey was secluded in his lab at the FBI Behavioral Science Services in Quantico, Virginia. His long, lean legs were aching. He'd run hard that morning, trying to relieve the mounting stress that he was feeling. He hadn't been sleeping well. His team of "mind hunters" and "monster fighters," as they referred to themselves, was hard at work profiling what they now called the "Pandemic Predator." They compared his killing spree with other serial killers such as Albert De Salvo (the "Boston Strangler"); John Wayne Gacy, Jr. (Chicago serial killer); Andre Crawford (South Side Chicago killer); Charles Ng (Sierra Nevada); Henry Lee Lucas (Texas); and Dennis Rader (the "BTK" killer in Kansas City). Jeffrey took a break from database analysis and walked into the "pit" where his team assembled to brainstorm.

Most criminal profilers agreed that serial killers, despite their wide variety of motives, have a few common traits, such as huge egos. Most are men who reside in the United States and share an indifference for anyone but themselves. They rarely make an abrupt, impulsive decision to kill. Instead, it is more likely for a serial killer to be driven by dominant sexual fantasies that lead to increasingly violent acts.

"We need to focus on the modus operandi," one of the mind hunters said, as he walked to the white board and wrote the words in large, red capital letters. "How is this guy committing the crime? Do we even know for sure? We know that he is leaving his signature. What does it mean? What is he trying to tell us?"

A woman, dressed in a tan, pressed uniform stood. "What is the killer's need? Revenge? Sex? Notoriety? Has he been rejected by women in general or did a Romanian woman do him wrong and he is now on a mission to kill them all?" Discussions broke out.

"You all seem to think we are dealing with one serial killer," Jeffrey interrupted. "What if this is some kind of biological warfare? This might be biological terrorism. We can't overlook the possibility." The possibility of terrorism had prevented Jeffrey from sleeping the two previous nights. He'd been online in the middle of the night, reading about World War II and Water Purification Unit 731.

Despite the 1925 Geneva Protocol which prohibited the use of chemical and biological weapons in war, Japan developed and used biological weapons up until the end of World War II. It is documented that the Japanese government authorized the Imperial Army to conduct human experimentation on Chinese and American prisoners of war. The unit in charge of these studies, Unit 731, set up a camp in an isolated area of the Manchurin Peninsula in northern China. The Japanese soldiers at the camp, named "Water Purification Unit 731," used aerosolized *Bacillus anthracis,* or anthrax, on prisoners by exposing them during open-air procedures. It is undocumented as to how many thousands of war prisoners died as a result of this particular experiment, but nearly one thousand of the victims were autopsied for the purpose of understanding the pathology of anthrax as a biological weapon. Anthrax was not the only agent that Japan tested.

According to surviving witnesses, many tens of thousands of people from China to Bangkok were killed in field tests in which Japanese troops distributed food tainted with deadly pathogens such as *Vibrio cholerae* (cholera) or *Salmonella typhi (*typhoid*)*. The field tests created epidemics by injecting microbes into unsuspecting victims, who were told that they were being inoculated against diseases. The Japanese government also used airplanes to spray villages with plague-infested fleas, killing thousands of nameless, faceless victims, all for the purpose of biological weaponry.

"Think BioThrax," Jeffrey said. Members of his think-tank team grumbled out loud.

"Not that again," one said, shaking his head. Some of the newer team members looked confused, unaware of the significance of BioThrax.

"Why not?" Jeffrey continued. He gave a brief summation of the BioThrax investigation for the uninformed team members. "In 1998, BioThrax was granted an exclusive multi-million dollar contract with the U.S. Department of Defense to manufacture, test, bottle and store the anthrax vaccine. BioThrax was a failing company at the time the contract was awarded. Many of the major stockholders of BioThrax were big political players in America and world-wide. Some feel that the anthrax mail mystery of 2001 will never be solved because it was fabricated in order to launch the anthrax vaccine."

"How does BioThrax apply to the avian flu deaths?" asked one of the mind hunters who was taking copious notes.

"Consider this scenario," Jeffrey said. "What if a drug company that is not regulated by something like the FDA has come up with a vaccine for a certain strain of the avian flu? How best to test the product?"

"By injecting victims?"

"Precisely," Jeffrey said. "They send out the 'inseminator' to various parts of the world, probably highly-populated places with limited medical resources. Launch the virus, and monitor its spread and containment. Then launch their vaccine. Some say that this is how the smallpox vaccine got its start. Why not the avian flu vaccine?"

"Playing devil's advocate," the woman in uniform said, "wouldn't this be too obvious? I mean, don't we always begin investigations by asking who profits most by murder? Closest kin and wealth recipients are typically scrutinized first. Wouldn't the 'hero vaccine company' be the first place we looked?"

"Yes," Jeffrey said, "they would. But I've seen the cover-ups in the past, and my mentor, who unfortunately is no longer alive, told me about cases like this with Bayer and other large companies dating back to the 1950's. These kinds of scenarios have happened in history before, and like I always say, 'history tends to repeat itself.'"

"But it doesn't appear that anyone is being injected in this case. The autopsies results show that these women ingested some form of duck right before they died. If a drug company was testing a vaccine, wouldn't they be using a syringe?"

"I've thought about that a great deal," Jeffrey said. "If victims were being injected with a virus, it would be more obvious that a pharmaceutical company might be involved. What better way to throw off authorities than to have the virus connected to birds? Birds are known to carry the H5N1 virus. By forcing women to drink a duck cocktail spiked with the H5N1 virus, it causes the scientific community to divide, which is exactly what has happened."

"With all due respect, it sounds a little far-fetched, Dr. Plattenburg."

"That's precisely why we've been hired. It is our job to consider all possible scenarios and then rule them out scientifically. You each have your respective assignments in the folders in front of you. Let's get to work."

* * *

The Evros Delta, located about ten miles south of Alexandroupolis, Greece, is ecologically one of Europe's most important wetlands. Three hundred different species of birds have been recorded on site, and more than two hundred thousand migrating waterfowl spend part of their winter there. The wetlands are in a highly sensitive area, due to their proximity to Turkey and the fact that the Turks and the Greeks have long battled over this land.

Alexandroupolis is a modern city, with a vibrant maritime and military economy. There is one train a day from Istanbul to Alexandroupolis. Nicolai Petrescu slept most of the train ride. He did not feel well. Had Margareta infected him with her bite? He should have tightened her gag. He alternated between doses of Stiflu and Rescuflu, hoping that one of them would work its magic and keep him from falling prey to the flu.

He had terribly vivid dreams during the train ride. He dreamt about his time in Peru and Ecuador–running from the authorities and hiding in the mountains. In his dream, he recounted a time he spent in Macchu Piccu–an archeological site high in the Peruvian mountains. The image in his dream was clear and horrific–he saw dozens of young, dead girls in frilly, lacey dresses, arranged in a circle having a tea party.

A strong jolt from the train startled him from his dream. His head and chest were drenched in sweat, and he felt like he had a dangerously high fever. When he arrived in Alexandroupolis, he called Vladimir Checovsky, complaining about the bite. "How many doses do I take?"

"Take one pill every four hours," Vladimir said. "You must rest. The medicine needs time to get into your system."

"How much time? Do you not know how long it takes to work?"

"We are still testing it, Nicolai. We have only conducted lab tests on mice. It worked for them and it will work for you. Take one day off. Then hit the rest of Europe hard. We are ready to launch."

"What if I die?" Nicolai asked. "Don't you care about me?"

"Of course I care. But you are my prodigal son. You know your role in this. In fact, it was your idea, my dear Nicolai. So if you die, make sure you infect a lot of people on your way." The phone line went dead.

The pompous bastard. Sometimes Nicolai hated Vladimir. But, Vladimir saved his life when he was wandering the streets of St. Petersburg, drunk. He took him in and gave him a home and a job cleaning cages for test mice in his medical laboratory. Seeing that he was a smart young man, Vladimir promoted Nicolai often, and as Tarirescu grew more successful, Nicolai's responsibilities increased. Vladimir had always been arrogant, but ever since Tarirescu gobbled up its competitors and gained control of vaccine production contracts in Russia, he had become a monster. Vladimir's power- hungry attitude served him well, but he had few friends. He believed that Nicolai was his friend, but he was wrong. Nicolai had his own agenda for what they called "Project Rescuflu."

Rescuflu was Tarirescu's antiviral medication to fight a new strain of the H5N1-type of avian flu. The new strain had been genetically created in Tarirescu's lab, and had been tested on its stock of chickens. The medication had also been genetically created in response to the strain, and had been tested in laboratory mice. Vladimir needed humans to test his medication, but due to the explosive nature of the virus, it was impossible to test. So, Vladimir and Nicolai, after a night of too much vodka, came up with a plan.

* * *

Mac was working on a legal brief late in the evening when her back phone line rang. She pushed aside a stack of books and grabbed the receiver before the call went into her voicemail. She was pleasantly surprised to hear Gil's voice, but he sounded hoarse and tired.

"Are you feeling ill?" she asked. There was an echo on the international call, and she heard her question reverberate before he answered.

"I think I have a slight head cold. Nothing to worry about. I'm calling because I'm going to be delayed further. My boss is unhappy with my marketing plan and is insisting that I stay in Russia until he is satisfied."

"I'm sorry," Mac said, cradling the phone to her ear with her right shoulder. "I know that you are looking forward to coming back here. I completely understand your predicament. Harry, who is my partner now, used to be my boss. Sometimes I had to re-write legal briefs fifteen times before he would approve. But looking back, his demanding nature made me a better lawyer. I'm sure your boss has a good motive."

"You don't know my boss," Gil said.

Chapter 13

Nicolai slept during the second leg of the train ride from Alexandroupolis to Thessaloniki. When he awoke in the Greek city named by the Macedonian general in 316 BC, he felt much better. Either the Rescuflu had worked, or he was so overly exhausted that sleep was the only remedy.

As the train came to a lurching stop, he fumbled through his backpack, looking for the name of his next victim. He had done his homework well, so far. He washed his hair in the train depot sink and shaved his beard. He would have to look good for this woman who went by the name of Demette Dimitrios. In her photograph, she appeared very attractive. Her prostitute mother had been attractive too, until her mutilated body was found on the outskirts of Bucharest.

He set out on his mission to find Demette Dimitrios, now a curator for the Museum of the Macedonian Struggle. He walked into the museum and pretended to read the story of the liberation of Macedonia from the Ottomans. Demette Dimitrios sat at her desk, reading. Her dark hair was loosely swept back from her face in a chignon. Her skin was creamy and soft-looking and her eyes were heavily made up. She wore tortoise-shell reading glasses, which she occasionally took off and replaced again, as she spoke to museum visitors. Her red, lacquered nails matched her red lips, and when she spoke, Nicolai noticed that her lips barely moved. She was extraordinary looking—better than he remembered from her photograph. Nicolai approached her research desk and asked her a question. She responded with a factual answer, not paying much attention to him. Nicolai was used to women finding him attractive. He did not like the way she shrugged him off, as if he were a peasant. He asked her a few more questions about Ottoman history. She glanced at him briefly, and then referred him to a particular display in the museum which contained placards with the information he requested. She did not make eye contact with him. She hardly looked up from her reading material when delivering her curt answer. He could feel heat radiating up his neck as she continued to ignore him. He had planned on courting her and enjoying her a bit. But his anger overtook him.

He reached deep into his backpack and retrieved a small, wooden mallet. He waited until no one else was in the foyer of the museum, and then he simply struck her in the head with the mallet. She fell to the floor and began to bleed from her right temple. He grew angry at himself for his petulance. Now he would have to stop the bleeding and carry her, without being noticed, to the White Tower. In a bustling city in broad daylight, this would draw attention. He would have to wait until dark.

He hid with her body in the janitor's closet until the museum emptied out. He poured a slightly different version of the brown liquid concoction down her throat, and listened to her gargle, as her reflexes tried to save her. "To hell with Vladimir. I was going to give him one more victim, but I've changed my mind," Nicolai said out loud to himself. "My mutuations will make Vladimir's virus look like the common cold."

His anger escalated as he explored beneath her stockings. She had a lovely body. And now he had poisoned it. He did not dare penetrate her. What a waste. He took his time drawing his pictograph sketch on her inner thigh, adding more details than he had in the past. He had time to kill.

When it was dark, he quickly carried her body across Poxenou Koromila to a 15th-century tower in the center of Thessaloniki. During the 18th century, it was used as a prison for insubordinate janissaries, soldiers of an elite corps of Turkish troops, who became servants of the sultan. Many of the janissaries were massacred in this tower, which caused it to be known as the bloody tower. Later, the tower was white-washed as a symbolic gesture and made it into a place of worship.

Authorities found Demette Dimitrios's bloody body in the stairwell the following day. Soon after, the people of Thessaloniki began recalling the janissarie massacre of centuries-past. The tower was bloody once more.

The European Commission requested that Greek authorities immediately send tissue samples to the Community Reference Laboratory in Weybridge, England.

As a precautionary measure, the Greek Ministry of Agriculture instantly restricted the dispatch of live poultry and poultry products, and insisted that every bird in the region of Thessaloniki be eradicated.

Bird watchers, who spent much of their free time enjoying the variety of birds in the Evros Delta, were horrified to learn that the birds were to be killed. Both Turks and Greeks who treasured the delta protested wildly. The Greek Minister of Agriculture was found floating face down in the water, in a cesspool of duck excrement.

* * *

The President of the United States was not happy to learn that Ralph Nader had sent him another "public letter" in response to the world-wide avian flu panic attacks. The letter criticized the administration's failure to act upon the warnings from top virologists and medical associations.

Once the criticism was public, politicians all over America got on the pandemic bandwagon. One particular headline was telling: "America Must Raise the Profile of Pandemic Preparedness as a Matter of National Security." In quick response, the President issued a Pandemic Preparedness Plan, which included the "Pillars of National Strategy." The strategy described the three pillars to dealing with the avian flu: Preparedness and Communication; Surveillance and Detection; and Response and Containment. But the administration placed the burden of carrying out the strategy on the states and localities, rather than at the national level, which led to a great deal of finger- pointing. A quote from the Pandemic Preparedness Plan read, "The success of these measures is predicated on actions taken at the individual level and in states and communities. Our communities are on the front lines of a pandemic, and will face many challenges in maintaining continuity of society in the face of widespread illness and increased demand on most essential government services."

The Governor of Wyoming was furious. "How can we adopt a strategy like this when our federal government cannot supply its people with a vaccine or antiviral medication to combat the spread of the disease? What are we to do? Words are words and strategies are strategies, but without real-life solutions they mean nothing to us plain-talking Wyoming folk."

Officials in many other states agreed with Wyoming's Governor and launched their own verbal attacks against the administration's strategy. Americans were in a state of panic because they could not get a sufficient supply of Stiflu. People protested on the streets and bombarded the government with massive amounts of phone calls and emails, logging their various complaints.

Leaders in Washington were feeling the squeeze of unhappy citizens. The President, who was in Switzerland, meeting with world leaders to try to solve the avian flu crisis, was warned by his Secretary of Health and Human Services that if he didn't act fast, there was going to be national insurrection.

Chapter 14

United States (Ana Bontierre); Hong Kong (Elena Costeau); Bangkok (Lucretia Sudea); Mumbai (Florentina Ursa); Syria (Rozalie Oana); Turkey (Maria Montea); Romania (Margareta Canja); Greece (Demette Dimitrios). At the CDC in Atlanta, Dr. Sharp added Demette Dimitrios's name to the flowchart that decorated the wall in her office. She had plastered a giant world atlas alongside the flowchart, with pins stuck in the cities where the outbreaks had occurred. She connected string from the name of each victim to their location on her atlas. She stood quietly, her five foot three inch frame clothed in a well-heeled suit, pondering where the next outbreak might occur. She was particularly concerned about an outbreak in Africa.

Dr. Fahrid walked into her office without knocking, and studied the chart alongside her. He had been overseas for weeks dealing with quarantine. He was home on a medical leave, suffering from fatigue.

"Dr. Ito called. He wanted to make sure that we'd been briefed on the Greece situation," Dr. Fahrid said. Dr. Sharp nodded to him, acknowledging the statement. "Dr. Kokinda called as well. She is sending you updated migration pattern analyses. She knows that you are worried about northern Africa. She is worried too."

"She still hot on the ducks?"

"Yes. She's convinced that the ducks are to blame. Although, based on the current migration, she's backing off the falcated teal and is focusing on a few sub-species."

"What else did Dr. Ito say? Did he mention antivirals? He *has* to make a decision regarding Reich soon. If he doesn't, my fear is that second- world countries are going to take matters into their own hands and produce whatever antiviral they can cook up. If they do, and it turns out that they've created an ineffective drug, all hell is going to break loose. We have eight dead women in fifteen days. We have a collateral death toll of at least eighty thousand people so far. If we don't have antivirals shelved all over the world soon, we are going to be at a death toll in the millions."

Dr. Sharp turned her back to the atlas-clad wall and paced her office. She was frustrated with Dr. Ito and with the WHO's response. She was more frustrated by the fact that few nations were willing to pony up the requisite financial aid to address the crisis. Chinese officials were culling poultry by the thousands, but hadn't offered to contribute financial aid to the WHO fund. Worse yet, the Chinese were refusing to share samples of bird flu that its scientists had collected from prior outbreaks, claiming that her most recent bird flu publication failed to give Chinese scientists credit for their portion of sample collecting and research. In the competitive world of vaccination research and licensing, hoarding of samples is not uncommon. But hoarding samples does not help innocent victims, especially when a virus is spreading like wildfire and only one company in the world owns the rights to produce an effective antiviral.

Dr. Ito knew that he had to make a decision that day about Reich. Rumors were circulating that two private pharmaceutical companies were producing a generic form of Stiflu and selling it to countries such as Canada. The generic forms had not been adequately tested, and could give people a false sense of security. But perhaps a false sense of security is better than no security whatsoever.

Other health food companies were advertising herbal remedies made from mushrooms, berries, and humic acid–claiming that the concoction would guard against the avian flu. Consumers continued to buy into any kind of preventative remedy that was touted as an effective flu fighter. A consumer could even buy an avian flu survival kit on EBay.

* * *

Ana Bontierre–Elena Costeau -- Lucretia Sudea -- Florentina Ursa - - Rozalie Oana -- Maria Montea -- Margareta Canja -- Demette Dimitrios. Mac was online doing a global person locator search, trying to determine what these victims had in common. Other than their Romanian heritage, Mac could not connect the dots. While it was true that some were prostitutes; that fact did not hold true for all of them. She asked Jacqueline to send her a copy of all documents that related to Ana's adoption and her Romanian heritage. Perhaps Mac could find a common link in the paperwork. After looking through Jacqueline's adoption file for Ana and her sisters, she noted that Ana was adopted from the Ploiesti Orphanage in Bucharest. Mac tried to contact the orphanage, but the head minister spoke broken English and refused to provide any information.

Although it was possible that Ana died from a mysterious virus and there was no foul play involved, Mac had agreed to help Jacqueline gain some closure with respect to Ana's death and in that light, compiled a list of possible suspects who might have wanted to harm Ana. Mac had been snooping through the backgrounds of Ana's former boyfriends, but most of them were ruled out because they were either serving time for drug dealing or their whereabouts were unknown. Mac wanted to give Jacqueline answers, but every lead turned into a dead end. It was frustrating.

Jeffrey had called Mac a few times recently and Mac expressed her frustration to him.

"Isn't that the county or district attorney's job to find out what happened to Ana?" Jeffrey asked.

"She needs closure. The county attorney found the autopsy results conclusive that Ana died from the avian flu. He does not feel that there are grounds for an investigation and he has closed his file."

"Maybe he is right."

"Maybe he isn't. If Jacqueline is willing to pay me to look into it, then I will."

"Why doesn't she hire a detective?" Jeffrey asked. "She could hire one a lot cheaper than what she's probably paying you?"

"She trusts me," Mac said. Before Jeffrey could make a wise crack about a client trusting her lawyer, Mac quickly changed the subject.

* * *

Julianna Latini was a lucky woman. She was born unlucky, to an unknown woman at Ploiesti Maternity Hospital in Romania, the same place where Lucretia Sulea was stolen from her mother's womb. Julianna was not stolen. Her mother gave birth and walked away, albeit without her daughter. Julianna was also sold, but fortunately, she was sold to an adoption agency in Milan, Italy. There, a prominent family adopted and named her, and raised her in an affluent lifestyle.

Julianna had been raised by a shopaholic mother on Via Montenapoleone, in the "golden triangle" of the showcase-studded streets of Milan. Luckily, Mr. Latini earned a vast living in the marble and granite business. Mrs. Latini worked daily to spend it. Milan, a fashion mecca, was center stage to every designer label in the world. Interior design, architecture, food, wine and fashion were front-stage conversation pieces among the rich and famous. Every Thursday, Mrs. Latini joined her lady friends for shopping and tea at the Four Seasons Hotel, and rested in the afternoon before joining her husband at Aimo e Nadia for dinner.

Julianna was spoiled, by most people's definition, yet she maintained a very practical side. Her grades were always top-notch in school, and she was self-educated in music and architecture. Architecture was, by far, her greatest passion, and she was confident that some day, when she convinced her mother that women should attend a university regardless of their shopping schedule, she would get her degree and become a famous architect. Mr. Latini loved the idea. He knew that Julianna had a special gift.

Julianna loved to sketch Milan's Duomo. As the world's largest Gothic cathedral, the Duomo is comprised of one hundred thirty five marble spires and over two thousand marble statues. Sometimes Julianna took the elevator to the top, just to draw a particular flying buttress, or to see if she could get a glimpse of the Swiss Alps, some fifty miles away.

One afternoon, as she was on the roof of the Duomo sketching various angles of the buttresses, a handsome, Zegna-suited gentleman approached her and asked her for a light. Julianna was one of the few Europeans who did not smoke, and so she quickly apologized and continued with her sketching. The gentleman did not relent.

"Your work is lovely," he said. "You have an eye for angles."

"Thank you," Julianna said, without looking up this time.

"Yet the angles of the buttress are not nearly as beautiful as the angles of your perfect face. You must be on the runway."

"No, I'm not a model. I'm training to be an architect. That is why I am here."

"You are here to study architecture, yes. But you are here, now, because it was destined that I meet you. You are the loveliest woman I've ever seen. Are you Romanian? You have that look about you."

Julianna pulled back, surprised by his statement. "No, I am Italian. My parents are Milanese."

"Of course. You are so lovely. I apologize. Perhaps you can help me. I am in Milan for a short visit, and it would please me if I could see Leonardo da Vinci's *Il Cenacolo*. Could you please direct me to Santa Maria della Grazie?"

Julianna relaxed a bit, sensing that this man was more interested in sight seeing than she initially presumed. She gave him specific directions to the piazza, and explained that the best time of day to see *The Last Supper* was between seven and nine o'clock in the evening. "You will enjoy it," Julianna added. "I think that the depiction of Jesus is the prefect embodiment of treachery and heartlessness."

Treachery and heartlessness. How delicious, he thought to himself.

"I can show you the way. I was about to meet my parents for theirrather boring Thursday night dinner."

"That would be delightful."

Chapter 15

Mary MacIntosh had not heard from Gil in nearly a week. She figured that he was busy with his work, but she felt slightly disappointed each day when she checked her email and there was nothing from him. She was pleasantly surprised, however, to receive another email from the Jeffrey. He continued to keep her updated on his cases, which was bold for Jeffrey, but she stirred something deep within him—a forgotten sense of confidence, or a pardoned desire for acceptance. He couldn't put his finger squarely on his emotions—which was unusual for him, but he knew for certain that if he buried his feelings for her, a garden would never bloom. In that light, he sent numerous emails to her, like the one he sent to her after his first visit to Wyoming.

> *I never break my solitary running protocol, but am so happy that I did with you. Thank you for sharing the Big Horn trail with me. The mountains formed a picturesque backdrop, and our conversation made the time go by too quickly. Thank you, also, for going with me to the Medicine Wheel. Your excellent directions and wonderful conversation made the trip enjoyable, despite the sad reason for going. I hope that we can meet in person again very soon. Good luck with your investigation. Let me know if I can be of any help. I might be back in Wyoming for work-related follow- up. If so, I will give you a call. -- Jeffrey*

Mac responded, offering an invitation to run again, but that he might want to bring a hat and gloves. Winter was setting in. And she asked how things were going with his investigation.

Jeffrey was usually not impulsive about responding to personal emails while on the job, but something about Mac intrigued him. She was attractive and independent and smart. He liked that about her. Then again, he liked those same characteristics in his ex-wife, before she dumped him for the intern. He shrugged the thought of his ex-wife out of his mind and hit the "reply" button.

> *I will take you up on the invitation to run again when I return to Wyoming. The investigation is going forward. Of course, I am not at liberty to discuss it, but I'll admit that it is one of the more fascinating cases that I've worked on this year. Any word regarding David Thrift?*

Mac filled Jeffrey in regarding David Thrift and the ongoing lawsuit in which she represented his estate. However, Mac knew very little regarding whether David Thrift remained a suspect in Ana's death. The sheriff's death and the quarantine slowed the gossip chain somewhat. Mac poked her head out of her office and asked Megan if she'd heard anything. Megan was younger and often went to the Mint Bar after work. If there was gossip to hear, the Mint was the place to be. Set in the middle of Main Street, it was advertised by a huge, neon-lit bucking bronco out front. Inside, the bar was a taxidermist's dream come true. Trophy heads of deer, elk, buffalo, moose, mountain lion and other scraggly mammals adorned the walls. A seven-foot long rattlesnake skin was plastered above the various bottles of liquor, and the patrons tended to consume more than they should.

Megan said that the rumor was that David Thrift killed Ana Bontierre, and that he committed suicide somewhere in the Cloud Peak Wilderness. "He was always a little wacko in high school," Megan said. "In the yearbook, his departing quote was, 'Theodore Kaczynski is my hero.'"

"The Unibomber?"

"No other. Anyone who has a hero like that is a little weird, in my book."

Mac agreed. Just as she was about to turn and walk back to her desk, the phone rang. Megan answered, and then cupped the phone with her right hand. "It's Norma Roberts from *The Sheridan Press*." Mac took the call in her office. She'd met Norma during her class action case against the methane gas industry. After the case was over, Mac and Norma had remained friends, and tried to have lunch together once a week. Norma was the eyes, ears and pulse of Sheridan, and if Mac *really* needed to know something, she asked Norma.

"I know that you represent the Bontierres," Norma said in her always matter- of-fact way. "I just got word that a group of hunters might have found David Thrift's remains on the slope crest of Antelope Butte. His backpack was alongside the corpse, and it was an area he was known to hike. I'll keep you posted if I hear anything further."

Mac thanked Norma and then reminded her that they were scheduled for lunch on Friday. Norma confirmed. After she hung up, Mac emailed Jeffrey and explained what she'd heard about David Thrift.

Jeffery was conflicted when he read Mac's email. A part of him wanted David Thrift to be on the lamb—at least he was a tangible suspect. If he was dead, then they were back to square one. Jeffrey was intrigued by Megan's remarks about David in high school. Often times, serial killers adopt a "mentor" or an "idol" who is also a killer. They frequently fantasize about the other's killing sprees, and sometimes even copy them. The fact that David Thrift admired the Unibomber raised suspicion. He would have one of his research scientists follow up on the tip.

Meanwhile, Jeffrey had scheduled a meeting with his top mind hunters to go over the commonalities of the victims. He had a team of FBI geologists studying the tattoos. The tattoos were the obvious common trait, and a digital photograph and an artist-enhanced reproduction of the sketching on each victim had been scanned into the database. They were comparing the drawings, looking for common edging and details. No two etchings looked exactly the same, but they all shared very similar traits. Each had a stone staircase that led to a partially dilapidated stone hut or structure. The structure had only a partial roof. There was short grass surrounding the structure, and behind the structure, in two of the more elaborate etchings, was a valley and in the distance, a large mountain peak. Point-to-point comparisons were being made and entered into the database. Hundreds of matches had been identified, most of which were

Indian ruins in Mexico, and Central and South America. Some matches included partially dilapidated structures in Europe and Asia, too. So, it was fair to say that the scientists had a heavy burden to narrow the scope of the search.

Jeffrey turned to his profiler team, pouring over the common traits among the victims. Like the geologists, the profilers had not turned over any magic stones, other than the fact that all the victims were Romanians, and that most of them were either orphans, prostitutes, or both. The documentation was quite sketchy—some of the women did not have birth certificates or other legal documentation. It did not appear that any of the girls were related to one another by blood or by marriage, nor did they seem to have crossed one another's paths. No commonality could be found among the people they knew. Other than heritage and the Ploiesti Hospital and its neighboring orphanage, there didn't seem to be a clear-cut connection.

The only remaining commonality was that they all had ingested some type of duck product prior to their death. But even this detail triggered doubt in the scientists. Due to the combustive nature of the victims' intestinal track, and the liquidity of the vital organs, it seemed suspect to Jeffrey, and to his team, that each of the victims actually ate duck before they died. It seemed more likely that they'd come in contact with an infected bird. On the other hand, autopsies performed by different doctors in diverse regions of the world must be taken at face value, until proven otherwise.

Jeffrey was certainly suspicious of the "duck factor," especially since Dr. Karen Kokinda was hot on the trail of every victim, likely poking her nose into every medical examiner's laboratory, making "suggestions" regarding causation, as she was known to do. He did not like Dr. Kokinda. The feelings were mutual.

Chapter 16

Almost immediately after learning about their daughter's death, Julianna Latini's wealthy parents began launching a no-expense-spared attack on the World Health Organization's lack of preparedness for the avian flu. The night prior, when they waited for over an hour for their daughter to arrive at the posh restaurant on Via Montenapoleone, the avian flu was not among their worries. Julianna sometimes got caught up in the craft of her art and lost track of time. But as the night grew longer, and they had not heard from her, Mr. Latini called the police. A search team was sent out looking for her. The next morning, a janitor working at Santa Maria della Grazie reported that he found a bleeding woman on the floor under Leonardo da Vinci's *Il Cenacolo*. The janitor was frantic. "So much blood," he kept repeating to the police. By the time the janitor had discovered her, the medical examiner later termed a "cytokine storm" had overtaken her body, destroying her lungs and other organs. The doctor had never seen such massive hemorrhage.

Within a day, dozens of medical personnel who had witnessed or assisted her progression of death at the hospital came down with flu-like symptoms. As seemed to be the case with this particular strain of flu, it spread quickly, and carriers of the virus were highly contagious before symptoms broke out. The virus spread swiftly through Milan, and the Italians had almost no Stiflu stockpiled.

Canada, on the other hand, had plenty of Stiflu and oseltamavir, the generic version that was being produced in India. They began stockpiling when the outbreak in China occurred in 1997, and they had been openly purchasing oseltamavir, despite the fact that doing so unquestionably infringed Reich's patent, and could cost the Canadian government tens of millions of dollars. But, Canadian officials refused to share their stockpile with other nations.

Mr. Latini personally paid for a loud BBC broadcast, condemning nations such as Canada for refusing to help. "We Europeans act collectively through the EISS to help reduce the burden of disease associated with influenza. We assist one another by gathering and exchanging timely information on flu activity, contributing to the development of vaccines, and providing information to health professionals and the general public, all of which significantly enhances European flu pandemic preparedness. I understand that there are twenty-eight countries in the EISS. If Canada refuses to help us now, forget the future when they need help. Europeans stick together. Our Euro is getting stronger by the day. And if the World Health Organization doesn't step in and insist that countries such as Canada help other nations, then we will be forced to go behind their back and buy drugs on the black market. And if this is the case, forget asking the EISS to contribute to the WHO fund!"

It was a heated interview. Mr. Latini was very angry. The broadcaster noted that Mr. Latini was not an elected official and therefore did not speak on behalf of the people of Italy, but remarked that his sentiments were widely shared across the continent. Shouldn't other countries assist those in a state of pandemic? Didn't it behoove the WHO to stop the virus from spreading, even if it had to force the hand of a few companies and a few nations?

Wearing a surgical mask, Dr. Ito took center stage at the summit meeting in Hong Kong. Thousands of people continued to die every day from the avian flu, and he felt that, in this time of crisis, he had to allow drug companies to produce oseltamivir in violation of Reich's patent rights.

"Let me be clear," Dr. Ito said to world leaders and pharmaceutical company CEO's, "I make this decision with a heavy heart. The WHO neither tests nor sponsors these new generic versions of oseltamavir. We have no way of knowing whether they are effective or safe. The WHO is simply declaring a world-wide emergency and defers to the right of nations under international trade treaties to break Reich's patent for Stiflu under this global health emergency. This is a temporary declaration on behalf of the WHO, and when this world health emergency is over, the WHO will issue a cease and desist order regarding the patent rights concerning generic oseltamivir. There have been eight uncontained outbreaks that we know of within the last ten to fourteen days, and we believe that there have been over one hundred thousand casualties thus far. In this time of crisis, we must ask that any pharmaceutical company ready, willing and able to make oseltamavir do so prudently, safely, and within the precautions normally undertaken when manufacturing a drug. The people of the world are dependent upon safe and effective medications. Please act accordingly."

Cheers erupted in the Hong Kong high-rise meeting room. World leaders flipped open cell phones and made calls. Reporters clicked photographs and wired the news.

* * *

In an industrial office park in Moscow, Vladimir Checovsky read the wire that he'd just received from Hong Kong. "Patent broken," was all it said. Vladimir knew that "his time had come." He would be a very rich man by the end of the week. He called Nicolai on his cell phone.

"Our time has come, my son. Dr. Ito has caved in, just as I predicted he would. Here is what I want you to do." Vladimir detailed his plan to Nicolai in excruciating detail. Per Vladimir's protocol, Nicolai repeated the plan back. "You understand exactly what I expect you to do, correct?"

"I understand."

"Then you are wasting time. Get moving."

Nicolai intended to get moving. However, he had a plan of his own.

* * *

Normally, Mac did not carry her cell phone with her when she went out for a run but today was an exception to her rule. Her cat had been throwing up for two days and she'd taken him to the vet for evaluation. Mac was awaiting a call from the vet. Her cell phone rang as she was taking on a hill in the fifth mile of her run. Her breath was heavy as she answered.

When Gil heard her winded hello, he was concerned. "Are you okay?" he asked.

"Fine. Just out for a run," she panted. "Big hill. Fifth mile. How are you? Where are you?"

"Warsaw. My boss finally accepted my marketing plan and has allowed me to present it to my team in Poland. After that, I have to make the rounds in Scandinavia. I should be back in Wyoming in a few weeks."

"At least you can see the light at the end of the tunnel now."

"I don't understand," Gil said. Mac realized that as a foreigner, he might not understand her reference. "What I mean is that you probably feel better knowing that you will be finishing soon."

"Oh. Yes. I will be finishing soon. That makes me very pleased. You have no idea how pleased I am."

"Actually, I understand completely. When I am preparing for a trial, it seems endless. Once the trial starts, I feel like my hard work starts paying off and I know that it will be over soon. It gets me through the late nights."

"I must hang up now. My boss gets mad if I am not on task. I will call you in a few days."

Mac zipped her cell phone back into the pocket of her Nike jacket and descended down the steep hill. As soon as she reached the parking lot where she'd left her Equinox, the phone rang again. This time it was the vet explaining that Ted had a massive hairball and needed a stricter diet. Mac was relieved. She had been worried that her cat might have contacted the avian flu.

Chapter 17

"No Containment in India." "Italian Virus Unresponsive to Stiflu—Thousands Dead." The headlines across the world were a telltale sign that Dr. Jocelyn Sharp knew what she was talking about. From day one, she'd been convinced that this particular strain of the H5N1 virus had mutated just enough to make it different from the outbreaks recorded in 1997 and 2003. Her published work explained that the natural progression of the virus invited some amount of mutation. Still, she was somewhat surprised by the intensity of each breakout, and the severity of the symptoms. In the past, patients did not die as quickly or as violently.

In the 2003 outbreak in Bangkok, a young girl developed a suspicious fever and stomach ache, and her health rapidly deteriorated. Her mother rushed to her side, kissing her and whispering to her that she would be alright. The daughter died, and the hospital listed the cause of death as "dengue fever." She was cremated before any tissue samples could be taken. A few days later, the mother came down with similar flu-like symptoms, and also died. An autopsy was performed on the mother, and the doctors suspected bird flu. When the mother's sister came down with similar symptoms, the doctors quickly administered oseltamivir, and the sister recovered. Nevertheless, the 2003 outbreak was striking in that it was the first recorded person-to-person transmission of avian flu. The WHO and the Thai government tried to downplay the situation, but Dr. Sharp knew then that the avian flu could mutate. This particular transmission prompted her blueprint studies of the 2003 outbreak in comparison to the 1918 Spanish flu.

When Dr. Sharp read the present-day headlines that had been downloaded and sent directly to her BlackBerry, she knew trouble was brewing. If Stiflu was ineffective in curtailing the flu symptoms, the world was going to be a radically different place. She'd predicted this, in her Nostradamus-sort of way.

Meanwhile, Dr. Sharp learned that in China and North Korea, new regulations were in effect that mandated fifteen days in jail and fines of up to two hundred yuan (equal to twenty five dollars) for anyone who failed to immunize their birds from the flu. This "plan" was in response to the world- wide criticism of the culling of birds. Millions of birds had already been killed, yet not one had tested positive for the H5N1 virus. Not one! Ambitious poultry vaccination was considered a good option for those who were radically opposed to the elimination of free-range poultry. The problem with the immunization plan, according to Dr. Sharp, was that it was difficult to distinguish between vaccinated and infected birds, since their antibodies were otherwise identical.

The issue of financial aid was even more daunting. Most of the chicken farmers were poor. And the law applied not just to farmers, but to anyone who owned poultry. Economic subsidies to support vaccination were scarce, primarily because most of the poorer countries were using their funds to purchase vast quantities of Stiflu for their people–not their poultry.

Do we send money to these poor countries to vaccinate their birds, or do we send them antiviral medicine that is in short supply and is also needed in other countries around the world? Neither option seemed to be viable. If no birds had the virus, the vaccinations were unnecessary. And the medicine, according to the headlines, was ineffective to this particular strain of flu virus. Not one to sit back and contemplate a notion for long, Dr. Sharp flipped open her laptop and began writing an article containing her opinion on the subject. She stated that it was wasteful to cull millions of birds without first testing them for the virus. It was also wasteful to vaccinate poultry when there was a short supply of the medication available to the public.

Dr. Sharp sat alone in her office, wearing a mask on her face and gloves on her hands while staring at a pile of medical journals. She thought to herself. *What makes the bird flu so deadly to people?* Her medical training told her that it was the human immune system itself that was to blame.

Strong immune systems usually defend humans against bad cells like germs and tumors. But in some cases, like asthma and allergies, strong immune systems work against the body, sparking inflammation, which exacerbates the symptoms. The unusual virulence of H5N1 causes the immune system to unleash a flood of inflammatory cells and chemicals which causes a "cytokine storm." Good cells go crazy and trigger an overreaction by the immune system, killing not just virus-infected cells but healthy cells too. The lining of blood vessels weakens, allowing fluid leaks, which causes blood pressure to drop and organs to fail. The lungs fill with fluid and hemorrhage.

Dr. Sharp decided to include this information about the overzealous human immune system in her article. She then faxed her finished expose to rivals at the National Influenza Center in Rotterdam.

In a research scientist's version of a tennis match, the NIC lobbed a quick response.

"How can Dr. Sharp, on behalf of the CDC, criticize any other agency's response to this bird flu nightmare when it was her fault that it started? Not only did she publish the blueprint to the 1918 strain, but over the last few years, her agency has systematically mishandled the virus. It has been documented that a Cincinnati bioscience firm lost thousands of samples of the H2N2 "Asian flu" virus that killed one to four million people during the 1957 pandemic. During the time that the CDC was supposed to have control of these samples, they were mislabeled as H3N2 test kits and were sent through the United States mail service. Of course, the CDC quickly claimed that it did not have regulatory authority over the distribution of the H2N2 virus because, at the time, it was not classified as a dangerous bioterrorism agent. The CDC can't have it both ways! They claim that it is perfectly fine to disseminate H5N1 information, regardless of its bioterrorism implications, yet deny any responsibility for the H2N2 foul up. That position is inconsistent, as are Dr. Sharp's quip statements with respect to bird vaccinations in Asia and the effect of Stiflu."

Dr. Sharp did not respond to NIC's statement because she did not want to address the H2N2 mistake.

Chapter 18

Within three weeks of the Hong Kong outbreak, nearly three hundred thousand people had been confirmed dead in China, Thailand, India, Syria and Turkey. Current numbers had yet to be reported for Romania and Italy. Stiflu, which had helped contain the outbreaks in China and Thailand, had proven ineffective in India, Syria and Turkey. The virus was the headline in every newspaper–everyday. The public outcry was vociferous.

Since the outbreaks, governments had worked hard to increase Stiflu stockpiles. The generic version of Stiflu had been much easier to purchase after the WHO allowed the patent to be broken. Experts wondered why the drug was effective in eastern Asia, but less effective in central Asia. Some claimed that people were growing resistant to the antiviral. Other experts believed that the virus had mutated. "It is classic, age-old chemistry at its finest. 'Be careful what one inoculates, for it might come back with a bite.'"

Dr. Ito's head was spinning. He was being briefed on the effect of the drug resistance being experienced with Stiflu. Had he broken patent protection on a drug that was ineffective in treating the strain that the WHO was fighting? He would certainly lose stature among colleagues, but more importantly, what was going to happen to those individuals who believed that they had purchased an antiviral that would keep their family safe? Would they be less careful around poultry, further subjecting their families to peril? Would lawsuits break out due to false assumptions that oseltamavir would protect individuals from the spreading virus? What would Reich do? And how would the small pharmaceutical companies in India and Thailand deal with the fact that their generic drug, whether in violation of a patent or not, was not working? Dr. Ito had a migraine. And Ibuprofen was not strong enough to help him.

* * *

Vladimir Checovsky, the tall, gray-haired, debonair CEO of Tarirescu, felt that the time was perfect to launch his company's new avian flu antiviral medicine. He purchased a two-minute satellite commercial broadcast regarding his H5N1 antiviral drug, "Rescuflu." A man blessed with good looks and a kind of preacher appeal, he carried a certain stage-presence during his global network broadcast.

"The avian flu is real, and we at Tarirescu understand the world's fears and concerns about having necessary antiviral medication available to protect your country. We, at Tarirescu want to protect you. That is why Tarirescu has been working for years to research and develop various antiviral medications and vaccinations for various strains of the flu, including the H5N1 strain. We have a new product called Rescuflu that we believe is the precise antiviral drug for the current mutation of the avian flu. Rescuflu has been successfully tested in the laboratory. In light of the current global crisis, we at Tarirescu are offering vast supplies at a discounted price. We are offering an open-bidding process, meaning that whoever wants to purchase it can. Rescuflu can be ordered on-line, telephonically, or by fax. We can mass- produce the drug on short notice and will do everything within our power to get the medicine to your doorstep as soon as possible. We are even willing to grant licenses to any government or private company interested in manufacturing Rescuflu, for a fee."

The commercial broadcast hit the media and caused a circus-like frenzy. Every major network and internet source ran the clip, over and over. Mac, who was sitting in her office in Sheridan, Wyoming, doing on-line legal research, listened to Vladimir Checovksy's speech. *Tarirescu. Where have I heard this before?* She thought to herself. Maybe it had been in the news. She quickly picked up the phone, called the pharmacist and asked that he place an order for Rescuflu.

"I'm on top of it, Mac," he said. "They promised delivery with second-day air service, so I will call you when it arrives. All of my lines are blinking. I need to go." Mac thanked him and hung up. She imagined that half of the world was on-line in one form or another, trying to get their hands on the new flu drug.

* * *

"How would Vladimir Checovsky know whether this so-called Rescuflu is effective on the current strain of avian flu?" Dr. Ito asked Dr. Sharp. He phoned her from Geneva the minute he heard about the network clip.

"My question exactly," Dr. Sharp said in response as she paced the confines of her office at the CDC in Atlanta. "To my knowledge, the CDC has never sent tissue samples to Tarirescu, and I doubt that any of my colleagues have either. I'm going to make a few calls to branch leaders on the CDC team, and to other scientists, and see if anyone knows how Vladimir Checovsky could have access to the blueprint of a *new mutation*. This is highly suspect."

"Agreed," Dr. Ito said. "Imagine my predicament. Everyone and their brother wants to get their hands on this new miracle drug, yet I cannot substantiate whether it is safe, or whether it works, or how it works, or if there is enough supply to meet demand. If I put a halt on the drug, pending further testing, chaos will erupt. I already look like a fool for breaking Reich's patent. This is a nightmare."

"It is only the beginning, I'm afraid. I keep getting reports from my quarantine teams that containment is getting more difficult with every outbreak."

"Make your calls and get back to me as soon as possible. I need to call my intelligence group and have this guy checked out. His company seems to surface every time there is an avian flu outbreak. During the 2003 outbreak, they had an excess chicken supply and sold supplies to Hong Kong at a premium."

"Either he is a very lucky man, or something peculiar is going on."

Chapter 19

"Vladimir Checovsky sent samples of Rescuflu to hospitals in Syria and Turkey two days ago," Dr. Fahrid told his boss, Dr. Sharp, over the cell phone. "Doctors from both hospitals called me to ask whether they should administer, and I told them to go ahead. People are dying every hour. I didn't see the harm in trying whatever was available under–"

"You authorized the use of a new antiviral without checking with me first?" Dr. Sharp yelled. "That is not protocol, Dr. Fahrid. All you had to do was pick up the phone and tell me about it. I was blind-sided today with the Tarirescu broadcast, and then by a call from Dr. Ito wondering how Checovsky got the blueprint for the current outbreak. Imagine what it is going to look like when I tell him that the CDC authorized the use of Rescuflu on victims in Syria and Turkey! Ito is going to think I was hiding the ball from him! I just got off the phone with him ten minutes ago. You've put me in a terrible predicament by–"

"The drug is showing promise, Dr. Sharp. Victims are responding. Symptoms are diminishing. It seems to be working so far."

"You are kidding me, right? Not only have you not told me that you are using an experimental drug, but you've also not communicated with me that this drug is successful in the preliminary stages? Your job is to–"

"This is an emergency," Dr. Fahrid said, agitated. "I've been working twenty-four-seven for three weeks straight around the world setting up complex biosafety labs, working in a deadly environment around terrified medical personnel who do *not* want to be there, doing everything within my power to quarantine and contain this monster of a virus. I've watched hundreds of thousands of bloody corpses being zipped up into body bags, and you are worried about your image–"

"Whoa. Watch your step, Dr. Fahrid. This is not about image. This is about communicating vital information for the safety of the public at large. My image has nothing to do with this. I have a responsibility to the President of the United States, the Department of Health and to other world leaders to get them the most accurate, up-to-date information so that they can, in turn, help their people make informed decisions. Do not for one minute confuse this with some kind of ego gratification–"

"I'm sorry," Dr. Fahrid said in a more calm tone. "I am exhausted and frazzled and jittery. I didn't mean to offend you. I'm just trying to put a finger in the hole in the dyke over here. You are right. I should have called you. But now that I have you on the phone, let me tell you what we have been experiencing here in Turkey." Dr. Fahrid filled Dr. Sharp in.

"What about the woman in Milan?"

"The rich man's daughter? You haven't heard the last of him. Mr. Latini is going to stop at nothing in his efforts to find out what happened to his daughter. Did you see his BBC interview last night?"

"No."

"He said on international television that he is convinced that America was at fault for his daughter's death. He stated his belief that the avian flu outbreaks were probably a CDC cover-up. In fact, he said something like, "Leave it to an American agency to create and then cover-up bioterrorism.""

* * *

"Do not proclaim ignorance with me, Dr. Sharp," a renowned scientist said from her office at the National Influenza Center in Rotterdam. "The CDC published the blueprint for this virus. Don't cry foul now! I'm sure that the Tarirescu scientists have been tinkering with your recipe for a year, and have probably cooked up a few varieties of antiviral medicines for slight mutations created in the lab. This is *exactly* what I have been complaining about for years. We have been issuing statements to–"

Dr. Sharp put her hand over the phone speaker and took a deep breath. She should have known better than to expect anyone at the NIC to put down his or her sword and offer constructive solutions to a problem.

When she put the phone back to her ear, the line was dead. Good thing, she thought to herself. She reached over and picked up the picture of her two kids. When she felt the weight of the world on her shoulders, like she did right then, she tried to focus on her children, and what they meant to her. Of course, she loved them dearly, like most moms love, but they also represented hope to her. Hope for the future. Hope that the world would continue to learn how to work together to solve problems, instead of the constant barrage of finger- pointing. If there was one lesson she could teach her children, it would be to focus on solving whatever problem came their way, and not worry about who was to blame. Dr. Sharp had a number of screen savers that flashed on her computer throughout the day. One was, "The Local is Always Global." Everyone who worked for her had heard her say it a thousand times. Another was, "Solve, Don't Blame." And another read, "Where's the Silver Lining?" She read her screensavers, one by one, and then dialed Dr. Ito's number.

* * *

"You cannot tell me in good faith that you had no idea that Rescuflu was being used?" Dr. Ito's migraine was back, in full force, as his blood vessels enlarged on his forehead. Dr. Sharp had to hold the phone a foot away from her ear, and even then, she could hear him take a deep pull from his cigarette. She silently chanted her mantra about solutions instead of blame. She hoped that he would calm down after he got it out of his system. She explained the situation, acknowledging the miscommunication, and suggested that other quarantine doctors should also be admonished. An argument ensued.

Meanwhile, shipments of Rescuflu were arriving at ports all over the world, except to the United States of America. The FDA would not allow importation of a drug that had not been tested on an adequate scientific scale. Americans were furious. Thousands flocked to the Canadian border from places like Montana, Michigan, New York, and Washington State, to purchase Rescuflu. Despite the fact that it was against the law to buy Canadian pharmaceuticals and bring the drugs back into the United States, Americans stockpiled. "I don't care about that law," said a Montana rancher's wife to a news reporter. "It was set up by them politicians in Washington after their pockets were lined with money from drug companies. Anyways, when that avian flu breaks out in my neck of the woods, them lawmakers might be knockin' at my door for medicine." On camera, the woman, who was in the cab of her green '57 Chevy pickup truck, held up the *Billings Gazette* and pointed to the headline. "Rescuflu is Rescuing the World." The article, which documented the success of the drug so far in Syria and Turkey, recommended that each person in the world have at least one dose on hand. "Heck, if I buy enough of this stuff, I might get myself elected mayor of my town by the end of the year." She flashed a smile, revealing a partial set of teeth encased by dark receding gums.

Nationwide, Americans were furious that the FDA would not allow the drug to be imported. Telephone lines to local, state and federal government offices were jammed with complaints and threats. Politicians in Washington did their typical song and dance with their constituents, agreeing that the laws should be changed in a time of emergency.

The President of the United States could not be reached for comment.

Chapter 20

Brewing beer was the most important thing in the world to Silvia Ursu's boss. In a country barely the size of New Jersey, Belgium's beer-brewing tradition dated back for centuries. Most of the local beers were not found anywhere but Belgium, and could be traced back to secret formulas created by the Trappist monks during the Middle Ages. In the forested mountains and valleys of the Ardennes region, where the Battle of the Bulge was fought, lies the ruins of the Abbaye D'Orval. This stunning abbey was built in the 17th century, and is now part of the grounds of the Orval brewing company. Orval beer is famous in this region and is sold warm, along with a hunk of cheese and a loaf of bread. Hikers often carted it around in a picnic basket while looking for the perfect place to take in a vista.

Silvia Ursu did not like Orval beer. The smell of it made her want to vomit. It was the same smell that summoned childhood nightmares of a hooded man forcing himself inside of her. She wanted to forget that memory, but it was impossible. Every waft of beer recaptured her subconsciously repressed thoughts, and made her wish that she could go far, far away from this place.

Silvia didn't remember much else from her childhood, except that at one point, she lived with her mother in a small apartment in Brussels. Her mother was beautiful, she recalled, with flowing red hair and dark eyes. They would lay together in the early morning, with the sun streaming through the apartment window, her mother telling her stories about the train ride from Romania to Poland. The stories sometimes gave conflicting versions of how they got from Poland to Belgium, but Silvia didn't care. She just loved to hear the stories.

Her mother entertained men every night, and she would make Silvia hide in the closet when the men were in their apartment. Silvia could peek out the keyhole and watch, if she wanted, but she didn't like seeing the fat-bellied men on top of her mother.

Unfortunately, one night, while a man was with her mother, Silvia needed to use the bathroom. Normally, the men did not stay long, and Silvia knew better than to interrupt. But this time, the man stayed for a very long time. Silvia was in tears in the dark closet, trying to hold her urine. Her mother would beat her if she peed in the closet, but she would beat Silvia if she interrupted too. She had no choice.

The man was grunting loud. She figured that she could quietly open the closet door and sneak out of the apartment and down the hall to the community bathroom. She could stay in the bathroom until the man left. She grabbed the wobbly metal door knob and slowly turned it until it unlatched. Then she gradually nudged the wooden door, bit by bit, to open it far enough for her to squeeze out. As she gave it one last nudge, the door made a loud creaking sound. The man jumped up off the bed. He bent over, grabbed his pants and quickly put them on. He then grabbed his coat that was draped over the chair, and retrieved from it a small, black pistol. He fired twice into Silvia's mother, and once toward the open closet door. He then ran out of the apartment and into the night.

With urine streaming down her legs, Silvia ran from apartment to apartment, trying to summon help for her mother. It was too late. Her mother lay dead in a pool of blood-soaked sheets.

The Trappists monks learned that there was a Romanian orphan in Brussels, and they sent for her. For room and board, she could help with the arduous burden of keeping the garden tended. The grounds of the Abbaye D'Orval were famous for the medicinal herb garden, and legend had it that the fragrance of the Orval beer was somehow tied to the herbs.

Silvia liked being outdoors, raking and sowing and digging with her hands, and grew accustomed to living in the hills. She would have been a happy child, had it not been for one monk, Father Jerry, who visited her every so often with beer on his breath and rape on his mind. Father Jerry told her that if she tattled on him for having sex with her, he would let the man who killed her mom get her.

Silvia grew numb to his visits and never said a word to anyone about him. Eventually, Father Jerry moved away from the Abbey, and the only time she thought of him was when she smelled the beer.

One day, when she was on her way from the garden to her loft, she heard a man's voice call out from down the road. Silvia walked to him. He had a basket in his hand, and asked her where the Auberge du Moulin Hideux was located. He had missed a turn somewhere. Silvia did not know where the Auberge was, but suggested that he go to the brewing area and ask one of the monks for directions. The man thanked her, and asked her a few more questions. He said that she looked familiar to him and wondered where she was from. She shrugged at first, not wishing to talk to a stranger. But the man seemed genuinely nice, and he even told her about his travels around the world. When he mentioned that he'd been to Romania, she perked up. She told him that she wasn't entirely sure where she was from, but imparted some of the stories that her mother had told her. The man seemed truly interested, and told her how sorry he was that she was so far away from her homeland. He told her that he had pictures of Romania in his car, and he wanted her to come and look at them. Silvia followed.

A monk found Silvia in the chapel the following morning. It was unclear to him whether she was alive. She had blood seeping from her nose, mouth and vagina. They drove her to Brussels, where she was admitted into the hospital. After throwing up black vomit, she was given a dose of both Stiflu and Rescuflu. Neither drug seemed to help. She died a few hours later.

In an abundance of caution, the monks who brought her to the hospital were also given doses of both antiviral medications. The doctors did not know what caused Silvia's death, but based on the symptoms reported to be associated with this strain of the avian flu, they thought it best to follow the hospital's newly adopted protocol. Both monks were admitted for supervision.

By that evening, both monks developed a high fever and severe stomach cramping. Additional doses of both antivirals were administered. Again, neither drug helped. By morning, both monks had died of internal hemorrhaging. Medical personnel who had assisted any of the three patients were also given the drugs. Unfortunately, the antiviral medication didn't seem to have the same kick that it did in Turkey. Doctors complained that perhaps they received a faulty batch of the antiviral medication. However, the complaints fell on deaf ears because Rescuflu was saving lives in Eastern Europe and western Asia, and the rest of the world was clamoring to stockpile the new drug. All the while, Vladimir Checovsky sat in his Russian laboratory giving orders to his employees regarding the constant shipment of Rescuflu. The money was rolling in faster than he could count it. He quickly made deposits to his off-shore accounts. He summoned one of his women from the harem and bedded her in his office suite. *Oh, the life of a rich businessman.* He was pleased with himself. His plan was working well and Nicolai Petrescu was performing his task perfectly. Life was good for this self-made man. Or so he thought.

Chapter 21

"No bells tolled, and nobody wept no matter what his
loss because almost everyone expected death And people
said and believed, 'This to be the end of the world.'"
–Agnolo di Turo, a chronicler of Sienna, Italy

The Black Death–a combination of the bubonic and pneumonic plagues–killed over twenty million people in Asia, Europe and Africa in the 1300s. At the time, physicians believed that the cause of the plagues was "planetary influences." There was no medicine available to stop the spread of disease.

* * *

Bells rang out in the mosques and churches of Istanbul, Turkey, as word spread that Rescuflu was working. People who had checked into the hospital with severe flu-like symptoms were responding well to the drug. This was very good news to Turkish leaders because thousands of people had already died in Istanbul, and it appeared that the virus had crossed over the Bosporus and was heading into the Asian side of Turkey. The Turkish people were frenzied, crying out about the Black Death. People refused to leave their homes and hardly anyone reported to work. "I run a Persian carpet business. My sole income is based in exports. If no one shows up to work, I have no one to take orders or deliver goods to the port. I will not be able to feed my family," an elderly man said to an English reporter on location to cover the spread of the avian flu. "I am told that a large shipment of Rescuflu is on the way. Maybe workers will show up if I offer them a dose of medicine."

Syrian leaders rejoiced in the fact that Rescuflu seemed to be causing the avian flu to subside in Damascus. With over nine thousand deaths in Damascus, neighboring regions such as Lebanon and Jerusalem exulted after hearing the news that containment could be a reality.

Tarirescu was being praised around the globe for its amazing capacity to handle the sudden and voluminous orders of Rescuflu. However, not everyone was impressed with Tarirescu's ability to respond to what most felt was an unforeseeable outbreak. "I don't see how a small company could have such a massive supply of an antiviral that was previously not even on the market," the Prime Minister of Great Britain said. "Don't get me wrong. We are happy to have the medicine, but it seems rather dubious." The press reacted wildly to the Prime Minister's comments. Some of the media agreed, questioning how a private company could afford to amass an unproven drug. But the majority of the media expressed shock and alarm at what it characterized as a callous and ridiculous accusation.

"The world is lucky to have private enterprises still willing to anticipate world needs and respond accordingly," reported one newspaper in France.

Meanwhile, in America, the FDA continued to refuse to allow the sale of Rescuflu within its borders. "This drug has not been adequately tested in humans and it would be very risky by FDA standards to use humans infected with a flu virus to test the antiviral's safety and efficacy. And that is exactly what Tarirescu is doing. They are using this near-global pandemic to test the safety and effectiveness of their drug. When the FDA believes that the drug has been sufficiently tested and it is clearly established that the drug is safe, we will welcome it within our borders."

While Americans felt angst and frustration over the lack of antiviral mediation, Nicolai Petrescu continued on his mortal crusade.

Chapter 22

Victoria Vlaicu spent her nights behind bars in Picadilly Circus. It was a different kind of incarceration—one thrust upon her by a series of unfortunate events. Born to political refugees from Bosnia, she'd lived all over Eastern Europe. When her father was arrested and detained for murder charges at the Poland border, she and her Romanian mother escaped to London. Her mother was an excellent seamstress and was able to earn a decent living in the Picadilly garment district. But when her mother couldn't sleep unless she was sitting, reclined in a chair, Victoria knew that something was desperately wrong. She begged her mother to go to the doctor, but her mother claimed that she was fine, that they couldn't afford expensive doctors. Her mother died that year, when Victoria was eleven, from stomach cancer.

Victoria had never mastered her mother's craft of sewing, despite her efforts to learn. She'd spent years in the "attic room," where her mother sewed for Louise, a dress maker in London. Victoria regularly offered advice to Louise about design. Victoria loved fashion, and had a distinct eye for vogue fads. She spent afternoons in Louise's design room making sketches and mixing fabrics. Louise took her in after Victoria's mother died, but instead of sending her to school, like her mother would have wanted, Louise allowed Victoria to window shop during the morning and design couture the rest of the day.

Louise was not, as they say, a traditional woman. When she was younger, Louise made a living in the escort business. As Victoria blossomed into a young lady, Louise encouraged her to dress more provocatively, and suggested that she seek evening employment in the neon-lit backstreets of Picadilly. At first, Victoria, a tall, lanky, long-haired beauty with iridescent blue eyes, disliked modeling lingerie in the window of a peep-show bar. She had led an isolated life, and it made her feel cheap to be behind glass, separated from the world, stared at like some monkey in a zoo. She decided that she would rather dance to a live audience, with or without clothes.

Louise had never paid Victoria for dress design. She received room and board, in exchange. Once Victoria started making good money as an exotic dancer, she decided that she wanted to go to design school. After saving enough money, she enrolled in a fashion institute. She went to school and designed during the day, and danced at night. She had only Sundays off. On most Sundays, she picked a new place she'd never seen, like a museum or a church or a park, and traveled there. She found that she loved visiting old castles around London—she was in awe of the architecture and exquisitely unique design of every structure.

One day, Victoria took the bus to the Salisbury Cathedral in the Wiltshire countryside, south of London. The Gothic-style cathedral was a feat of thirteenth-century architecture and engineering, and, at the time of its completion, the tallest structure in the world. Victoria climbed the tallest spire's steps and stepped out on the veranda, enjoying a breathtaking view of the entire Salisbury Plain. She spotted the Stonehenge boulders miles away. Curious as to the significance of the large rocks in the middle of the plain, Victoria inquired about them to a handsome man who happened to be standing near her in the spire. He had taken the same bus with her from London to the cathedral, and she'd noticed that he'd been staring at her. When she asked about Stonehenge, he perked up, quickly offering her a good deal of information.

"I come here just for the view of Stonehenge. It is a magical formation, is it not?" he replied. His voice sounded familiar, as if she'd spoken with him before. "No one knows who placed the rocks out there, but some theorists believe that King Arthur had it built as a monument to his greatness." Victoria stared at the huge boulders, which from a distance seemed like huge dominos stacked in a complex pattern. She wanted to see them up close.

"Is there a tour that goes there?" she asked the man. He smiled awkwardly, and told her that there was. His uneasy smile looked familiar to her. She wanted to ask him whether he had been in a certain bar in Picadilly, but she knew better. That kind of a question would probably embarrass him, and would certainly make her look bad. She decided against it.

"There is, in fact, a tour going to Stonehenge later," he said. "It is one of my favorite places in the world. I know quite a bit about the history. Would you like to join me?"

Victoria hesitated at first, concerned about her round-trip bus tour, and getting back to London in time to get a good rest before morning classes. She expressed her concerns to the gentleman.

"I know for a fact that you can take the late bus back. I inquired when I got here. There is plenty of room and your ticket is interchangeable."

After confirming that she could take the late bus back to London, Victoria agreed.

* * *

The dramatic collection of gigantic rocks looked like a massive army of soldiers huddled together in the middle of a battleground. Victoria couldn't believe her eyes. From the cathedral, the rocks looked huge, but up close, they were enormous.

"It is uncertain who built Stonehenge or why, but most hypotheses conclude that they were placed this way for use in rituals or ceremonies pertaining to the sun or the calendar," the man, who'd identified himself as Nicolai, said to Victoria.

"Why are there two upright stones with one on top?" Victoria asked.

"It is called a trilithon. Scholars believe that they were assembled four thousand years ago in a circle. Perhaps it was for mathematics or engineering. Or astronomy. Follow me. I have a favorite statue I'd love to show you." Victoria followed him.

Chapter 23

Jeffrey sat in a meeting at the Pentagon with his boss, FBI Director Diana Weiss. She was preparing for a trip to Moscow to join intelligence agency directors from around the globe, and needed last-minute information from all of her direct reports. There was a consensus among world intelligence organizations that Rescuflu was too good to be true. They had agreed to join an informal alliance and share information before interrogating Vladimir Checovsky.

Jeffrey informed Director Weiss that he had narrowed his list of suspects to approximately seventy people, but that there was no direct link to any one person. The only clue left behind by the perpetrator was the tattoo- like drawing. Each rape kit had proven inconclusive for DNA due to the nature of the virus and the tissue disintegration. If the victims had been raped, the perpetrator either used a condom or used some other object to penetrate the victim. No semen was left behind. Nor was there a sign of spermicidal jelly. There was bruising on the genitalia of each of the girls, but it was impossible for any medical examiner to conclusively determine the suspect's identity.

Jeffrey told Director Weiss that he had assigned Dr. Laura Weckesser to work on computer-generated matches comparing scanned copies of each of the tattoos. Commonality points had been measured, extracted and processed through the FBI's mainframe. Jeffrey showed Director Weiss his PowerPoint presentation of the various victims' tattoos on the widescreen in the center of the room. "We have identified approximately one hundred and fifty structures that show a strong resemblance to the tattoos, and while we continue to narrow our list with each 'patient zero,' we are still far from a direct hit," Jeffrey reported. "I believe that our suspect has an agenda, and he is deliberately leaving out details in the drawings to keep us in the spin cycle. For now."

"Isn't this unusual for a serial killer?" Director Weiss asked, as she sat cross-legged in the back of the double-doored conference room in the Pentagon.

"Yes and no," Jeffrey said. "Most serial killers who leave clues do so for power and control. This guy is giving us just enough to keep us guessing. When he's ready, he'll give us more."

"Ready for what?"

"That's the question of the millennium. We don't know what his message is. Maybe his message is that the world is in the Dark Ages and that we should have been better prepared for the avian flu."

"That suggests that he is deliberately infecting these particular women."

"Yes. I believe that this is the case."

"Motive?" Director Weiss asked, with raised eyebrows.

"Medicine, if this is the design of a person somehow connected to Tarirescu," Jeffrey said.

"But if it is not for financial gain? Who would do this if it is someone not connected to Tarirescu?"

"It could be a number of profiles. Perhaps a 'visionary,' which is someone who hears 'voices' in their head, telling them to do something. Or, it could be a 'missionist,' who is a serial killer trying to rid the community of a certain type of human. A missionist is a strong possibility in this case. All of the women murdered are of Romanian descent, and most seem to have been prostitutes or orphans."

"Why would someone want to rid the world of underprivileged Romanian girls?"

"Mission killers typically find the type of person they are seeking to eradicate to be particularly repulsive. Maybe he feels like he is doing them a favor by sparing them of a life of pain and misery. Or, he was mistreated by someone like that in his past and he is getting revenge."

"Can we link anyone at Tarirescu to Romania?" she asked.

"We are working on it."

"Anything else?" she asked, noting the time on her watch.

"It could be a 'hedonistic' killer, who kills for the pleasure of sex or mutilation, or for financial gain."

"That's my vote," said Director Weiss. "I think it is someone who stands to get rich. Let's focus on that."

Jeffrey was beginning to respond when Director Weiss turned her attention to Dr. Jocelyn Sharp of the CDC, who had just entered the meeting room, late.

"My apologies," Dr. Sharp said. "I was summoned to D.C. from Atlanta on short notice."

"I know that you are not one of my direct reports, but I've gained special permission to include you in today's meeting. I am running short on time. What is the CDC's position with respect to the causal link between the 'patient zeros' and the avian flu?"

Dr. Sharp had her own PowerPoint presentation. She quickly put on latex gloves so that she could disassemble Jeffrey's laptop and hook up hers. After she connected, she began by explaining the differences in the hemagglutinins for each flu virus. "I'm afraid I don't have time for physics and chemistry today," Director Weiss said.

"Yes, I understand. But for a clear picture of the antiviral that Tarirescu is producing, I need to show you one very important protein. Ask Vladimir Checovsky about this," Dr. Sharp said. Director Weiss looked carefully at a slide showing the difference in the protein strain of the current virus as compared to the 1997 and 2003 outbreaks. "Now compare these," Dr. Sharp said, bringing up a slide showing the current virus and the 1918 Spanish flu.

"They look the same."

"Yes, they are remarkably similar. Except for this," Dr. Sharp said, pointing to one molecular strand. "This genetically altered polymerase is the key."

"And you think we will find that it will unlock doors in the Tarirescu lab?" Director Weiss asked.

"If it doesn't, then we are in a world of trouble."

"Why don't you walk with me to the heliport and explain what you mean. I'm late for my flight." Dr. Sharp gathered her laptop and followed Dr. Weiss to the helicopter that was waiting to transport her to the airport. Along the way, she explained the scientific issues in as simple terms as she could. "There is no way that I can process what you are telling me in such a short period of time. I need you to accompany me to Russia."

"But you are leaving right now, Director Weiss. I have two young children at home and I left to meet you here in D.C. on a whim. I have not made arrangements for the children beyond today's daycare."

"Make whatever calls you need, but make them right now. I will see that my aide packs an extra suitcase for you and a warm jacket. It is freezing this time of year in Moscow."

Chapter 24

"You will not be granted permission to enter my laboratory!" Vladimir Checovsky shouted to Director Weiss and the twelve other intelligence directors from around the globe, all seated in a Tarirescu conference room in Moscow. "Our research and development documents are top-secret and Tarirescu owns the exclusive rights to them."

"The 1925 Geneva Protocol prohibits the use of chemical and biological weapons as warfare. It was ratified by Russia on April 5, 1928," said the United Nations Secretary-General, who was seated next to Director Weiss.

"And how does that affect me and my company?" asked Checovsky, as he rocked back in his leather chair. His silver hair shone in the modern high-beam spotlights that criss-crossed the ceiling of the room. The oval, black lacquer table gleamed in the light. The only paper on the table was that which Director Weiss had in front of her. Checovsky rested the back of his head in his cupped hands as he continued to rock.

The Secretary-General exchanged glances with intelligence agency directors from around the world before speaking again. "The Convention on the Prohibition of the Development, Production and Stockpiling of Bacteriological and Toxin Weapons, signed in 1972, also applies here, and this agreement has a genuine disarmament measure. We have the right to inspect and destroy weapons."

"Again, I fail to see what these agreements have to do with me. The only thing that Tarirescu is stockpiling, and disseminating as quickly as we stockpile, is Rescuflu. There is nothing in the Geneva Protocol, or any other multilateral arms control treaty, that disallows the stockpiling of antiviral medication in the event of world disaster. You are wasting my time, and the time of these world leaders, who should be working hard to ensure that the people of the world are protected from this horrible epidemic. Now, if you'll excuse me," Checovsky said, as he stood and started toward the conference room doors.

"It is not that simple," the Secretary-General said. "We have the right to make inspections, and we intend to do so."

"I'm afraid that's not possible. My lab is operating at capacity. We have no time to conduct an investigation. Sick people are waiting for their medicine and we have an obligation to get it to them. I have made a promise to the world, and I intend to keep it."

"Although I am not sure that you are as altruistic as you claim, I understand your desire to continue production," the Secretary-General stated in a calm tone. "We do not intend to interfere with the workings of your laboratory. However, the thirteen other people seated in this conference room feel that an inspection is reasonable and necessary under the circumstances.

We will use our best efforts not to interrupt your business any more than is reasonably necessary."

"Of course you won't, because you are not going to enter my laboratory. Now, if you'll excuse me. I have important matters to attend to."

"So do we," the Secretary-General stated, as he pressed a few buttons on his cell phone. Within a minute, units of military soldiers in riot-control gear surrounded the building and took control of the Tarirescu lab. Inspections commenced, as did interrogations of all Tarirescu scientists.

* * *

As the Tarirescu lab was invaded by world-renown scientists, a taxi dropped off a young woman at the curb outside King's College Hospital on Denmark Hill in central London. She was throwing up and crying out for someone to help her. A family, who was rushing their one-year-old toddler to the emergency room after he'd fallen down the stairs, heard the young woman, and the father ran inside to get her help.

As the emergency room staff attended to her they tried to talk with the young woman to find out what was wrong, she repeatedly cried, "Nicolai.

Nicolai." The nursing staff had no idea why she was calling out a man's name. They asked her if someone had hurt her, but she did not coherently respond. Instead, with a guttural heave, she spewed a brownish-red substance all over the staff assisting her. They rolled her over on her side, allowing her vomit to collect in a bedpan on the floor. With each heave, the fluid splattered from the center of the pan and sprayed out in all directions.

"I found identification," one nurse claimed. "Her name is Victoria Vlaicu and she lives in Picadilly." Another nurse made notes on the medical chart.

Meanwhile, the injured toddler was lying on the next gurney, being evaluated for a large laceration above his right eye. His three-year-old sister was curious about the noise she heard in the next partition. She crawled under the white dividing curtain and took a peek at the woman who was throwing up into a bedpan on the floor. To the three-year-old, this was rather interesting to watch. The red stuff was making a polka-dot pattern on the floor. She took her petite index finger and smeared the dots together, until her mother found her and pulled her back to their side of the curtain. Focused on her son's hysteria, the mother did not notice that her daughter had blood smeared on her fingers, and did not think much of it when her daughter put her index and middle fingers into her mouth to suck. The habit was annoying and hard to break, but was not her prime focus at the time. As they wrapped her son into a papoose to restrain his movement while stitching his head, the mother lost sight of her three-year-old for a second time. The precocious child had crawled back under the curtain to play with the polka-dots again.

* * *

Mary MacIntosh had come into her office on Sunday afternoon to get caught up on paperwork. It was one thing to be a busy lawyer, but it was another thing entirely to run her own firm and play junior detective on the side. She had worked for Andrew Harrison for a decade in Jackson Hole, first as his associate, and then his junior partner. When they agreed to open a satellite office in Sheridan, Mac was put in charge of running the show. She'd never dealt with the accounting and personnel issues of law practice management, and found the paperwork both overwhelming and tedious. Nevertheless, it was part of the price of independence, and despite the fact that she would rather have been hiking in the Big Horn Mountains on such a beautiful late-November day, she was stuck in the office. Her desk was a mess. She collected pleadings and letters and stacked them on top of their respective files, so that Megan could organize them the following day. One stack consisted of the documents concerning Gilbert Bonita's farmhouse purchase. She opened the redwell file and looked through the papers.

When Sheridan National Bank had asked her to handle the legal issues regarding the sale of the farmhouse to Gil, she perused the loan application, but did not pay particular attention to his financial matters. It was Mac's job to ensure that the liens were properly extinguished so that the property could be sold. It was not her job to determine whether or not Gil could afford the property. Where he worked and his sources of income hadn't registered with her. Now that the deal was done and she could close the file, she decided to take one last look at his application. It wasn't like she was snooping on him, really. The information had been provided to her for a legitimate reason, she thought to herself. Her feline nature kicked in, curious as to his financial condition and curious about his employment. He'd been so vague about what he did for a living.

She flipped through the paperwork and escrow documents until she came to the portion of the file containing the financial data. He listed a few accounts, but not much supporting information. It was noted in the "comments" section that he was paying cash for the farmhouse, eliminating the necessity for full financial disclosure. She lifted the front page of the loan application and stared at his employment history. In the left-hand column, in bold print, where the document requested current employment, Gil had printed three words. "Tarirescu, Moscow, Russia."

Chapter 25

"Rescuflu Not Working." "No Rescue by Rescuflu." The headlines on the news and in the Belgium papers injected terror into the Brussels community. Hundreds of people had died within four days at the Saint-Pierre University Hospital, and thousands more complained of flu-like symptoms. At first, local doctors wondered whether they'd received a faulty batch of the antiviral that had worked so well in Turkey, Syria and India. But when the hospital administrator called Tarirescu headquarters, he learned that the facility was under investigation and production had been halted until further notice. This news caused shock-waves throughout the community.

In Bucharest, Romania, Rescuflu had proven unsuccessful as well. Over three thousand people had died, and there was no sign that the quarantine was effective. The virus did not respond to any antiviral medication, and carriers of the virus were contagious within a short period of exposure. The CDC had never seen anything like it. It was beginning to make the Ebola virus look like the common cold.

* * *

Dr. Kokinda had not given up on her theory. She felt strongly that migratory birds were somehow connected to the spread of the virus, but even she had to admit that no clear migration pattern was being followed. She had published many papers on the changing migration habits of wild birds, comparing the patterns to global atmospheric changes that were due, in part, to global warming.

Dr. Kokinda turned her attention to outbreaks in modern history for clues. The 1918 Spanish flu had swept through army camps like a wildfire. Poor sanitary conditions were a major contributing factor. Dr. Kokinda analogized the spread of the 1918 pandemic to the present one, realizing that so far it had spread quickly in the highly globalized areas, such as Mumbai, Bangkok, and Hong Kong, but that the two antivirals were effective in those areas. She was puzzled by the fact that the antiviral had been effective in India, where globalization was at its height, but ineffective in a country like Belgium, where sanitary conditions were at their finest. What was so different between the 1918 virus and this one? It didn't make sense to her.

She struggled with different theorems, considering them both as a scientist and as a statistician. She constantly had to keep a check on her ego and her desire to prove that she was correct about migration. She knew for certain that bird migration was a factor in the common cold and flu season. What she hadn't proven, to a scientific certainty, was that bird migration could spread avian flu. It was difficult for her to see it any other way, but she did try. She thought back on her published works regarding the "pig factor." Had the recent outbreak proven her wrong? Or was Jeffrey right? Was there a killer on the loose infecting people with a highly lethal, contagious virulent? She half hoped that Jeffrey was correct, because if he was, her scientific theorems could still prove to be true.

* * *

The London outbreak caused a giant tsunami-like splash in the headlines around the world. Not only was the virus spreading like a bullet train, but there was no effective antiviral. Stiflu did nothing for the strain, and Rescuflu only prolonged the agony of death. Both medicines were in desperately short supply. Critics lambasted the United Nations and the CDC for shutting down the Tarirescu plant at such an incredibly inopportune time. The BBC talking heads asked, "Why wouldn't they wait until after the world crisis was over to investigate the propriety of the drug maker? Isn't it more important to save lives right now?"

Meanwhile, in Bogotá, Columbia, Nicolai Petrescu climbed down the steps of a Boeing 737 and onto the tarmac of the international airport. He produced his passport and eased through customs without claiming any luggage. He was traveling light these days. He hailed a cab to Girardot, a town south of the capital. He knew exactly what he was looking for, and when he found his old stomping grounds, he selected the appropriate target and lured her to his favorite park. He was born in this region of Tolima, Columbia, and knew the ins and outs like the back of his hand. After taking care of business in Girardot and leaving one woman infected and on the verge of death, he continued south on the train to Popayan, and then to Pasto, and then further south into Ecuador's mountainous Napo region. He continued making his selections, careful not to leave any trace evidence behind, as he made his way to Quito, and then back up the Pacific Coast and into the Gulf of Panama. These women were so ignorant! They deserved to swallow every last drop of duck pudding.

Nicolai had never enjoyed Panamanian women before. He wondered whether they would be as gullible as the Ecuadorian women. He hoped that they would be gentle and trusting and innocent because he was running short on time.

Travel by train or bus was important to a terrorist, because it generally did not require as much documentation. But the train or bus would have taken too long to get through Central America, and so, after Nicolai had taken care of business in Panama City and in Colón, he commissioned a gentleman with a speed boat to take him to Limón, Costa Rica, and then on to Nicaragua. He tipped the boatman heavily and then set about on bus through Honduras, El Salvador, Guatemala, and into the Chiapas region of southern Mexico.

Nicolai's victims in Asia and Europe had all been premeditated. He chose Ana Bontierre and all of the rest of the Romanian women because they had all once been orphans at Ploiesti in Bucharest. He hated Ploiesti orphans–he being the progeny of one.

Now that he was in South and Central America, he had no specific victim in mind. He was killing the way he used to kill–randomly. The spontaneity of it all was most delightful and refreshing. He had not lost his allure to women, he'd discovered, and he was pleased to see how quickly and easily a certain type of woman responded to his Casanova jargon. He continued north until he rampaged through Mexico City, and then chartered a small plane which landed him in Culiacán. He knew that he could make a connection in this drug capital, and it did not take much time or money before he was on another charter–this one landing him on an unmarked airstrip in southern Arizona.

He was saddened by the fact that he would likely never again have the privilege of killing Latin women. In consolation, he thought to himself, "Welcome to America."

Chapter 26

Dr. Peter Mills worked with Dr. Jocelyn Sharp in the Special Pathogens Branch of the CDC. He was her brightest virologist, and they had worked side-by-side decoding the genetic blueprint of the H5N1 gene. He was not popular among his coworkers because of his competitive nature, and it was rumored that he performed "special favors" for Dr. Sharp in order to gain access to her research.

When Dr. Mills learned that Dr. Sharp was en route to Tarirescu's Moscow plant to conduct genetic blueprint comparisons of the Rescuflu antiviral formula, he begged to join her. At first she hesitated, but after consulting with Director Weiss and considering Dr. Mills' extensive knowledge of the genetic blueprint, she agreed that he should meet them there. He had to settle for a commercial flight and was several hours behind Dr. Sharp's arrival. When he finally got to the Tarirescu lab, he wore his field suit, which was fully hooded, along with goggles, gloves and a mask. He brought with him the scientists who had worked with him on the 1918 Spanish flu blueprint. Together, they were hopeful that they could decipher whether or not Tarirescu had the blueprint for this particular strain of hemagglutinin, the protein that allows the virus to latch onto human cells before invading them. If they could prove that Tarirescu had the blueprint, and that the blueprint matched the current outbreak, then they could prove that the virus had come from the Tarirescu lab. The project was painstakingly laborious, but after working for nearly a decade to decode the 1918 virus, they knew what they were looking for. "Don't let this take ten years, Peter," Dr. Sharp said to him as he entered the Tarirescu lab. He looked back at her and winked, his crystal-blue eyes shining behind his goggles.

It was no joking matter. Dr. Sharp was quite serious. European nations depended on a quick answer. Little did they know that Nicolai Petrescu was on a spree in Latin and South America and that soon, these nations would join the ranks decimated by powerful and ferocious avian flu.

* * *

Mac did not know what to do with the information in Gil's loan application file. Should she call Jeffrey and tell him? She felt like that might be over-reacting. She had read that Tarirescu was being investigated because of Rescuflu. But just because Gil worked for a company under investigation didn't mean that he was somehow involved in any alleged malfeasance. It seemed a bit presumptuous to call an FBI profiler with this information. Surely, members of the FBI could find out anything they wanted to know about an employee of Tarirescu, or any other company in the world. Why should she meddle in their investigation? And, besides, wouldn't Gil feel betrayed if she turned over the information? Could it be considered an ethical violation, based on the manner in which she came to know his employment information? If he was falsely accused of wrongdoing based on her suggestion that he be investigated, he could sue her. She decided not to say anything for the time being.

Maybe she was just looking for an excuse to contact Jeffrey. Something about him intrigued her and she found herself quite smitten over him. He wasn't the most handsome man she'd ever known, but he seemed sincere and gentle and kind. His intellect was captivating to her. She'd always been attracted to smart men. And she liked the fact that he was a runner. Non-runners did not understand runners. Even people who were exercise maniacs in some form other than running did not understand the mentality of a runner. There was something pure and powerful that took place each time Mac's foot met the pavement, and she felt free and alive with each stride. When she was running, her thoughts grew sharp and her breath grew deep and she felt invincible. She knew that Jeffrey felt the same way–she could tell by their conversation when they ran together. He opened up and confided in her about his marriage that ended in divorce, and how that made him feel, and how he poured himself into his work.

She doubted that he would have ever told her such things if they were having coffee or lunch. The cathartic momentum of running opened up channels of communication. She decided to give him a call.

Mac had agreed to chaperone a group of high school students to Washington, D.C. for a Close-Up program study of the U.S. Supreme Court. Her itinerary noted that they were staying in a hotel in Alexandria, Virginia. Jeffrey said that he lived and worked in Virginia. Perhaps they could meet again. She picked up the phone and dialed his direct line at the FBI's Army Medical Research Institute of Infectious Diseases in Quantico, Virginia, just a few miles south of Alexandria. "YouSamRid, Dr. Plattenburg," he said, answering her call. After exchanging initial pleasantries, Mac told him about her trip.

"After a few days with rowdy teenagers, I might need a break," Mac said. "Would you like to get together for a run? Or coffee? I know that this is short notice, and I should have told you about it earlier. If you are busy, I completely understand. I know that you are swamped with this investigation—"

"I would love that!" Jeffrey said, almost embarrassed by his zealousness. "I have been working around the clock here and could really use a break. There is an amazing trail that follows the western banks of the Potomac. I think you would love it. It is pretty chilly in the morning, but you must be used to that. If we went early enough, we could watch the sunrise over the Atlantic as it illuminates the foggy banks of the river. The trees still have some fall color."

"Sounds beautiful."

"After a good run, I know of this great coffee house in Woodbridge, where I live, and we could have a quick bite before you need to get back to your rowdy kids."

"That sounds like a good plan."

"And then, if you can talk one of the other chaperones into covering for you one night, I could take you to a play in D.C. Or to dinner. Or both," Jeffrey said. He paused for a moment. Mac did not know if he was finished, so she hesitated to answer. He interpreted her pause the wrong way. "Or if you are busy, I understand. Maybe just the run and a quick bite will be good."

"No, no. I would really enjoy taking in some culture. I don't get much of that in Wyoming. Let's plan on it." Mac and Jeffrey firmed their plans and exchanged cell phone numbers before hanging up. She felt almost giddy with excitement. His voice was rather sexy, and she liked the fact that he had some boyish nervousness to him. Gil was the opposite, and although his gregarious nature was intriguing, it was also a bit too bold for her tastes.

Mac leaned back in her wing-tipped leather chair and looked out the top frame of her office window. It was going to be fun to be back in Washington, D.C. She had not been there in years, since college, and she looked forward to seeing it through the eyes of high school-aged people. With the Close Up program, they would get to tour a portion of the White House and Supreme Court building. She looked forward to standing at the Lincoln Memorial, looking down The Mall, to the Capitol. It was November, and she anticipated cold weather. She contemplated an evening out with Jeffrey, bundled in her long, leather coat and a warm, wool scarf. She pictured his arm around her, protecting her from whirling snow, as they entered the theatre. She thought of them sitting by a roaring fire, sipping wine and talking.

She logged onto her computer to check the weather forecast in the D.C. area, and to see what was playing on stage. She noted that she had several emails in her mailbox, and one of them was from Gil. She clicked on it and read his message.

I anticipate being back in Wyoming by mid next week.
We shall dine on vegetarian cuisine on Thursday at my house.
See you then. GB

Mac responded, informing Gil that she would be in Washington D.C. until Saturday, so he would have to wait a few days for their dinner date. She would be in touch.

Chapter 27

Central and South American countries were not at all prepared for the avian flu. They had not stockpiled much antiviral medication because it was expensive. Perhaps more importantly, because the avian flu had never before broken out in Central or South America, medical personnel had no experience or training in dealing with it.

When the first victim arrived in the Bogotá hospital, the medical staff did not see the warning signs that perhaps a doctor or nurse trained in China or Malaysia might recognize. When she spewed black mucus-like vomit, they thought that she had typhoid fever or malaria or some other jungle bug. No special precautions were taken, even when blood started to ooze out of her private parts. The medical staff assumed that she was having a miscarriage, and her bloody discharge lay dormant on the hospital bed. Once the blood had soaked through to the mattress, a kindly nurse gathered the soiled sheets and placed them in the laundry pile.

A resident doctor, who was making rounds, performed a vaginal examination on her, noting the swollen nature of her uterus. He diagnosed a second trimester miscarriage and ordered a D&C. Her uterus was scraped clean, and the blood and uterine lining was left intact in a metal pan in the hallway of the emergency room. It was a busy night in the hospital. Clean up would have to wait.

The resident who performed the D&C on the young woman left the hospital just in time to get to the Museo del Oro's opening night of the El Dorado gold exhibit. His wife loved golden figurines, and he was anxious to meet her there for a night of viewing. He felt out of breath upon arrival, but at eight thousand six hundred forty feet in elevation, it was hard to acclimate to Bogotá's altitude. They'd only lived in the city a short while, and he wanted his wife to have a night on the town. As the night wore on, he felt worse and worse. But, he managed to make love to his wife before he collapsed on the soft sheets of their bed. By morning, he could barely lift his head off the pillow, and he could not make it to the hospital for rounds. By the following evening, he was admitted as a patient to his own hospital. Two days later, he, and several hundred other Columbian residents, lay dead.

Similar outbreaks occurred in large and small towns in Columbia and Ecuador. Dr. Karen Kokinda immediately surmised that the Galapagos Islands were to blame. Six hundred miles off the coast of Ecuador, Charles Darwin developed his theory of evolution among the incredibly diverse wildlife that thrived on the fifty-eight island archipelago. "It is exactly what I figured would happen," Dr. Kokinda claimed. "Canadian birds carry a cesspool of virus. They infected a few people in Wyoming on their journey south, and have made a mess of things in Columbia and Ecuador on their descent over the Galapagos. Only God knows what is in store for the southern tip of Chile, which is exactly where these birds are headed. You know that those people haven't even heard of Stiflu or Rescuflu, or the avian flu for that matter. It is bound to get worse before it gets better."

Meanwhile, on the Archipelago de San Blas, off the Caribbean coast of Panama, a naval officer landed on the shore of an idyllic tropical island, ready to take in some rest and relaxation after being commissioned on a submarine for six months. He'd enjoyed the company of a beautiful Latin woman the night before while in Panama City, and wished that he'd paid her just a few more dollars so that she would accompany him to his island getaway. But he figured that he could find another woman on the island. The women wore vividly colored skirts and gold jewelry, and a black line tattoo down the length of their nose. To the officer, the women looked exotic and fun. The island women were part of the Cuna Indians, a self-governing community living within their ancient customs. The Cuna were proud, timeless people, famous for their colorful dress and woven fabrics.

When the naval officer came down with severe flu-like symptoms, he sought the Cuna's assistance. Not educated in modern medicine, the Cuna practiced old-fashioned bleeding techniques, meant to free the demons from the impure soul. However, the more blood they let from the naval officer, the faster the virus spread, and within a few days, nearly all of the residents of San Blas were infected with the avian flu.

* * *

Nicolai's quest through the green mountain- and volcano-rimmed valley of Guatemala turned out to be quite successful. One of his victims lived in Antigua, one of the oldest and most enchanting cities in Latin America. Antigua's colonial past is fascinating and portrays the charismatic heritage of Spain's capital city during the time when She ruled the Americas. Despite a massive earthquake in 1773, Antigua is home to many Spanish Renaissance and Baroque churches. On an epic day in November, while preparing for the feast day celebration of the patron saint Nuestra Señora de la Merced, a nun found a young woman curled up in the fetal position inside one of the confessionals of the church. The woman must have been there for a few days, as the small, four-by-four-foot dark room smelled horrifically. The ambulance took her fifteen miles to Guatemala City, where an autopsy was to be performed. The nun who found the young woman asked that the church janitor clean the confessional prior to the feast day celebration, as there would be hundreds of church-goers in need of confessing their sins. Unfortunately, the janitor did not do a thorough job in the confessional, and each time a sinner got down on his or her knees, they acquired small pieces of the young girl's innards on their clothing. As they reassembled in the church to say penance, children swarmed them, hopping onto their laps, touching their skirts and pants, and then putting their hands in their mouths, as children do. The virus swarmed Guatemala like a plague.

Chapter 28

Nicolai Petrescu hated cacti. They looked like deformed genitalia to him. And he hated the desert. It was hot and sandy and barren. Southern Arizona was like a moonscape to him, and he was cursing the day that he had agreed to Vladimir Checovsky's plan. Luckily, the end was in sight, and soon he would be back home.

He wondered how Vladimir was enjoying his new-found riches. While he was in Europe, Nicolai had read in the newspapers while he was in Europe that Rescuflu's sales had topped those of Stiflu. But Nicolai knew that the bubble would soon burst, and the man who had taken him under his wing would be humbled. The thought of Vladimir in handcuffs excited Nicolai.

Nicolai needed to focus on the task at hand. He stood next to a giant saguaro cactus on Old Spanish Trail and stuck his thumb in the air. He only needed a ride into Tucson–from there, he'd made arrangements for transportation. He hoped that it would not be long before someone would pick him up. Hitching a ride in Europe or South America was much easier. Americans were so paranoid. Knowing this, earlier in the day he had washed his hair in the men's room sink at the Rincon Mountain visitor center at Saguaro National Park. He shaved off his beard and mustache too. He hadn't been clean-shaven in nearly a month, and in the desert heat it felt good to be rid of the facial hair. He examined himself in the mirror and was pleased. He had not slept much in the last month, and was afraid that his life on the lamb was catching up with him. But upon close examination, he felt like he had cleaned up fairly well. He purchased a baseball hat and a clean t-shirt at the visitor center, and tried to look the part of an all-American guy.

One by one, cars zoomed past him until finally, a group of high school-aged boys in a pickup truck pulled over to the side of Old Spanish Trail. They allowed Nicolai to ride in the back of the truck until they reached the outskirts of Tucson. It was illegal to have a passenger in the back without a seatbelt, so when they arrived at the intersection of Broadway and Camino Seco, they dropped him curbside.

Nicolai walked into the Tucson Historic District and made his way to the Barrio Historico. He knew a woman there, and today she would join him and imbibe on his special duck pudding cocktail. Chills ran down his spine just thinking about her, and how he would enter her adulterated body as she lay choking on his concoction. He planned to take her to a secluded area of Sentinel Peak Park so that he could draw an even more detailed picture of the Temple of the Condor on her inner thigh, and then drop her off at the Mission San Xavier del Bac.

Chapter 29

Mac felt small, standing next to the five hundred fifty-five-foot Washington Monument. It was a crisp, calm November morning in the nation's capital. With her digital camera strapped around her neck, she tried to arrange the twelve high school students so that the reflected image of the Monument would show in the narrow pool of water, with the Lincoln Memorial in the backdrop. It was a beautiful shot.

The students followed her down the banks of the Tidal Basin to the tranquil nineteen-foot bronze statue of President Jefferson. She had each student read aloud from the passages of the Declaration of Independence etched on the columned rotunda in the Jefferson Memorial. Mac was enjoying her time with the energetic teens, and she felt like perhaps she had missed her calling as a teacher. It was great fun to walk through history with them, instead of simply reading about it in a book. While watching the students interact, she wondered whether she would ever have children of her own. She felt the pang of her age, knowing that the possibility of conceiving a healthy child declined each year after she turned thirty-five. Now at age thirty-seven, her time clock was ticking louder. She had considered adopting a child, but felt that the timing wasn't right due to the stress and long hours commensurate with heading the satellite office. Perhaps in a year or two her life would settle down a bit and she could seriously consider adoption.

After several full days of sight-seeing, Mac told one of the other chaperones that she had a breakfast meeting that she had to attend, and that she would catch up with the group that afternoon when they visited Georgetown University. She called Jeffrey on his cell phone to confirm their meeting place.

"Change of plans, I'm afraid," Jeffrey told her. "I wanted to take you on a run near my home in Woodbridge, but I was summoned last night to an emergency meeting at the Pentagon. It lasted almost all night, so I'm here, in Arlington. Why don't you meet me at the Peirce Mill in Rock Creek Park?" He gave her directions.

When Mac arrived, she spotted Jeffery near a gorgeous stone bridge. He was standing next to a giant maple tree, wearing black running shorts and a white long-sleeved t-shirt. He wore a fleece hat and wool gloves, and was stretching his legs. It was chilly, and Mac could see puffs of mist with each breath he took. She zipped her jacket, pulled her hat over her cold ears, and trotted over to where he was waiting. He looked more attractive in his running gear. He wasn't wearing his thick reading glasses, and his cheeks were flushed in the cold morning air. She noticed his lean, muscular legs.

"They let you out of the think tank for a few hours a day, I see," Mac said as she approached.

"If they didn't, I'd be loonier than I already am," Jeffrey joked. "We've been burning the midnight oil in Quantico ever since I last saw you in Wyoming. If I didn't get fresh air in the morning, I don't think I'd ever see the light of day. You ready to go?"

Jeffrey took off over the stone bridge, and Mac followed. "This place is amazing," Mac said.

"This place is a gem. The President runs here sometimes, as do most of the folks who work on the Hill. I'm usually stuck in Virginia, so I don't get up here enough. I'm glad that I could show you around here." Jeffrey took Mac on a six-mile loop of the southern half of the park. They talked mostly about their jobs, and the bird flu.

"Do you still think that there is some serial killer out there spreading the flu?" Mac asked. She didn't mean to use a mocking tone, but perhaps it came across that way. Jeffrey picked up the pace and grew quiet. Mac had to push herself hard to keep up with him. "I'm sorry if that came out wrong. I didn't mean it that way."

Jeffrey slowed a bit and let Mac catch him. "I'm a little touchy about my work. I take it very seriously. If you knew what I know, you would be terrified. Obviously, I can't tell you anything top-secret, but suffice it to say that the spread of this virus is no accident."

"I've been reading the headlines about it on-line," Mac said, trying to recover her breath. "It sounds like they think that the CEO of Tarirescu might be deliberately spreading the virus so that people buy his medicine. Is that possible?"

"Anything is possible," Jeffrey said. "The question is whether it is probable. A week ago, my answer was probably a 'yes.' But the Rescuflu drug doesn't seem to be working. It worked at first in some parts of the world, but it hasn't been effective in Western Europe. So, either the strain has mutated and Tarirescu was just lucky that they had an effective antiviral, or something else is going on. I'm really not sure what to think of that angle of the investigation. That's one of the reasons that I spent the evening at the Pentagon. We were discussing Tarirescu's involvement. Of course, this is strictly confidential. I trust that you won't say anything about this to anyone. Especially the press."

"Runner's Privilege," Mac said.

"What?"

"Runner's Privilege is the axiom that anything we discuss during our run stays confidential. For me, running is like therapy. So, anything we talk about during the run is between us. It's like the saying, 'What happens in Vegas stays in Vegas.' I promise to keep it to myself."

Jeffrey liked Mac's attitude. She was smart and confident, and she looked good—even with sweat dripping down her forehead. When they headed over the Bluff Bridge, back toward Peirce Mill, he said, "Are we still on for the theatre tomorrow night?"

Chapter 30

Dr. Peter Mills had been in the Tarirescu laboratory for many, many hours trying to decipher the Rescuflu code. He was getting close. He was testing the antiviral against samples of the various strains of the avian flu that had been collected in areas where outbreaks had occurred. Rescuflu, like any other antiviral flu medicine, worked by blocking a certain protein that is present in every type of flu, neuraminidase. Neuraminidase is the "N" in the formula "H5N1." In order to block the "N" from invading a healthy cell, the antiviral must be taken within forty-eight hours after symptoms appear. If the antiviral is ingested within this time, the severity of the symptoms is reduced and the length of the illness is shortened. The antiviral is most effective if taken within twelve hours of onset of symptoms. The problem with Stiflu is that the medicine must be taken for at least a week, and even then it only protects an individual for as long as they are taking the drug. Once a person stops taking Stiflu, they are just as vulnerable as someone else who has not taken the medicine.

Dr. Mills noticed that Rescuflu was a much more potent neuraminidase-inhibiting drug. It appeared to be tailor-made to a specific genome of the H5N1 virus, and it not only blocked the neuraminidase from entering the host cell, but it acted like an antibiotic, treating secondary bacterial pneumonias. He shared this information with Dr. Sharp and Director Weiss. They agreed to question Vladimir Checovsky.

"I do not understand why you think my medicine is sinister," Vladimir Checovsky said in a spiteful tone. "The purpose of developing it was to address the shortfall that I've seen with competing drugs. Stiflu only works as long as you are taking it. If you are the only person in Hong Kong taking the drug during a bird flu outbreak, you are not in much better shape than the next guy. You cannot take the drug forever, and eventually you will stop. Once you do, you are as vulnerable, if not more vulnerable, than your neighbor who did nothing, assuming that your neighbor is not dead. I have developed a highly effective drug. I should be getting awards and honors, not questions and ridicule."

"The problem, as I see it," said Dr. Mills, "is that Rescuflu is tailor-made to a mutated strain of the H5N1 virus that none of us in the scientific community has ever seen before. How could you know the exact compilation of the genome, and how to create the correct formula for the neuraminidase inhibitor, if you did not create the virus in the first place?"

Vladimir Checovsky looked defiantly at Dr. Mills and let out a large sigh before speaking. He ran his stubby fingers through his gray hair, and then shook his head. "I do not deny that I have tinkered with the genome. That is what scientists do. If you asked me directly, 'Dr. Checovsky, did you create a genome?' I would answer affirmatively. If you asked me, 'Dr. Checovsky, did you spread a virus so that you could sell your new drug?' I would answer negatively. Why not just ask what you want to know? I have nothing to hide. This is the problem with the world. No one is smart enough to ask the right questions. It is really quite simple."

"Did you set this virus loose on the world?" Dr. Sharp asked, leaning forward over the table toward Vladimir.

Vladimir rocked back in his seat with a smug look on his face. "Did I? No. I did no such thing. I have nothing to hide."

Dr. Sharp pulled Director Weiss aside and recommended that they take a short break from the interrogation to speak to Henry Lewis, a CIA operative who had been busy hacking into the Tarirescu computer system. They found him in the mainframe typing quickly on several keyboards. Henry Lewis was a petite Chinese man with frameless glasses and spiked, black hair. He was a genius at cracking pass codes and had been hired by the CIA after serving time in prison for wire fraud.

"What have you found?" Director Weiss asked.

"He has a partner in crime." Henry Lewis did not turn in Director Weiss's direction when he spoke with her. He kept typing as quickly as his fingers would allow.

"Does this partner have a name?"

"Several names, I think. I am decoding still. I will have your answer in five minutes or less."

Director Weiss looked over Henry Lewis's shoulder and read a series of deleted emails between Vladimir Checovsky and Nicolai Petrescu that Henry had been able to retrieve.

"What do we know about Nicolai Petrescu?" Director Weiss asked. Henry Lewis quickly wheeled his chair across the floor to another computer system and frantically typed.

"Employment file. Work history. Love history. It is all right here."

Henry Lewis pushed his chair back to the system where the emails had been retrieved and continued working. Director Weiss read the information about Nicolai Petrescu. She flipped open her cell phone and made a few calls to the Pentagon before rejoining the interrogation of Vladimir Checovsky.

Chapter 31

Nicolai Petrescu hopped on a bus heading north to Phoenix. He had picked up a newspaper at the bus station and now, seated in the back of the Greyhound, he perused the headlines to see if there was any mention of the avian flu. To his utter delight, a front-page story covered the outbreak in Columbia and Ecuador. "At least three hundred people have been confirmed dead from the most recent outbreak of the avian flu," reported the *Arizona Republic*, "and hospitals in Bogotá and Quito are under strict quarantine." Nicolai grew hard with the exciting news. He readjusted his pant zipper and grinned to himself, content with the fact that these worthless women were creating havoc by spreading their deadly germs to innocent people. He thought of his own mother, and how much he enjoyed watching her slowly die, some fifteen years ago. He hated her with unspeakable passion.

Nicolai took a deep breath, pulling in every molecule of filthy desert air. He much preferred the mountain air–it was clean and crisp and full of promise. The desert air felt dry and dead to him. His thoughts drifted back to his prostitute mother. When Nicolai was eight, she kicked him out of the house for fondling his younger sister. He didn't know that it was wrong to do that sort of thing. He watched other men fondling his mother all of the time, and she seemed to like it. When his mother walked into his bedroom and found him touching his five-year-old sister's private parts, she went crazy with anger, shouting profanities and slapping him. Her rage intensified, and she took off her high-heeled shoe and started beating him in the head with it. He begged her to stop, and tried to hide under the chair, but she dragged him out and continued to wail upon him until blood trickled down his forehead. When she finally got some control of herself, she told him to put on his socks and shoes, which he did, and then she marched him down to the park and told him to never, ever return to their home. She told him that if she ever saw him again, she would let one of her boyfriends kill him.

Nicolai never returned to his mother's house. He slept on the park bench for a few days and rummaged for food in an alley behind a local restaurant. On the third evening after being banished from his home, he curled up on the same park bench to go to sleep. An older man approached him and asked him where his home was. Nicolai told him that he had no home. The man, who appeared well kempt and friendly, told Nicolai that he could sleep on his couch in the warmth of his home. The man promised to feed him a hot meal and allow him to take a bath. Not knowing better at age eight, and hungry and cold, Nicolai agreed. He followed the man through the back alleys of town to a one-bedroom apartment. After eating bread and soup, the man took him by the hand to the bathroom. There, he disrobed Nicolai and sodomized him against his will. Nicolai screamed out in pain, but no one heard him. He cried himself to sleep on the couch that night, and escaped before the sun came up.

Nicolai spent his adolescence in and out of group homes, and his teenage years were filled with gangs, drugs, and violence. He was arrested on drug-related charges at age eighteen and was sentenced to prison. He was a pretty boy, by all accounts, with soft, full lips and sparkling eyes. Within a day of being assigned to cell number eleven, he was gang-raped by five prisoners. At that moment, something snapped in his brain, and all the rage and anger from his childhood exploded within him. He killed three of his assailants with his bare hands.

Upon his release from prison in his mid-twenties, he started killing young girls with impunity. Killing excited him sexually. He strangled his victims, and then raped them post-mortem, often mutilating their genitalia before burying them in a mass, hidden cave near Macchu Piccu, Peru. He sometimes went back to the burial site and dug up a few victims, assembling them for a "tea party," like the kind that he and his little sister used to have.

Nicolai thought back to his tea parties and grinned again, and then continued reading about the spread of the deadly bird flu virus through

Panama, Honduras and Guatemala. It annoyed him that the articles did not mention the clue that he continued to leave on each of the victim's inner thigh. Had they not noticed? He wanted the authorities to discern the pattern and be perplexed by it. Surely, some high-tech doctor was comparing the drawings, seeing the extra details that he left with each additional victim. He wanted the game to begin, for without the game, it was no fun. Why didn't the papers mention the drawings? All that the newspapers discussed was whether the world had enough antiviral medicine and how people and companies could prepare for a pandemic. "How boring," he thought, out loud. "They are focusing on the wrong issue. I am practically giving them a map of how to stop the pandemic, and all they care about are drugs. Vladimir is probably in heaven over this. The son-of-a-bitch."

He read about Microsoft's plan to allow telecommuting in the event of quarantine in Redmond, Washington. The article detailed Marriott's stocking of respiratory masks for hotel guests. 3M was boosting production of respiratory masks, making a huge profit, of course. And United Airlines was carrying masks and biohazard bags for flu-stricken passengers. What fun it was to know that the entire world was being turned on its ear, just because he could pour a little viral pudding down the throat of some no-good whore.

Soon, he thought to himself, *the hunters will be after me. But by the time they figure it out, I will be gone.*

Chapter 32

Phoenix was as dreadfully phony as Tucson, thought Nicolai. Almost everything around him was a man-made jungle. He longed for pristine, green mountains, lush valleys, snow-capped peaks, and fresh air. Soon he would have it. But for now, he had a job to do, and his job was to locate his next victim and lure her to Papago Park in Scottsdale, not far from the Good Samaritan Regional Medical Center, one of the largest hospitals in the Valley of the Sun.

The Greyhound dropped him off in downtown Phoenix, and it didn't take Nicolai long to stalk his victim. She was standing at the corner of Washington and Central, and looking the part of a naturalist, he asked her for directions to Papago Buttes. She rattled off something in Spanish, and looked the other way. He decided to find another unsuspecting victim, but thought that he might have better luck along the running trail near the Hole in the Rock at the park. He hailed a cab and was dropped off at the Desert Botanical Gardens. There, he found a woman asleep on a park bench, and he knew that his luck was good. She was an easy target to lure to the red-rock butte with a large hole in the center. In her severely hung over state, she probably did not appreciate Nicolai's forceful manner. The cocktail he served her would be the last she'd ever have.

* * *

The four-mile stretch of Las Vegas Boulevard is the world's hub of flashing lights, high-rise hotels, wedding chapels, and cheap buffets. At the heart of all of this glamour and glitter and man-made excitement is gambling–anytime–anywhere–anyhow. For Nicolai, it was the essence of sin, and his hedonistic nature was tremendously aroused. He would not just pick one victim and move on. The choices were endless, and he intended to wipe out the population of this overly indulgent city by spreading his victims around. He checked his black bag to see how many vials of duck pudding cocktail he had left. Nine. He thought about using all nine of them on the Strip. He could get more vials when he got home, if he needed to. He had left a few in the basement refrigerator. He contemplated his plan. If he used all of them up in Las Vegas, he would deprive himself of the West Coast, which was not fair. He settled on five.

Nicolai's favorite place in the world was Lake Como, Italy, and his favorite town in his favorite place was Bellagio. Bellagio, Italy, located on a promontory point where the fjord-like lakes of Lecco and Como meet, hosts breathtaking alpine vistas second to none. Vladimir Checovsky took him there once, and they checked into the Grand Hotel Villa Servelloni, a neoclassical, bastion-like palace on the water's edge. It was Nicolai's first experience with the finer things in life, and he would not soon forget the luxurious suite in which they stayed, or the view of the Alps when they boated on the lake.

It seemed befitting, therefore, to take his first Las Vegas victim to the man-made Italian turret modeled after his favorite place. He checked into the hotel, paying cash and using a false name. Nicolai had purchased an Italian business suit earlier in the day from one of the hip shops in the Venetian. He brought his new duds back to the Bellagio, where he shaved and trimmed his hair so that he could look the part of a rich businessman. It worked.

She was easy prey, standing on the strip in a dazzling red-sequined dress and stiletto red pumps. Her man-made, inflated breasts jettisoned out of her halter-top and her shiny red lips matched her long, red fingernails. He approached his first target and asked her if she would join him for dinner at the chic Le Cirque. She hastily agreed. He informed her that the reservation was set in an hour, and recommended that they have a drink in one of the casino bars while they waited.

It had been a long time since Nicolai had been with a blond, and he was enjoying her giddy company. She talked endlessly about nothing over two glasses of chardonnay, and when she was sufficiently tipsy, he offered her a shot glass of a brownish-red concoction. Without the blink of an eye, she agreed to do a "duck-shot," and with a quick tip of the glass, emptied the thick liquid down her throat. She'd done shots before, he surmised. After tasting the liquid, she let out a loud moan, followed by several expletives. "It is like Ouzo, without the licorice taste," Nicolai teased. She wasn't amused, and asked for a glass of water.

It wasn't long before her stomach became upset and she complained that she felt flush. He recommended that she lay down on his hotel room bed for a bit. She agreed. He escorted her through the lobby and up the elevator to the twenty-sixth floor. He slid the card key through the slot, and helped her to his bed. As she lay there, moaning about a stomach ache, he parted her legs. "This will make you feel better," he said. He touched her until her moans of pain turned into moans of pleasure, and then he sketched the Temple of the Condor on her inner thigh. This time, he wrote "Condor" underneath his artwork. As he finished, his victim started writhing in pain. She grasped her stomach and mumbled something about throwing up. Nicolai quickly escorted her to the bathroom and then backed away. He did not want her to vomit on him. He told her that he would wait for her back in the bar. As soon as the hotel room door closed, Nicolai bolted toward the Mandalay Bay.

He made his rounds selectively on the Strip, enjoying poisoning beautiful prostitutes with his duck cocktail at Paris, New York, New York, and the MGM Grand, before boarding a bus heading southwest, to Los Angeles.

Chapter 33

Mary MacIntosh's cell phone vibrated silently in her pocket while she sat in an auditorium at Georgetown University. The students were listening to a speaker discuss the nuances of politics and literature, so without being noticed, Mac flipped up her silver cell phone and read the text message from Jeffrey. It read, "Dinner at Marcel's at 6:30. *Les Miserables* at National Theatre at 8. Shall I pick you up at your hotel?" She sent him a text message back that said "Yes. I'll meet you in the lobby at 6."

Mac didn't get back to her hotel room in Alexandria until five-thirty and was rushed to get ready. She slipped into a black Versace dress she'd purchased in San Francisco a few years back and slid on her black pumps. She pulled her long, auburn hair up into a French twist and reapplied fresh make-up. When she stepped off the elevator, Jeffrey was standing there in a dark business suit with one long-stemmed white rose in his hand. He commented on her dress and then escorted her to his silver 930 Porsche Carrera convertible. She complimented his car.

"It's a little over-the-top," Jeffrey admitted, "but I don't have anything else to spend my paycheck on. It is fun to drive to Quantico in the early morning when no one else is on the winding roads. I always wanted a car like this, so I guess it was my consolation prize to myself when my wife left me." Mac was quiet for a moment. Jeffrey felt that maybe he'd said too much. *I should have just said thank you*, he thought to himself. She had complimented his car. He didn't owe her an explanation as to why he bought it. He was embarrassed now, wondering if she thought that he was a bumbling baboon. He tried to think of something else to say, but was afraid to open his mouth. He was about to tell her about the restaurant where they would dine when she broke the silence.

"You got the nice car. I took off for Paris when Greg and I broke up. At least you have something to show for it. All I have are a bunch of pictures of cathedrals and castles and artwork." She smiled at him and winked. He took a deep breath and smiled back.

Dinner at Marcel's was incredible. The tuxedo-clad waiter recommended an amazing French-Belgium special that was delicious. They enjoyed a variety of wines that the waiter paired with each course. The conversation came easy for them, like they had been friends for a long time.

Mac had only been to one Broadway performance, with her mom in New York City when she was in college. She was in awe during *Les Miserables*, thoroughly enjoying the music and the stage show. Jeffrey actually forgot about his work for a few hours. It was divine.

Jeffrey had such a great evening with Mac that he didn't want the night to end. After the performance, he thought about asking her to join him for a nightcap, but he didn't want to be too forward. As they made their way to his car, Mac said, "Why don't you take me for a drive? I'd love to see the area where you live. Maybe you can show me the route you take to work, since you like driving it so much." He quickly agreed, and accelerated down the Jefferson Davis Highway toward his home in Woodbridge.

As they drove through the meandering hills, they talked nonstop and laughed hysterically. Jeffrey pulled over near the entrance gate to his office. "This is YouSamRid."

Mac read the block-lettered sign. UNITED STATES ARMY MEDICAL RESEARCH INSTITUTE OF INFECTIOUS DISEASES. She thought about the acronym. USAMRIID. It finally made sense to her. "So, this is where you spend most of your working hours."

"Unfortunately. I love my job—don't get me wrong. But I do spend too much time in the lab." Mac asked him about his career and how he had ended up working for the government. "After I got my Ph.D. in Behavioral Sciences, I taught at Georgetown for several years. I liked working with the students. In fact, I loved teaching, but my wife was dissatisfied with my salary and my hours and felt like I wasn't being promoted quickly enough. She had a friend who worked for *America's Most Wanted* and talked the producer into allowing me to do a segment on Ted Bundy. So, I did. It was fun, actually. More interesting than I thought it would be. Not long after the broadcast of the show, I got a call from Director Weiss, and eventually I was hired as a profiler. I guess I can credit my ex-wife for my job. She'd like that."

"She didn't interview with the FBI for you, did she?" Mac asked. Jeffrey shook his head. "You got the job because you are smart and talented." Mac put her hand on the back of Jeffrey's hand. He felt a shockwave throughout his body from her mere touch. It was not like him to be so forward, but something inside told him to bend over and kiss her. He started to lean in her direction when Mac said, "Would you mind terribly if I test- drove your car?"

"Uh, s-s-sure," Jeffrey mumbled. He could feel beads of sweat forming on his forehead as he answered.

Mac had never driven a sports car before. She loved the power and control of the car. After gaining comfort in her driving ability, Jeffrey relaxed and loved watching her drive. She was confident and daring and the look on her face told him that she was having a great time. After maneuvering the Quantico road, he directed her back towards his home in Woodbridge.

* * *

Jeffrey lived in a one-story bungalow-style home in a quaint neighborhood along the Potomac. His street was lined with large oak trees, which, in the evening light, cast dancing shadows over the well-manicured lawns. He told Mac that he was the only single man on his street, and that during the afternoon, the street was filled with kids on bikes and scooters. Boys set up their hockey nets in the middle of the street and played lively games. Driving home was sometimes a bit of an obstacle course, he said. Mac liked that thought.

He walked her through the front door and into the hallway of his neatly kept home. To the right, there was a living room with a large fireplace and a long, leather sofa in front of it. To the left, a dining room with a beautiful, antique oblong table. "The table belonged to my grandmother," Jeffrey explained. He showed Mac his exquisite china collection. He explained that his grandmother's family was in the glass and china business, and that when she passed away, she bequeathed a few sets of her finer dinnerware to him. Mac could tell how much he must have treasured his grandmother by the way he described each set.

He showed her the rest of the home, and then sat her down on the sofa and offered her a glass of port. He poured a snifter for her, and then got busy building a roaring fire in the fireplace. The room immediately felt warm and cozy. He put on some soft music and then joined her on the couch. He gently removed her heels and began massaging her feet as they talked.

Jeffrey refilled her glass when it was empty, and then lit a few candles on the mantel over the fireplace. He sat back down on the couch, this time sliding behind her, and began massaging her shoulders and back. Mac's heart beat faster as a tingling feeling filtered through her body. She could feel his chest on her back, and it sent electrifying pulses through her. *Too much wine*, she thought? She turned toward him, her lips nearly brushing his.

He guided her to her feet and held her tight as they swayed to the music. As the melody changed beats and a new song started, he pulled back from her and looked her in the eye.

"You look tired. Why don't you stay here tonight? You can sleep in my bed. I'll take the guest room."

Jeffrey held Mac's hand and guided her back to his room. He gave her an oversized t-shirt to sleep in and gently tucked her in. He lay there beside her and they talked until Mac finally fell asleep, mid-sentence. He watched her settle and listened to her heartbeat slow until the wee hours of morning. Finally, he went to the guest room and fell into a deep, restful sleep.

Chapter 34

When Mac awoke, Jeffrey was sound asleep in the guest room. He looked so peacefully happy that it made her smile. She thought back to their evening, and smiled again. She never dreamed that she would spend the night at his house, but she had no regrets. He had been a complete gentleman.

She quietly slid out of the bed and slipped into his terrycloth bathrobe. She found her way around his kitchen, making him coffee and breakfast. He awoke to the smell of eggs and toast, and joined her in the kitchen. He kissed her on the forehead, and then sat down next to her at the table. They each grabbed a portion of the paper and read while sipping hot coffee and eating. He loved having her in his home, and was delighted to abandon his traditional early morning run just to spend time with her.

"The bird flu is spreading like wildfire through Central America. Thousands of people are feared dead," he said to her as he perused the front page. "And officials think that there may be a case in Tucson!" Jeffrey read the articles quickly, and then excused himself from the table. He went into his home office and picked up the phone. Mac could hear his tone of voice rising as he talked. "It shouldn't be taking this long!" he yelled into the receiver. "We are overlooking something here. I need you to get on a plane this morning and get digital overlays from the Tucson victim. If this guy is doing what I think he's doing, we are in big trouble, Laura. Big trouble. I am running late this morning, so before you get to the airport, please re-run the digital images and I'll do the point comparison myself this morning." There was a pause in the conversation, and Jeffrey's voice seemed to calm down some. "Send it to the Pentagon. They are expecting it."

When she heard Jeffrey replace the telephone receiver, Mac went into his office. He was busy typing on his laptop and didn't notice her. She looked in amazement at the giant corkboards on the wall, essentially constituting a wall-length atlas of the world. The atlas was covered with information on each "patient zero" victim of the avian flu, with an arrow pointing to where the victim was found. Next to the information sheet for each victim was a ten-by-twelve blowup of the pictographic tattoo that had been drawn on their thighs. Common features were marked on the blow-ups in red ink. Mac read about each victim, noting that most of them were Romanian. She saw the location of Romania on the atlas and noted that one of the victims was found in Voronet. That name sounded familiar to her, but she couldn't remember why. She remembered Gil saying something like it, but he was talking about Russia, she thought.

Under each victim's picture was her name and date of birth. Under the birthday was a release date from either the Ploiesti Hospital or the Ploiesti Orphanage in Romania. Mac thought back to the information Jacqueline had given her. Ana and her sisters had been adopted from the Ploiesti Orphanage.

Jeffrey caught her movement out of the corner of his eye and quickly turned around. "Oh, Mac. I didn't hear you come in." He looked a little wide- eyed, as if in a frenzy. He stumbled over his words. "Y-y-you can imagine that my work is classified. That means that I cannot share certain information with anyone who isn't cleared. It's not that I don't want you in here, it's j-j- just that this case is—"

"It's okay, Jeffrey."

"No, it's not okay," he shouted. "This is highly confidential."

"I should have knocked. I'm sorry for the intrusion." Mac quickly backed out of his office and ran to the bathroom to get dressed.

She heard a knock on the bathroom door. It was Jeffrey, apologizing. He offered to drive her back to Alexandria.

"No, just call me a cab," Mac said. She was hurt and angry.

"Really, I'll drive you," Jeffrey said, as Mac opened the door to the bathroom. "I'm sorry."

Mac wanted to tell Jeffrey about the Ploiesti Orphanage, but after his abrupt and rude reaction, she was afraid to. She again declined his offer to drive her back to DC, insisting that he had important work to do and that she could call a cab. He seemed relieved by her offer and quickly dialed for a taxi.

Jeffrey acted awkwardly as he tucked Mac into the cab. They exchanged quick and awkward good-byes.

Chapter 35

The giant, white letters claiming the hills of Hollywood glistened in the late afternoon sun. Nicolai slept on the bus from Las Vegas, and felt rested and ready to find his next victim on the corner of Sunset Boulevard and Vine Street. He was pleased with his performance in Las Vegas, knowing that he had infected people from all around the world. He was confident that hundreds of gamblers were boarding airplanes at that moment, unknowingly taking his viral contagion back home to suburbia, U.S.A. He pictured it in his mind: a beautiful woman falling ill on a casino floor. Men would rush to her side to see if they could help her. She would gag and be sick, spreading the virus on them. Others would rush to help. A cocktail waitress would bend over to see what the commotion was all about, followed by a pit boss from the casino. Some of them would touch the victim or try to help her to the bathroom. Eventually, about the time that she started to bleed, the ambulance would arrive, and she would be wheeled away to the hospital. In the meantime, dozens of onlookers would have the undetectable genomes floating through their bloodstreams. It wouldn't be long until they infected others.

Yes, five victims in Vegas was a good call. And each victim's leg got a little bit more detail on the pictograph. Nicolai wanted them to find his Peruvian mass grave—he was leading the FBI there, one victim at a time. It gave him a deep thrill to think that soon, investigators would discover all the women that he killed years ago. He just wanted to finish his sojourn through America before they figured it out. And then, he wanted to escape deep into the backwoods of Wyoming, and eventually into Montana and up into the territories of northern Canada. He had vanished from the radar screen once before, and he planned to vanish again. But not before using up his final few vials of viral duck pudding.

The bus came to a stop on Hollywood Boulevard. Nicolai gathered his black bag and ventured onto the streets of Los Angeles. He stopped at the Sun Palace to eat some chicken before beginning his task. He knew that it would be easy to find a woman here–as easy as it had been in Vegas. He saw many wearing short skirts, high boots and slinky tank tops. The mere sight of them turned his stomach. They were not classy, like the Vegas hookers. To him, these women were scum. They didn't even deserve the death he would give them. They were unworthy. But time was running short and he didn't want to waste it being choosy about a Hollywood hooker. He didn't bother putting on his nice clothes. He wouldn't need them. All he would need is some money–of which he had plenty, thanks to Vladimir Checovsky–and a good, centrally located place to dump her ravaged body when he was through with her. He would have liked to have been able to dump his victim in a religious place, like most of the rest of them, but he was running short on time. Therefore, he chose the courtyard of the Chinese Theater, near the west end of the Hollywood Walk of Fame.

* * *

The rugged Pacific Coast between Los Angeles and San Francisco boasted some of the most scenic panoramas in the United States. Nicolai Petrescu, however, was not taking in the gorgeous scenery. He was fast asleep on the Amtrak train, as it rolled toward his final destination city–San Francisco. He was down to one last vial of his viral duck pudding, and he would need to go back to his lab before he could continue his killing spree beyond Northern California. His partial-world tour had been a success. He figured that he'd killed close to a million people thus far, and the virus was still doing its trick. He hoped to restock, disappear for a while, and then, in a few years, head for Africa, where he assumed that he could kill over ten million in a few weeks.

It was early morning when his train pulled into the depot in downtown San Francisco. Street cars whirred past him as he walked around Union Square. It was a crisp, clear, blue-skied day in the City, and despite the fact that Thanksgiving was still a few days away, Christmas decorations were being displayed in storefront windows. Nicolai was hungry again, as he always seemed to be, and so he stopped in a local coffee shop for a bagel and some strong coffee. American coffee was distasteful to him. He'd been spoiled by thick, darks roasts from Columbia. But some coffee was better than no coffee. Nicolai bit into his plain, toasted bagel and chased it with a slurp of what the waitress considered dark roast. In the corner, the coffee shop had a television and the local news was airing coverage of the avian flu outbreak.

"The avian flu continues to spread swiftly through Arizona and Nevada," the news reporter announced. "Despite quarantines, the flu seems to have no boundaries, nor does it appear to be selective with its victims. Healthy individuals are dying as quickly as the elderly and young. The CDC has issued strict warnings regarding sanitation and hygiene, and has recommended that all Americans, especially those living in the Southwest, wear masks to protect themselves. The President has ordered that all stockpiled Stiflu be sent to the American Red Cross in those areas. Americans continue to voice their anger about the low supplies of Stiflu, and the fact that the FDA refuses to allow Rescuflu to be sold within the U.S. Thousands of people continue to flock to the Canadian and Mexican borders in hopes of purchasing both antivirals.

"The World Health Organization and the National Institute of Allergy and Infectious Diseases believe that the avian flu outbreaks are the result of infected wild poultry migrations, and that fastidious precautions should be in place in every community regarding the handling and vaccinating of poultry.

"However, in sharp contrast to the WHO, the FBI believes that a serial killer is responsible for the continued outbreaks. Although it is difficult to identify the alleged perpetrator, based on surveillance cameras in casinos in Las Vegas, it appears that the suspect is a man in his mid-to-late forties, and has dark hair and dark eyes. He might go by the name of Nicolai Petrescu."

Nicolai stood in shock. He looked around the coffee shop, wondering if anyone was watching the broadcast. No one appeared to be paying much attention. He hadn't considered that video cameras would be running at all times in a casino—a major oversight on his part. He was angry with himself for being so stupid. He would have to quickly change his appearance. He dashed out of the coffee shop without eating the rest of his bagel, and headed up Market Street, in search of a pharmacy.

* * *

The Castro is the gay center of San Francisco, and also one of the most interesting places to watch pornography in action. Body piercing and tattooing are a top form of entertainment among the clientele who frequent this part of the City. Nicolai, looking quite like rock star Billy Idol because he was now sporting stark, bleached-blond hair, wandered up Castro Street, in search of his final victim. He was feeling edgy after viewing the news broadcast, and wanted to get his business done and get the hell out of Dodge.

He met her in front of the Phoenix Club. She said that her name was Flo. He didn't care that she lied about her name or her age. Recognizing the needle tracks on her arms, he asked if she wanted to join him for a little smack in the park. He told her that he had a connection near Kezar Stadium, and Flo readily agreed. He would have liked to have taken her to more sacred grounds, but time was an issue, and after the news report, he didn't want to be seen in a densely-populated or touristy place. They hopped in a cab and headed to a deserted area of Golden Gate Park.

When they got to the stadium, Nicolai told her that she needed to drink his magic potion before he would shoot her up. Flo objected. She was sassy and angry, and told him that she needed her hit now. After a half hour of arguing, Nicolai was losing his patience. He yanked her by the hair and dragged her behind a pine tree. She screamed and kicked at him, calling him every name imaginable. He decided to force the liquid down her throat, but when he tried, she fought back hard. She was a strong girl. He threw her to the ground, put his knee into her chest and cranked her mouth open. As he was dumping the duck pudding in her mouth, she kneed him hard in the groin. This infuriated Nicolai.

He shoved her skirt up, intending to savagely rape the bitch. When he looked down, he saw that she did not have a vagina. She was a "he" in the process of becoming a "she." Nicolai grew enraged. He grabbed Flo by the throat and strangled the life out of her. He did not bother tattooing her.

Chapter 36

Dr. Laura Weckesser was an expert at computer-generated comparisons. She had a double Ph.D. in quantum physics and psychology, and nothing escaped her analytical and logical mind. She was arguably the smartest person that Jeffrey had ever known. Still, he was greatly concerned that she could not decipher the pictographic code left behind by the "Pandemic Predator," as they had recently tagged him.

She had spent a painstaking number of hours scanning and digitalizing the tattoos drawn on each victim, comparing and contrasting each nuance. The problem was that every picture was significantly different–so much so that nothing matched.

At first, she thought that the Pandemic Predator was leaving a clue as to the next place he planned on striking, but she soon realized that her hypothesis was incorrect. The killer was certainly leaving a message, but that wasn't it.

She decided that she needed to reconsider the killer's plan. This particular serial killer was very methodical: he picked a certain type of woman–in this case, mostly prostitutes–and he killed her by feeding her a viral concoction. He wanted to rid society of a certain type of person, and he wanted her to endure pain while dying. He was obviously angry with women, particularly weak women, or women that he perceived to be victims.

What was his message? Did it have something to do with birds? Was he a bird freak? She didn't think so because so many chickens and ducks had been senselessly slaughtered as a result of the outbreaks. Did the pictographs represent somewhere that he was planning on going? Or his messiah?

When Jeffrey walked into his office at the FBI's Behavioral Science Services, he found Dr. Weckesser pacing the room, talking out loud to herself.

"You need a friend, Laura. You are talking to yourself again." Dr. Weckesser grinned at Jeffrey. He had ordered her to go to Tucson that morning, but she knew that he was just frustrated, and that the digital downloads sent to her from the medical examiner made the trip unnecessary. She would have wasted half a day in travel time.

"I have a friend. You are the one who needs a friend." Jeffrey let out a big sigh. He'd met a friend in Mac. And he was such an inconsiderate jerk to put her in a cab back to her hotel room in D.C. How could he have been so daft? He'd been beating himself up the entire drive into Quantico. Ever since his ex-wife had left, he had been a very lonely man. He resigned himself to living out his life alone, until he met Mac. The first time he laid eyes on her, he felt his heart skip a beat. He never dreamed that she would agree to have dinner with him in Wyoming. But she did. And then, she took him out on a run. They shared common interests, and she was beautiful and funny and engaging and smart. They drove to Medicine Wheel together and he learned quite a bit about her. The more he got to know her, the more he knew that he needed to be with her. He felt so connected to her.

To convey his deep feelings toward her, he'd somehow managed to tune her out, focus on work, and offend her within six hours of tucking her in to his bed. How could that be? Was he a complete and utter idiot, destined to live his life on a deserted island called the FBI? Laura had a soul mate that she went home to every day. She didn't talk much about her relationship, but Jeffrey knew that they were happy together. He'd finally found the woman he'd been searching for his entire life, and yet he had thrust her into a cab because of his job. He wanted to bang his head on his desk, repeatedly. But fortunately for him, Dr. Weckesser was busy using his desk to plot common pictograph points.

"Either he is trying to tell us where he has been, or where he is going. Either way, I'm completely at a loss. The pictographs match up with dozens of Mayan and Incan ruins throughout Central and South America.

The only new clue is 'Patient-Zero-Tucson' who had the word 'Condor' beneath the pictograph."

"Did you plug in 'Condor" as a focus term with your comparison analysis? He wrote it there for a reason."

"Yes," Dr. Weckesser said, in an exasperated tone, "but condors are a common theme in Mayan and Incan culture, so it hasn't prompted that 'Eureka' moment, if you know what I mean."

"Let's think about this," Jeffrey said, pushing his reading glasses up his nose a tad. "A condor is a bird of prey. Maybe that is how the serial killer thinks of himself. He is preying on victims."

"Simplistically, that is a good analogy, but he is going to painstaking efforts to draw us a map. If he just identified with a bird of prey, he would consistently draw us a picture of a condor or an eagle or something of that nature and leave it at that. The fact that this guy is giving us a detailed picture of what he wants us to see leads me to believe that there is much more to this."

"Like?"

"I'm not sure."

Jeffrey walked around to the bookshelf behind his desk and pulled out a large, leather-bound dictionary. He flipped through the pages until he found what he was looking for. "Webster's says that a condor is 'a very large American vulture of the high Andes having the head and neck bare and the plumage dull black with a downy white neck ruff and white patches on the wings.' Do you think that this guy views himself as bird of prey? Maybe he is dull-looking. Ordinary. And this is how he sets himself apart from the rest of the flock."

"Like I said, I don't think that this has to do with the bird. I think that the condor is a portion of the message." Laura turned and sat on the edge of Jeffrey's cluttered desk. She rifled through some printouts that she had and then quickly looked up. "Oh! I just thought of something," she said, as she dashed out of Jeffrey's office and into the data lab.

Chapter 37

Dr. Laura Weckesser was often crazy with enthusiasm, especially when she thought she'd figured something out. When her team found the final clue that helped them identify the BTK killer, she nearly did back flips down the hall to Jeffrey's office. Laura was not a very attractive woman. She had wavy, dark brown hair and large, thick glasses. She wore no makeup and made no effort to dress. Yet, when she deciphered something complex, she glowed like a full moon in June.

"Panorama," Laura said, as she burst back into Jeffrey's lab. Jeffrey was combing through the piles of information that she had left there.

"What?"

"Virtual tour," she said, rolling back and forth on the balls of her feet. "He has been giving us a virtual tour on each of the victim's legs."

Jeffrey furrowed his brow and stared at Laura for a long moment. He had no idea what she was trying to tell him. "Give it up, Laura. What are you talking about?"

"I think his pictographs are a virtual tour of wherever it is that he wants us to go. He is trying to show us exactly what the place looks like, one frame at a time." Jeffrey considered her hypothesis for a few minutes, while looking at his copies of each pictograph. She helped him place his set of pictographs contiguously across his corkboard. "If your corkboard was convex, I think you'd have a better notion of what I am talking about. Come to my lab and I'll show you what I think is happening."

* * *

In Russia, the name for the color red (*krasnaya*) is closely associated with the word *krasivaya*, which means "beautiful." Much of the artwork and grandiose architecture from centuries ago incorporates red for that reason. Of course, most people today associate Russian red with communism, and view the correlation negatively. But in ancient Russia, red meant beauty and power and honor.

Vladimir Checovsky was seeing a different kind of red as he sat behind the closed doors of his conference room at Tarirescu, being grilled by intelligence agents from around the world. He was haughty and arrogant when FBI Director Diana Weiss first interrogated him. Vladimir was not used to answering to a woman, and she was five steps ahead of his every answer. He felt that she was toying with him, and it made him angry. It also made him angry that several hundred men, all flanked with heavy artillery and riot gear, had shut down his lab. *How dare they march into my company and take over?* He thought to himself.

When Director Weiss and her team of agents first stormed his complex, Vladimir called the Moscow police, but they declined to assist him. Although the local police had been ordered to stand guard in case of an emergency, the Tarirescu raid had been approved by the Russian military.

Henry Lewis had been able to break the codes of the Tarirescu computer mainframe. He was busy comparing notes with Dr. Peter Mills, who was quite confident that Vladimir Checovsky had created a mutated form of the avian flu so that he could promote and sell large quantities of Rescuflu. Henry Lewis was reviewing computer correspondence to confirm his suspicion that Nicolai Petrescu was involved in creating the mutated form of the virus.

"Is Nicolai Petrescu an employee of Tarirescu?" Director Weiss asked Vladimir. She knew the answer to her own question. It was part of her interrogation skills to ask that type of question.

"I do not know to whom you are referring."

"Who is Mr. Petrescu?" Director Weiss's voice was growing increasingly impatient with Vladimir's evasive answers. "You can continue to play stupid with me, Mr. Checovsky, or we can get to the bottom of this and you can have your company back. The longer you play 'cat and mouse' with me, the longer you sit and rot in this conference room, and the longer your lab sits empty. I will instruct my men to go through this place with a heavy hammer and a fine toothed comb, and by the time we are done, you'll need to rebuild it from scratch. Don't mess with me. I am not a patient woman."

Vladimir sat up in his high-backed leather chair and took a resigned breath. He'd been locked away in the conference room for thirty-some hours, and he was growing increasingly anxious and irritable. He was furious with himself for not following his hunch a week ago, when Rescuflu stopped working in Europe. He suspected that Nicolai might have double-crossed him, and he considered shutting down his lab, destroying the evidence, and fleeing to his native Poland, where he had stockpiled plenty of money. His wife and children were there already, living with relatives. He could have easily vanished after cashing in on the first few mass orders of Rescuflu. But Vladimir had always been a greedy man. He had many lovers and excessive needs, and he assumed that the Russian military would back him up. He'd paid off so many officials over the past decade that he felt invincible. He never dreamed that it would come to this.

After thinking it over for a time, Vladimir could not believe in his heart that Nicolai would double-cross him. He'd taken in Nicolai nearly twenty years ago, giving him shelter and a good job. He felt sorry for the orphaned boy, and being an orphan himself, he wanted to help the kid.

Nicolai was smart, and he was willing to work hard to learn. He was also willing to risk his life for Vladimir.

Once, when Vladimir was negotiating a deal with Chinese officials for a large order of chickens after a H5N1 outbreak in 1997, a huge argument broke out. One Chinese official lost his temper and pointed a gun at Vladimir's head. Nicolai, who had been seated next to Vladimir at the meeting, bolted from his seat and stood between the armed Chinese man and Vladimir. When the Chinese official refused to lower his weapon, Nicolai attacked him with his bare hands and nearly put him, and a few of his colleagues, in his grave. It was then that Vladimir knew that he had a trusted "son," and also knew that Nicolai was capable of sadistic brutality. Nicolai looked crazed after the altercation, almost like he took on a different persona. It frightened Vladimir a bit, and it clearly frightened the Chinese businessmen into agreeing on a price for chickens.

"Who is Petrescu?" Director Weiss yelled.

"Nicolai Petrescu. He works for me," Vladimir finally answered in a shamed tone.

"Where is this Nicolai Petrescu right now?"

"I have no idea."

"You must have some idea. You spoke with him ten days ago. Where was he when you spoke with him?"

"I do not know."

"What did you speak about?"

"Business."

"What kind of business?"

"Poultry."

* * *

The one-word answer routine went on for several more hours. When Director Weiss had finally had enough of Vladimir's games, she called in the head of the Moscow police to confirm that all Tarirescu assets, and all of Vladimir's personal financial accounts, including his assets in Poland and in Switzerland, had been frozen. Director Weiss then placed another call.

"Your wife and children are being detained by the Polish police," Director Weiss confirmed. "We will take steps to ensure that they are not, and have not been, involved in your conspiracy. You will have to decide who means more to you—your family, or Nicolai Petrescu."

Chapter 38

*"If the epidemic continues its mathematical rate of
acceleration, civilization could easily disappear from the
face of the earth within a matter of a few more weeks."*
-- **Victor Vaughan**, head of the U.S. Army's division of
communicable diseases, 1918

A giant blow-up of Vaughan's statement was centered above the
podium of the United States Senate floor, where spirited discussions
were taking place about how to deal with the avian flu outbreaks in the
Southwest. The flu was spreading rampantly through Arizona and Nevada,
and initial reports indicated that at least ten people had died so far in Los
Angeles. A woman senator from California, who was wearing a surgical
mask on her face, spoke. "Southland cities survived the 1918 pandemic
by imposing strict quarantines within ten days of L.A.'s first case. Schools
were closed and parades were not permitted. We had 'flu squads' in place
that kept shoppers from congregating. The squads banned people from
gathering in public places and the local government strongly discouraged
people from attending weddings, funerals, or any other gathering. I'm
not saying that we should call in the National Guard like they did then,
but we need a plan in place in every municipality. San Francisco didn't
follow that same protocol back then, and allowed holiday parades and
such to take place, and the death rate in San Francisco was more than
twice that of L.A. We can learn from history. We can better protect
ourselves. Let's learn from our past and make sure that this flu doesn't
claim fifty million people."

While senators in Washington, D.C. worked on a pandemic plan,
Nicolai Petrescu boarded the Bay Area Rapid Transit and sped under the

San Francisco Bay. He then boarded the Amtrak, and headed north, high into the Sierra Nevadas.

* * *

A few miles south of Washington, D.C., at the U.S. Army Medical Research Institute of Infectious Diseases, Dr. Laura Weckesser showed Jeffrey her most recent discovery. Her entire office was wallpapered, literally, with a panoramic view of a village high on a mountaintop. "I used satellite imaging for these pictures," she said, pointing to smaller versions of photographs on her desk. "I plugged specific coordinates into the satellite's camera and had the views downloaded."

"Where is this?" Jeffrey asked her, still slowly turning in a circle.

"Peru. Machu Picchu, to be exact."

* * *

"I have never been to Machu Picchu, and I assume that you haven't either, so I got a copy of a *National Geographic* video on the 'Natural Wonders of Peru.'" Dr. Weckesser took the video cassette out of its yellow jacket and put it in the V.C.R. The tape started playing with a narrated aerial panorama of majestic, green mountains. The film focused on a ruin site in the saddle of one of the valleys, high in the Andes mountain range. The ruins appeared to be made of stone. The audio portion of the video tape began.

"South America is endowed with superb archaeological sites, and high in the Andes Mountains, deep within the sacred Urubamba Valley, are the ruins of Machu Picchu—the Lost City of the Incas." The film showed a variety of the dilapidated rock dwellings abandoned centuries ago by the Incan tribe.

"Machu Picchu is nearly invisible from below, tucked away on a small hilltop between two Andean peaks, carved into its natural surroundings. Majestic temples, fields, terraces, huts, and baths appear to be part of the hillside itself. Visitors hike the Inca trial from Cusco to Machu Picchu, where a small herd of llamas graze on the grass, keeping it efficiently mowed." Jeffrey watched with interest, but glanced at his watch. He was already late for a meeting, and was curious as to how long the documentary would last.

"Laura, I have a meeting to—"

"Just wait," she said, pushing the pause button. "The part you need to see is next and only takes a few minutes. After you see it, you'll understand what I am talking about when I show you the pictographs of the victims' tattoos." Jeffrey looked at his watch again and then nodded at her. He trusted her judgment and instincts. She pushed the play button again.

"Upon entry to the ruins, one first encounters the House of the Terrace Caretaker, where thousands of Incans lived and worked the terrace fields or corn. About a twenty-minute walk up to the left of the entrance, Funeral Rock provides the quintessential view overlooking Machu Picchu. Heading back down the trail and into the ancient city, the Dry Moat separates the agriculture and urban sections, where a series of sixteen small fountains link the Inca to their worship of water. Beyond the fountains is the round Temple of the Sun, a marvel of perfect Inca stone assembly where, on June twenty-second, the date of the winter solstice in the southern hemisphere, sunlight shines through a small, trapezoid-shape window and casts light into the middle of a large, flat granite stone."

"This was their calendar," Dr. Weckesser whispered to Jeffrey. "From this point on, pay close attention to the landscape," she said.

"Below the Temple of the Sun lies a small cave, called the '**Royal Tomb**' and although no human remains have ever been found here, it is thought to be a ceremonial structure, containing a stone-carved cross representing the three levels of existence in the world of the Inca. The first step represents death, or the underworld, and is symbolized by a snake. The second step represents the present, human life, and is symbolized by the jaguar. The highest step represents the celestial plane of the gods, and is symbolized by the condor.

"On the opposite side of the Temple of the Sun lies the Temple of the Condor, resourcefully created from a natural rock formation resembling the outspread wings of a condor in flight. On the floor of the temple is a rock carved in the shape of the condor's head and neck feathers, completing the figure of a three-dimensional bird. Historians speculate that the head of the condor was used as a sacrificial altar."

Dr. Weckesser stopped the video and turned to the photos of the tattoos on each of the victims, showing Jeffrey how the serial killer had been giving them a virtual tour of Machu Picchu.

"The Pandemic Predator started with Ana Bontierre, showing us the front view of the Royal Tomb. Next, he used Hong Kong's Elena Costeau to show us the side view of the tomb." Dr. Weckesser continued to paste together one autopsy photograph after another. "Now look at Bangkok's Lucretia Sudea. See how her tattoo shows the steps? And then there was Mumbai's Florentina Ursa—she has part of the Hitching Post of the Sun. Rozalia Oana from Syria has one of the pillars from the hitching post. The next three girls have the rest of the four pillars. Then we get to Victoria Vlaicu of London, who has some of the Temple of the Condor." Dr. Weckesser continued to piece the pictographs together, comparing them to the panorama in her office. She rewound a portion of the *National Geographic* video to the part showing the Temple of the Condor, and then froze the frame so that they could compare the pictograph and the natural version of the ruin.

"What is his message?" Jeffrey asked. "What is it about this place that he wants us to see?"

"The women from Tuscan and the Bellagio in Las Vegas both had the word 'condor' under her pictograph. So, I think he wants us to see something in the Temple of the Condor."

"Isn't that the one that has the sacrificial altar in it?" Jeffrey asked.

"Yes. That's the one." Dr. Weckesser pushed the play button again, pausing at the point in the video showing the sacrificial altar. Jeffrey studied the still frame on the television. He was quiet for a few moments before he spoke.

"You don't suppose that he–"

"That's exactly what I suppose."

Chapter 39

Mary MacIntosh did not know what to make of Jeffrey. They had shared a wonderful evening together in Washington, D.C., yet the next morning he had completely shut her out, literally thrusting her into a cab. He barely even kissed her good-bye before he darted back into his house. Was he hiding something from her?

What if Jeffrey wasn't who he said he was? He'd only showed Mac a business card with FBI information on it. What if he was an imposter? The business card could have been a fake. He never sent her an email from his FBI address–his emails came from his private email account. In his *home* office, he had photographs of all of the victims with their names, dates of birth, place of birth, and other pertinent information. Either he really was an FBI agent, or........Mac stopped herself. She was allowing her detective mind to get carried away. There was no way that Jeffrey was involved in the murders. Absolutely no way. He *couldn't* be. Mac felt bile rise in her throat.

Ploiesti. The word had been haunting her. Mac had asked Jacqueline about the hospital and orphanage.

"My husband and I traveled to Bucharest in 1990. Romania was in a state of chaos at the time. Up until 1989, the country was controlled by repressive communist dictator Nicolae Ceausescu. He was publicly executed on Christmas Day 1989. He was a terrible man, that Ceausescu. He had strict anti-abortion laws and he required that all women have five children by the age of forty-five before he would allow them birth control or abortion. He mandated large population growth, while, at the same time, he exported Romania's food. People were starving to death. Mothers were forced to take their kids to orphanages, which had horrific living conditions comparable to Nazi concentration camps.

"My husband and I were mortified. We were supposed to adopt through a Christian orphanage that our church had connected us with, but on our way to the orphanage, we met Ana. She was walking the streets. She was so young and innocent, yet she was selling her body so that she could eat. She showed us Ploiesti, and that is where we found her adoptive sisters, living in squalor. We made an offer to pay for the girls and the orphanage greedily accepted it.

"We signed the paperwork at the hotel, and the girls came back to America with us with only the clothes on their backs. They did not have toys or anything. We bought them each a toy at the airport."

Mac thought about Jacqueline's experience and researched a number of orphanages in Romania. There were many. Some were very large. The majority of American adoptions came from two orphanages in particular. Ploiesti was not among them—in fact, it was more a hospital for the destitute than an orphanage.

It could not be a coincidence that so many of these victims of the avian flu came from Ploiesti, but Mac had no way of connecting them. She had essentially come to a dead end in her investigation of Ana's death. She told Jacqueline as much. Jacqueline was not willing to let go just yet, and encouraged Mac to keep searching. So Mac did, but she was frustrated with her own lack of progress.

Mac sat in her second-story office in Sheridan overlooking Main Street and looked out the window as people drove past. It was the day before Thanksgiving and shoppers were out in the chilly morning air, getting what they needed for the next day's big meal. Mac especially loved Thanksgiving because the focus was not about giving or receiving presents—it was about being together with loved ones and sharing. But this year, for the first time in her life, she was going to be alone on Thanksgiving. For the past ten years, she shared the holiday with her law partner, Harry, and his family. Before that, she spent Thanksgiving with her family in Colorado. Mac remembered the holiday with her mother—watching her bustling around in the kitchen, giving Mac small tasks like putting butter on the table and filling water glasses with ice, more as a favor, to make Mac feel like she was part of the effort. Mac's mother was a gourmet cook, and took to the very last detail of the meal with prized passion.

This year, living in a new town, with Greg out of her life and no steady boyfriend, Mac knew that it was going to be a lonely day. Several people had asked her to join them, including the Bontierre family, but Mac didn't feel comfortable accepting their invitation. She would probably spend the morning at the office getting caught up on the work she missed while in Washington, D.C. and then volunteer in the soup kitchen at the Elks Club.

Just as she was about to get started on the stack of pleadings sitting on her dark, oak-stained desk, she heard her computer sing that welcomed tune, "You've Got Mail." Mac toggled her word processing screen over and opened her new message. It was a note from Gil's Blackberry.

I am making my way back in hopes of cooking a vegetarian Thanksgiving feast for you, like I promised. I will have to travel all night to get there. Do you have plans for tomorrow evening? I would love to dine with you. Gil.

Mac responded to Gil's email, agreeing to the dinner date, and feeling less melancholy about her day. She was still contemplating her time with Jeffrey, feeling confused. But instead of dwelling on her emotions, she decided to think positively. It had been too long since she had volunteered her time at a homeless shelter or soup line, and she looked forward to focusing on helping others and being thankful for the many blessings in her life.

* * *

"Three mice infected with H5N1 avian influenza virus apparently disappeared a month or so ago from the Siberian Health Research Institute, which conducts bioterrorism research for the Russian government. The mice were injected as part of an inoculation and vaccination experiment. What do you know about that?" Director Weiss asked Vladimir Checovsky, who was still under interrogation at his Tarirescu lab in Moscow.

"I know nothing about the mice disappearing," Vladimir responded.

"Dr. Mills checked into it a little deeper, and he learned that the mice were on loan from the Tarirescu lab."

"That's news to me," Vladimir said. "One can find mice anywhere. I doubt that they were from my lab. I have never *loaned* mice from my lab. There must be some kind of misunderstanding."

"And the virus that the mice were injected with matches the strain of H5N1 that is now killing people in Central and South America."

"Again, I don't see what that has to do–"

Vladimir stopped speaking mid-sentence. His eyes grew wide and his lips pursed. He shook his head back and forth. "That son-of-a-"

"What is it that you know?" Director Weiss said, leaning over the conference room table and peering into Vladimir Checovsky's eyes.

Vladimir's face grew red with rage. He shouted to himself in terse Russian.

Director Weiss decided that she should give Vladimir a break and allow him to collect his thoughts. Normally during the heat of an interrogation, she pushed harder–in an effort to make the witness crack. But something inside of her told her to let him have some time to stew. They had been interrogating him for days, and her orders from the President were to keep interrogating him until she had all the answers she needed, even if it took weeks. But, the interrogation team was growing weary.

A half hour later, Director Weiss stepped back into the conference room and calmly approached Vladimir. She took a seat next to him and continued the interrogation. "Now would you like to explain your relationship with Nicolai Petrescu?"

Vladimir sat in silence, shaking his head back and forth. He pounded his fist on the table, mumbling brusquely in Russian. "I should have known," he finally said. "I should have known."

"You should have known what?" Director Weiss asked.

"I should have known that I could not trust that boy."

"Are you referring to Mr. Petrescu?"

Vladimir rose from his chair and paced the room. "He stole from me once when he was young. I caught him. He did not lie to me about it. I admired him for that. He said that he would never do it again. I believed him. He proved to be my most loyal employee from that point on."

"Is this Nicolai Petrescu?" Director Weiss asked, pulling a photograph out of the manila file she was holding. It was a picture of Nicolai leaving the casino portion of the Bellagio. Vladimir took the photograph and looked at it closely.

"Yes, that is my boy."

"Your boy?"

"He was like my son. My wife, she only gave me daughters. Nicolai was my son, to me."

"Do you know where he is now?"

"No, I do not know."

"This picture was taken in a Las Vegas, Nevada casino. In the United States. Do you know what Mr. Petrescu would be doing in America?"

Vladimir looked away from Director Weiss. He did not answer.

"If you cooperate with us, we will cooperate with you, Mr. Checovsky. You need to tell us what you know, right now. Time is of the essence."

"I need assurance that my family will be protected," Vladimir said.

Director Weiss looked at the other members of intelligence agencies from around the world that were present in the interrogation room. They nodded in unison. "We can assure that your family will be protected, provided that you fully cooperate. We need to find this man immediately and stop him before he strikes again."

Chapter 40

Jeffrey stood in Dr. Laura Weckesser's office, staring at what she called the virtual tour of Machu Picchu, when her phone rang. She answered it in her customary fashion. "YouSamRid, Dr. Weckesser." He listened to Laura's side of the conversation, as she spoke of databases, scans and probabilities. Then she passed the phone to Jeffrey. "It's Diane Weiss." Jeffrey took the phone.

"Vladimir Checovsky has given us his formal statement. I will fax it to your attention promptly. In the meantime, I need you to listen closely. He claims that he and Nicolai Petrescu, his former employee and current business partner, cooked up a plan to mutate the H5N1 virus, and then create an antiviral medicine to counteract it. Essentially, that is how Rescuflu was created. Mr. Checovsky claims that Mr. Petrescu's mission was to hit China and Malaysia with the 1997 strain of the H5N1 virus, meaning that Stiflu would be the effective antiviral. Initially, they wanted to see how the virus would spread from human to human, using some kind of 'duck pudding' cocktail that contained the 1997 H5N1 virus. He admitted that they did not use a syringe to inject the virus because needles are difficult to get through security, and the duck element would keep scientists thinking that the birds were spreading the virus.

When they felt like they'd created enough of a scare, Mr. Petrescu then hit Syria, Turkey, and Romania with a new 'duck pudding'–which was a mutated version of the virus that they had created in the Tarirescu lab. They knew that the mutated genome meant that this version would not respond to Stiflu, so Tarirescu would then launch Rescuflu, and make an enormous windfall, which is precisely what has happened. Checovsky estimates that they've made close to fifty million dollars in the last month selling stockpiles of Rescuflu around the world."

"So, Nicolai Petrescu is our man?" Jeffrey asked. "He is the one spreading the avian flu?"

"Yes. But it gets more complicated. There is a long history between Checovsky and Petrescu, which I have documented in my report, but I don't have time to get into on this call. Right now we need to focus on finding and stopping Petrescu. We believe that Petrescu has created another mutated genome of the H5N1 in a Siberian lab. We believe that this 'Siberian genome' is what he is using now, and is what he spread through South, Central and Northern America instead of the version that responds to Rescuflu. Apparently, there is no antiviral for this genome, as far as we know."

"What is his motive?" Jeffrey asked. "If there is no antiviral, then his motive isn't money."

"That's your job. You need to tell me why this guy would spread a deadly virus to the population at large."

"He continues to leave us clues. Dr. Weckesser figured out that each 'patient zero' victim's tattoo on her inner thigh is part of a virtual tour of Machu Picchu, Peru."

"Ancient ruins?" Director Weiss asked.

"We think that he has killed before and that he wants to show us something. The last two victim's tattoo had the word 'condor' written underneath. The Temple of the Condor has a sacrificial altar in it. We think that whoever this guy is–and you say it is Petrescu–he has killed there before and he wants us to see it."

"Or he wants to lure you there. Has he communicated with you in any other way, other than the tattoos on the victims?" Director Weiss asked.

"No. Not that I'm aware of," Jeffrey said.

"Authorities think that they have a positive identification of him from a casino surveillance tape from the Bellagio. Surveillance tapes from a few other Vegas casinos show a similar image. It looks like we might have a positive identification of this guy. Once we have been assured that the surveillance tapes are authentic, I am considering issuing a bulletin."

"The last outbreak was in San Francisco. It is possible that he caught a flight from San Francisco International into Cusco, Peru."

"I'll issue an FBI dispatch and put together a reconnaissance team to go to Peru with you."

"You want *me* to go to Peru?" Jeffrey asked. He did not want to go. He wanted to fly to Wyoming, apologize to Mac in person, and tell her how he felt about her.

"You are the best person that I have, Jeffrey. If anyone can find this guy–it is you."

"But we have no idea where Petrescu is. For all we know, he is on his way to Canada. Or back to Russia. He could be crossing the Bering Strait. Why do you want me to go to Peru? Shouldn't we send in a search and recovery team?"

"Jeffrey. Listen to me. You are going to Peru. Take Laura with you. Decode the message so that we can find this guy before he wipes out half of the world's population. I don't know where Petrescu is, or where he could be going. But my fear is that he is going to either hit every major city in the United States, which would be horrible, or equally bad, he is going to escape our borders and hit a densely populated continent, like Africa. Can you imagine what will happen if he decimates Africa? Remember Ebola? This viral soup that Petrescu has will make Ebola look like a mild case of Typhoid Fever. This man has a message and it is your job to figure it out. Before it is too late."

Jeffrey took a deep breath. "I'm on my way," he said.

* * *

As he rushed to board the special reconnaissance plane at Bolling Air Force Base in the District of Columbia, Jeffrey desperately wanted to talk with Mac. He was nervous about the mission, afraid that something bad might happen. He wanted her to know that he cared for her and that she was the first person he wanted to see upon his return. Jeffrey had forgotten what it felt like to have feelings for a woman, and he knew that he didn't want to ruin his chances with her. He loved what he did for a living–being a mind hunter–but he knew his job was overly demanding when a crisis hit. Jeffrey wanted to assure her that the crises didn't occur often, and that under normal circumstances, he could and would be there for her. He wanted to tell her that she was the most incredible, beautiful, smart, sensitive, interesting woman he'd ever known, and that he wanted to get to know her better–much better. Unfortunately, he had only a few seconds before take-off, and the best that he could do was to send a text message to Mac that read, "I'm sorry that I didn't say good-bye better. My work has taken over my life right now. I hope to see you again when this case is . . .". The text message cut off.

When Mac received the message, she was annoyed. She felt like he owed her more than a phone text message apology. Her Irish temper flared, and she responded with a text message to his cell. "Happy Thanksgiving to you too." After she hit the 'send' button, she regretted the message. She wished that she would have thought about it longer. Her response was curt and she knew it. Her Catholic guilt set in about a minute later, and so Mac decided to call Jeffrey and apologize. "I'm sorry, but I can't talk right now," Jeffrey managed, as the G-force nearly stripped his cell phone from his hands. "I'll have to call you back........." The connection failed.

Chapter 41

Facial recognition software is one of the most innovative breakthroughs in law enforcement technology. It allows detectives to compare a composite sketch of a suspect to images in a digital mug shot database for possible matches. Within seconds, a search could display photos of similar composites from around the county, state, country, or even the world. The technology can be used at the international level to apprehend terrorists. On the local level, a suspect caught on a bank or convenience store video can be checked against a digital photo database for possible identification.

In an effort to stem a growing problem with methamphetamine dealers and users throughout the state, Wyoming's Department of Motor Vehicles recently replaced its digital cameras with face recognition cameras, so that when a person renewed or applied for a driver's license, their photograph was also stored in a centralized mug shot database for use in comparison with photographs of criminals.

After the avian flu outbreak in America, the FBI ordered all states that already had the new facial recognition databases to compare the photograph taken by the Bellagio surveillance camera to their mug shot database. Since the Bellagio tape did not use facial recognition software, the picture of Nicolai Petrescu first had to be converted to a sketch, which would not be as accurate for search purposes. Nevertheless, when the technician in Cheyenne's FBI office performed his comparison, one driver's license photograph popped up as a match. The technician quickly forwarded the information to Washington, D.C.

* * *

Mary MacIntosh woke up Thanksgiving morning in a spirited mood. She had terrible nightmares the night before about a client she'd once represented, Michael O'Connor. She dreamed that Michael was on the lamb for a crime he committed, and that he took her hostage while trying to evade the police. In the dream, Michael held Mac against her office window with a gun to her head, and told the police that he would shoot her if they didn't provide him with an airplane. The police refused. The sound of the gun firing into her right temple was really the noise of her alarm clock. She bolted upright in bed, and tried to shake off the bad dream.

After a cup of steaming black coffee, Mac slipped into her running clothes and hit the trail. It was a frosty morning, and as her feet crunched through an inch of newly-fallen snow, she thought about her dream. Mac had been plagued with night terrors since her father died when she was four years old. Most of her bad dreams involved car accidents, or being trapped alive in a burning car. Her father died in a car accident during a terrible snow storm, so she assumed that her dreams correlated to her loss. However, when she was practicing law in Jackson Hole a few years back, a methamphetamine drug dealer broke into her law office and tried to rape her at gunpoint. If her boss, Harry, hadn't come into the office that morning, Mac probably would not be alive. Since that episode, her dreams often involved staring at the cold, black metal of a gun. She attributed last night's dream to the attempted rape. Her psyche was apparently still dealing with the trauma of that incident, despite the fact that she rarely thought about it anymore. She picked up her running pace, thinking about her father and about Jeffrey. She was angry at Jeffrey for making her feel so safe and loved one minute, and then abandoned the next. She picked up her pace even faster, so that she was almost sprinting. She thought more about her anger toward Jeffrey. Was it really misplaced anger at her father for abandoning her as a little girl? Of course, her father did not mean to die in a car accident, but to a child, abandonment is abandonment, regardless of the reason. Did Jeffrey's reaction in his home office trigger Mac's defensive mechanism to protect herself from the feeling of being deserted? Was she being too hard on Jeffrey? She decided that she wasn't. He owed her a big apology. In person.

Mac looked up at the dark clouds looming over the Big Horn Mountains, and worried that another storm was on its way. She hoped that the weather wouldn't keep Gil from making his way back home. She did not want to admit it, but the thought of spending a holiday alone was depressing to her.

After her run and a long, hot shower, Mac went to the office for a few hours of catch-up. When it was time to go to the Elks Club to help in the soup kitchen, she walked across the street and up the steps of the old brownstone building. Mac put on an apron, affixed her long hair under a hairnet and slipped on the latex gloves before taking her position in the soup line. It was rewarding to greet each person with a warm smile and a steaming bowl of chicken noodle soup.

After hours of serving, clearing and cleaning up the cafeteria, Mac wanted nothing more than to go home, take a long, hot shower and curl up with a good book. But she had promised Gil that she'd meet him at his place. She tried to call him on his cell and email his Blackberry, but she received no response. She figured that he was still en route.

Mac drove home, showered and put on a nice pair of black pants and a shimmering silver blouse, and then headed to the grocery store. She presumed that Gil would be exhausted from a long, international flight. She was pretty sure that Gil's front door had not been fixed and that his house would be open. She decided to surprise him by making him a delicious Thanksgiving feast. She would make a turkey, as her little joke to overcome the lie about being a vegetarian. While the avian flu remained a global threat and was still the main story on the news, no further outbreaks had occurred in Sheridan, and she felt it was safe to eat poultry again.

Mac purchased everything she needed to make an incredible meal, and then drove south on U.S. 87, through the cottonwood-lined, rolling ranch country. She pulled up to Gil's front gate, got out of her Chevy Equinox, and unchained the large, metal fence. She pulled her SUV over the cattle guard, and then got out of her car again to secure the gate. She noticed that large flakes of snow were beginning to fall and that the air was growing very cold. She parked in front of the old, red barn and carried two large grocery bags to the front porch. She decided to try the lock first, to make sure she could get in the house, before carrying the heavy turkey inside.

The house was unlocked, and when Mac entered, she noticed that it was colder inside than it was out. She carried all the groceries inside and got to work building a giant fire in the fireplace before beginning to prepare her masterpiece meal.

Chapter 42

Jeffrey was out of breath after deplaning in Cusco, Peru. The city rests in a high mountain valley nearly twelve thousand feet above sea level. His reconnaissance team was met by members of the Unidad de Gestión Santuario Histórico de Machu Picchu, the organization that oversees the Incan trail. Eduardo, their guide, assembled the group into their respective Hummers, courtesy of the Peruvian government, and they swiftly departed on a very bumpy ride through the Sacred Valley, down the Andes Mountains. Eduardo had lived in Peru his entire life, and was quite knowledgeable about the region.

"Peru is the third-largest country in South America and lies entirely within the tropics. You probably do not feel like you are in the tropics now, because the elevation is so high. You may even feel a little dizzy or carsick at first. But, we will drop about one thousand meters into the valley, and you will start feeling a little better. When we get to Machu Picchu, remember that you are still two thousand five hundred meters above sea level, and you must be careful about acclimation."

As they drove, Laura and Jeffrey showed Eduardo the pictures of the tattoos left behind on each victim of the avian flu, and discussed their meaning with respect to the investigation. Eduardo agreed with Laura's interpretation that whoever left the clues behind was trying to depict various structures within the sacred city.

"I have been to Machu Picchu hundreds of times and I have never seen anything unusual in the Temple of the Condor. I do not know what you expect to find there. Thousands of tourists roam through there every day, along with many archeologists and geologists and astronomers. If there was something unusual there, our government would have known about it by now. I think you are searching for . . . what is it you Americans say—a straw in the haystack?"

"I don't think that the serial killer is done taking us on his virtual tour yet," Dr. Weckesser said. "There may be more victims out there that we have not learned about. We are hoping that we might find some clues in the Temple of the Condor that lead us to this guy."

Eduardo was sitting in the front of the Hummer. He turned his head quickly and glared at Dr. Weckesser. "You don't think that the killer is in the Temple of the Condor right now, do you?"

"It's okay, Eduardo," Jeffrey said. "I doubt that he is there waiting for us. Besides, we have a very well-trained team of soldiers with us. If something were to happen, you will be protected. You don't have to go to the temple with us if you do not feel comfortable. We do not know if we are even on the right track with this guy. This could be a ruse, for all we know."

"But you think it is possible that he is here, no?"

"It is possible. But Lima's airport is on high alert, as are all border patrol officers. It would be very difficult for this man to cross borders now, unless he is on foot or has private means."

"But it is possible that he is here?" Eduardo asked again.

"Anything is possible," Jeffrey said. As the words escaped his mouth, his thoughts went back to Mac. He was worried about her. He had a sick feeling in the pit of his stomach that she was in danger. He wanted nothing more than to talk with her. Assure her that he loved her and that he would take care of her. They would take care of each other. Instead, with no cell service and the Temple of the Condor looming, he had to focus on his job.

* * *

Mac stuffed the turkey with rosemary, sage, thyme, and garlic, and then put the giant bird in the old-fashioned oven at Gil's house. It was difficult to read the dials for the correct temperature, so she decided that she would have to frequently check on the turkey. Expecting that it would take three or four hours to the turkey to cook, she got busy peeling potatoes. Her mother was a gourmet, and had taught her the secret family recipes for the gravy, sweet potatoes, stuffing, and home-made bread, and she was having fun recreating her mother's great dishes.

An hour later, the potatoes were boiling on the stove and the stuffing was prepared. There wasn't much more for her to do for a few hours. She had no idea what time Gil would be home, and hoped that he wouldn't be upset with her for making the meal. What if he stopped on the way home and bought all the fixings? She hoped that wouldn't happen. She had left messages on his cell phone and email, but had not heard a reply from him.

A certain feeling of uncomfortable started seeping in and Mac began to second-guess her decision to cook an elaborate meal for him. Would he be offended by the fact that she let herself into his house? They didn't know each other that well. Perhaps this had been a mistake. Mac decided not to focus on the negative. What was done, was done, she thought to herself. Perhaps she needed to put on some nice music and relax for awhile. She walked around the living room, trying to find his stereo, but had no luck. There was only a small portable radio and a chair in the living room. Mac continued to walk through the house. The dining room was practically empty, only furnished with a make-shift wooden table and six old chairs. Mac contrasted Gil's dining room to Jeffrey's, remembering how much Jeffrey loved having his grandmother's antiques displayed. Gil's house was devoid of any past history.

She continued to tour his house. There was a den off of the dining room, but it was full of stacked boxes. Gil showed her the upstairs the last time she was out for dinner, but she couldn't remember if there were two or three bedrooms. She flipped on the hallway light and started up the stairs.

What if Gil comes home and I'm in his bedroom? That would be awkward. Her goal was to find a stereo. Even if there was one upstairs, she wouldn't be able to hear it in the kitchen. She decided to stay on the ground floor.

After checking on the turkey one more time, she went back to the living room and flipped on the radio. There weren't many radio stations in Wyoming, and the reception out in the country wasn't good. She twisted the dial back and forth, trying to hone in on a station, but all she could get was static. She slowed down, and finally found a station. She heard the weather forecast, noting that a terrible storm was on its way. She hoped that Gil wasn't delayed by bad weather. Before the sports update, there was a bulletin regarding the outbreak of the avian flu in the United States.

"Forty-seven people have been confirmed dead in Arizona so far. Another thirty-nine are dead in the Las Vegas area, plus ten more in Los Angeles. There is a possible suspect in the outbreak," the radio newscaster said, "based on surveillance videos in Las Vegas casinos. The FBI is about to release a composite sketch of the suspect. We are told that the FBI believes that the suspect is a serial killer who goes by the name of Nicolai Petrescu. The FBI believes that the suspect has been deliberately infecting women around the world with the avian flu virus."

If it was true that Jeffrey was in charge of the FBI investigation, Mac felt a pang of guilt for not being more tolerant about his present work demands. Hearing the radio bulletin made her more aware of the pressure he must be under and the importance of his role in the investigation. The world was depending upon his team of profilers to catch the killer. Maybe he was abrupt with her at his house, but perhaps something big had happened in the investigation and he needed to focus on it. She realized that she had overreacted and that she should have given him the benefit of the doubt at the time.

Mac looked around Gil's house once more, and realized that she shouldn't be there. She didn't know him well enough and in her heart, she knew that she was there because she was angry at Jeffrey and she was lonely. She paced the living room floor, contemplating her emotions, allowing the ripple of sentiment to wash over her. She'd acknowledged to herself that she had been suppressing her feelings toward Jeffrey since her trip to Washington, D.C. because she was so afraid of getting hurt. Thinking back on her time with him, it became clear that when she was in Jeffrey's arms, everything felt right. They fit.

She thought back on the morning in his home office, when he was staring at the pictographs of the avian flu victims, trying to figure out the commonalities among the drawings. He was probably under a great deal of pressure to stop the killer–this Nicolai Petrescu–or whatever the newscaster said was his name. Mac felt terrible for leaving him the petulant text message. How childish and rude of her.

She decided to take the Thanksgiving feast out of the oven, store it in containers in Gil's refrigerator, and leave him a note. She wanted to get home before it got too late and give Jeffrey a call.

Chapter 43

Jeffrey, Laura Weckesser, Eduardo, and the team of reconnaissance soldiers marched down the rocky slope leading to Machu Picchu. Jeffrey had never seen such beauty. The contrast between the sharp, rocky peaks and the lush, green valley was striking. It was easier to breathe now that they were at a lower elevation. He was in excellent physical shape, due to his daily running regime. Laura, however, was out of shape and overweight, and struggled to catch her breath as they traversed the steep grade of the uneven trail.

"Some people come here for a spiritual nirvana," Eduardo said, as they climbed the steps toward the caretaker's hut. "They believe that this place holds special powers. I believe that this was a place of worship for the Incas. They were very smart, industrious people. My ancestry is Incan."

"I have read a book about prophecies that have been performed or experienced here," Laura said to Eduardo. "I think I'm supposed to look for some yellow hue that glows around one of the temples."

"If you are here to experience spirituality, then we can focus on that. But I do not believe that you are here for that purpose. I will direct you wherever you wish to go," Eduardo said, as they breached the top of the agricultural terraces that separated the valley from the ruins.

The reconnaissance team crossed the dry moat that separated the terraces from the urban sector of the ruins. They looked up in unison at the hundreds of stone temples built into the hillside.

"The Temple of the Condor is up ahead on your left. If you will follow me, I will take you there, but if you don't mind, I will wait outside."

Jeffrey walked through the opening of the Temple of the Condor, somewhat apprehensive about what might lie ahead of them. The placard in front of the temple described the condor as a symbol of heaven in the Inca cosmos, but Jeffrey did not feel divinity at the moment. He was nervous and anxious that Nicolai might be lying in wait, ready to pounce like a hungry leopard at any moment.

Jeffrey asked that one reconnaissance soldier walk in front of him and one walk behind him as they entered the Temple. Inside, the air smelled musty, like the smell of death.

Chapter 44

After Mac finished cleaning up his kitchen and storing the food, she turned off the kitchen light and headed for the front door. While passing through the hallway, she noticed a light under the door that led to the basement. Gil had warned her that the basement had flooded and that it was infested with vermin, or something of that nature. How could a light stay on for three weeks straight and not burn out? Had the light been on when she got there? If it wasn't burning when she arrived, how did the light get switched on? Mac decided to check it out. She set down her grocery bags and slowly turned the knob, afraid of the rats charging out as soon as the door popped open. As she pulled back on the door, she could hear a suction-like noise, as if the room was vacuum sealed.

The wooden plank steps were solid under her feet as she descended the dimly lit staircase. She expected dry-rot and mold on the ground, but everything was desiccated and clean. Immaculate, in fact. The sharp smell of chemical cleansers permeated the air.

At the bottom of the staircase, there was a closed, metal door. Mac knocked lightly, but there was no answer, so she turned the handle and opened it. Inside, there was a small light in the center table of the room, and Mac could hear scratching noises. After her eyes adjusted to the dim light, she looked around for a light switch. When she flipped on the lights, she was nearly blinded by the glare. The room was stark-white and sterile, and had the appearance of a science laboratory. In the middle of the room, there was a large, square acrylic case, and inside it were dozens of chicken eggs. None of the eggs had hatched.

Along the far side of the room there was a long table with syringes, test tubes, and other laboratory equipment. It looked similar to what Mac saw on television when she watched crime scene investigation shows. One machine had around fifty sealed test tubes inside it, with red, yellow and green blinking lights next to each tube. There were notepads strewn across the counter with annotations written in a foreign language.

Screeeeeeeeeeeeeech. A loud squeal startled her, and she nearly jumped out of her skin. Her heartbeat amplified as she twisted around to see what made the noise. Over in the corner of the room, adjacent to the test tube table, was a four foot cage containing two white mice. Their noses twitched as she grew closer, as if they were happy to see her. "Hello there," Mac said. "What are your names?" The mice backed away as she pushed her hand toward their cage. "Don't be afraid. I won't hurt you," she said.

Mac looked to the right of the mice's cage, into a sealed vat. Inside, she could see the skeletal remains of other mice. Dead mice. Dead mice with coagulated blood all around them. "No wonder you guys are afraid of me," Mac said to the two mice hiding in their cage. "What happened to your friends?" Mac knew that Gil was a scientist, but she thought that he said that he worked in the pharmaceutical business. Maybe he was testing drugs on mice.

Next to the vat of mice carcasses, sat a refrigerator. Mac yanked on the door and looked inside, where she found dozens of test tube vials full of a clear liquid, each labeled in a foreign language on white tape. She pulled open the freezer compartment and saw what looked to be raw meat, individually wrapped in tiny, one-inch samples. Each sample was tagged, again in a language Mac could not identify.

Screeeeeeeeeeeeech. One mouse was making a racket in the corner of the cage, running on his mouse wheel. Mac closed the freezer door and approached the mice again, looking around their cage to see if they had any food. "Are you hungry, buddy?" she asked.

Her eyes rose above the cage to a giant corkboard that lined the wall. Attached to the corkboard, Mac saw dozens of photographs of women. Under each photograph, there were pieces of paper with words written in the same language that Mac did not understand. *Russian, perhaps,* she thought. It seemed as though Gil had been collecting information on these women for a long time. There were news clippings from a foreign press and copies of official documents with the women's names on them. She noticed numbers on some of the papers; birthdates and addresses, perhaps. She wondered why the pictures were displayed. Many of the images resembled one another. *Maybe they were his family from Russia or Poland? Or was it Romania?* There was a large atlas high on the wall, above the pictures of the women. Lines were drawn from each woman's picture to a place on the atlas. China. India. Thailand. Italy. Gil told Mac that he traveled extensively. Perhaps these were his past girlfriends.

She tried to think of where Gil said he was from. Mac couldn't remember for sure. She continued to look at the photos of the dozens of women . . . until she came to a face she recognized. Mac gasped as she looked at the very young-looking face. There were three pictures of her. One picture showed her as a little girl, another as a teenager and one current photograph. "Ana Bontierre!" Mac said out loud to herself. "Why does Gil have a picture of Ana?" Under Ana's photograph was her birthplace in Romania and the date of her adoption from Ploiesti, all written in English. *Why would he have this information?*

Mac's eyes grew wide and she sucked in a deep breath. "OH MY GOD!" she yelled.

Chapter 45

Jeffrey walked to the head of the giant condor, looking for signs of the Pandemic Predator, but the "sacrificial altar" looked sterile to him. He followed Laura through to the next small chamber, which some explorers claimed to be the "prison" within the ruins. Each chamber was connected to another and another, until they finally reached the back side of the ruins, bordered by a terraced hillside leading down into the valley. "I don't know what we are looking for," Jeffrey said to Laura. She pulled out her BlackBerry and punched the keys.

"I downloaded the digital tour from my office onto my hand-held. Maybe if we take another look at what *he* wanted us to see, we'll have a better idea of what to look for." Laura pulled up her downloaded file, and they looked at the pictographs that had been drawn on the victims' thighs.

"The last one we have is from the lady in Los Angeles. It shows this valley and that rock outcropping over there," Jeffrey said, pointing to a group of rocks at the bottom of the terrace. "Why don't we check that out?"

"My only concern," Laura said, "is that we are not supposed to be in the valley without a guide. Should we go back and find Eduardo? He'll know the best way to get there." Jeffrey agreed. They walked back through the Temple of the Condor and found Eduardo sitting with some other men. They explained the situation to him, and asked that he escort them down to the rock outcropping. He agreed. They climbed down the switchbacks of the green, terraced slope, descending to the valley floor.

"What are we looking for?" Eduardo asked.

"We don't know."

"How will we know when we find it?" Eduardo asked.

"We don't know that either."

"You told me about the Temple of the Condor. Why don't you tell me about this rock outcropping. What do you expect to find? If I know what you're looking for down here, maybe I can be of greater assistance." Eduardo's patience seemed to be growing thin. Laura looked at Jeffrey. He nodded. They told Eduardo the rest of the story, and showed him the virtual tour left behind on each victim. Eduardo had never heard of the avian flu, despite the fact that thousands of people had died from it in Columbia and Ecuador.

"This serial killer has caused the deaths of hundreds of thousands of people and he is leading us here. We have no idea why."

"I do not know either," Eduardo said. "We have had no deaths like that here in a long time. Twenty years now."

"What do you mean, twenty years?"

"The Monster of the Andes." Eduardo crossed himself in a religious fashion, as if the mere mention of this character made him feel the need for divine protection. "He killed with a bloodlust. I was quite young when it happened, but I remember how frightened everyone was. My mother wouldn't let my sisters out of the house for months."

"Who is the Monster of the Andes?"

* * *

Mac flipped open her cell phone and tried to call Jeffrey, but she had no cell service in Gil's basement. She started to type him a text message instead. Even if she couldn't make a call, her text messages usually went through. It said, "I think Nicolai Petrescu is . . ."

"I see that you have made yourself at home," said a voice behind her. Mac spun around. It was Gil. His hair was blond and his eyes looked green, but it was Gil. And he looked very, very angry. Mac felt shrills of terror run down her spine.

Mac held her cell phone behind her back and blindly tried to search for the keys to spell Gil's name. She typed what she thought might be

"Gilbert Bonita," but she could not be sure. She felt around for the "send" button, and prayed that she hit the right key. She flipped her phone closed while remaining as still as possible.

"I-I-I came out here to cook you a Thanksgiving dinner," Mac started to say. "I thought you would be home earlier and thought I would surprise you. The d-d-dinner is upstairs. Are you hungry?"

"Am I hungry?" Gil asked back, in a mocking tone. "Am I hungry? You ask if I'm hungry like I'm a child. I am not a child, Ms. MacIntosh. I am a grown man. If I am hungry, I will tell you. If I am hungry, I will feed myself. If I am hungry, I know how to satisfy my desires."

"I know you are a grown man, Gil. I was just trying to be polite. I haven't seen you in a few weeks and I missed you and wanted to spend the holiday with you. I thought it would be a great surprise if–"

"You thought it would be a great surprise to break into my home and snoop through my personal belongings. That's what you thought. I think that I made myself quite clear the last time you were here that you were not allowed down in the basement. Didn't I make myself clear?"

"You told me that there was a flood."

"Didn't I tell you to stay out?"

"I remember you saying that the basement was infested with vermin from a flood. I noticed a light on in the basement, and I came down to investigate. I think my actions were reasonable. I wasn't trying to snoop on–"

"Reasonable? You sound like a lawyer." Gil's upper lip curled back with his sneer. He took a few steps toward Mac. Mac tried to back up, but she had nowhere to go. As he got closer to her, she could smell his putrid breath, as if he hadn't brushed his teeth in days. Gil took a few more steps closer to Mac, and she could see by the look in his distilled eyes that his anger was intensifying. She felt her pulse accelerate and the adrenaline kick in.

The basement room was a rectangle shape with a table in the middle where the eggs were incubating. There was only one door out and it was behind Gil. Mac wanted to lure Gil further into the room, around the table, so that she could run out the door and make a break for it. The only way she could think of luring him was to keep talking to him, and slowly aggravate him. She didn't want to infuriate him too quickly, for he might lose his temper and do something forceful. She thought it best to keep chafing him, bit by bit, with slightly stinging comments–just enough so she could entice him to approach her with each baiting comment. Then, when she rounded the back side of the egg table, she could make a run for it up the steps.

"You've been lying to me. You weren't in Russia, were you?"

"I don't believe that I owe you an explanation as to my whereabouts. I told you that I had business overseas. And I did. That is all you are entitled to know."

"Actually, I think you told me that you had to go to Russia on business. But something tells me that you never made it there. My hunch is that you were in China first, and then Thailand." Mac nonchalantly pointed to the second and third pictures of the victims on the wall. "It occurred to me, as I stood here in your laboratory, that you have been premeditating this killing spree for a very long time. I admire your thoroughness in your research to find the 'right' victim. They are all Romanian girls, correct?"

Gil took another step closer to Mac.

"Ploiesti? Were you an orphan there too?"

His eyes darted to the corkboard on the wall and then back to her. He did not respond.

"It looks like you've gone to a lot of trouble to kill these poor women. What have they done to you? Did they turn you down? Is that what happens when a woman doesn't agree to dine with you? You kill them?"

Gil took another step closer, his eyes narrowing in anger. "You are smart, yes. But not smart enough. I held you too high on a pedestal, I'm afraid. I thought that maybe you were different. Better. But I was wrong. You're just like all the rest."

"I'm not like all the rest, Gil. I'm different. This time, I've tracked you down. I've prepared a meal for you. This time, I'm the hunter and you are the prey. You probably don't like that too much. You like to be the one in control. How does it feel to be out of control?"

Gil treaded another step closer, his eyes revealing pent up hostility. "You think you are in control, Miss MacIntosh? You look scared to me. And you should be."

Mac flipped open her cell phone, which remained in her right hand, behind her back. She blindly searched the keys again, trying to find the numbers 9-1-1.

Chapter 46

"You have never heard of the Monster of the Andes?" Eduardo seemed genuinely surprised that someone on the planet did not know of the dirty deeds of such a crazed animal.

"No. I have never heard of it," Jeffrey replied.

"Him. It is a him. The Monster of the Andes was a serial killer. About twenty-five years ago, young women started disappearing from the streets of Lima. Most of them were prostitutes, so not much was made of it at first. And then it started to happen in Ecuador. And then Columbia. The Columbian policía finally caught the guy. His name was Pedro Perez, I think. They found him in a cave in the Columbian mountains with a group of twenty or thirty dead girls, all set up in a circle, having a pretend tea party."

"He arranged the dead girls for a tea party? That is disgusting," Laura said.

"Yes. It is disgusting, but true. He is what we call a depraved heart."

"Whatever happened to the guy?" Jeffrey asked.

"He served about ten years in prison, and then when the Columbian government was overthrown, he was set free. At least that's what I heard. No one has ever heard of or seen the guy again, but mothers still worry that one day he will come back and take their little girls. Parents around here still warn their children to be careful of the Monster of the Andes. He is part of every ghost story. You can imagine. They estimate that he might have killed several hundred young girls. I am surprised that you have not heard of him. Didn't you say that you study serial killers?" On the long ride from Cusco to Machu Picchu, Jeffrey and Laura told Eduardo that they were mind hunters for serial killers, and that they studied their profiles, trying to link common traits among them in an effort to catch them quicker. Eduardo assumed that the Monster of the Andes would be someone they would use as a case study.

"I remember reading about that guy in college, I think," Laura said. "Jeffrey and I were both pretty young when those killings took place."

"So was I. I was just a young boy—but I remember it clearly. Pedro Perez was a young man when he started his killing spree, so he wouldn't be much older than forty by now. It sometimes frightens me to think that he could be roaming around. They found a few of his victims in the Temple of the Condor."

Jeffrey stopped walking down the terraced hillside. He could not believe what he'd just heard. He turned toward Eduardo. "He killed people in the Temple? Why didn't you tell me that?"

"It didn't occur to me that it could be relevant to your investigation. The killings happened so long ago that I didn't think to mention it before."

Jeffrey was growing irritated with Eduardo. It seemed that Eduardo was holding out on them. The altitude wasn't helping his mood either, as Jeffrey was feeling tired and had a headache. "So this serial killer left some of his victims in the Temple of the Condor? Tell us what else happened. Did they find more bodies around here? Did he admit to killing the women in Peru? Or did he just serve time for the killings in Columbia?"

"I don't remember the details that much. Like I said, I was a young boy when he was caught. I don't know if he admitted to killing the women in Peru, but the reason they think he did it was because all the girls were prostitutes, like the ones he killed in Columbia. The girls they found in the Temple of the Condor had been mutilated."

Just then, Jeffrey's cell phone buzzed twice, indicating that he had a text message. He noted from the digital display that it was from Mac. "Nicolai Petrescu is Gkgadrt bmnita." Jeffrey furrowed his brow while he re- read the message. He showed it to Laura. "What do you think it means?"

Laura shrugged her shoulders. "I have no idea. Must be a mistake."

Jeffrey sent her a text message back that read, "Nicolai Petrescu is who? Your message was scrambled. Are you okay?"

Within seconds of sending his message to Mac, his cell phone buzzed again. This time, Mac's text message said, "9-1-1."

Chapter 47

"I just got a 9-1-1 message from a lawyer in Wyoming," Jeffrey shouted into his cell phone to FBI Director Diana Weiss. "She knows the identity of Nicolai Petrescu. I think she might be in trouble. Can you do a global positioning satellite search and determine where her 9-1-1 transmission originated? This is an emergency."

Director Weiss, who was still in Russia working with authorities regarding Vladimir Checovsky's plea bargain, agreed, and immediately called the Pentagon. Both Jeffrey's and Mac's cell numbers were entered into the GPS system, and within ten minutes, Director Weiss had her answer. She called Jeffrey back.

"The call originated from a town in Wyoming called Big Horn. I'll have more information shortly. Do I need to send in a team?"

"Yes. Please do. I am worried about her. Please send the local police there right away to investigate. I am worried that this creep is going to —"

"Where are you?"

"Still in Machu Picchu. Ever heard of the Monster of the Andes?"

"The name rings a bell, but I don't recall the details." Jeffrey told her the story. "Do you think it relates to the Pandemic Predator?"

"I'm not sure. I just learned of him today, but it is interesting that the killer has been leading us back to Machu Picchu, and both killers have a vengeance for killing young prostitutes or women who have ties to prostitution."

"Good point, but it would seem unlikely that a serial killer who killed hundreds of girls in South America in the 1980's, or whenever this happened, would lie dormant for twenty years and then resurface in Asia and Europe. Seems like a stretch to me. Maybe the whole tattoo virtual tour thing is a ruse and the guy is sending us on a wild goose chase. I hear that there's a new outbreak in San Francisco."

"I heard about that. But my biggest concern is Mac."

"Mac?"

"The lawyer in Wyoming. Please, please send the police there right away, Diana. If something happens to her–"

"I will handle it, Jeffrey. Do you think that she is his next victim?"

"Yes. We have to stop him!"

"We will. You do your job and I'll do mine. Call me back if you learn anything."

Jeffrey ended his conversation with Director Weiss, and then asked Eduardo to continue their search down the terraced fields to the rock outcropping. The sun was beginning to dip behind the mountain and they wouldn't have much daylight left. He and Laura followed Eduardo down the emerald-green slope, traversing back and forth on the narrow foot path. When they got to the valley floor, they climbed over a group of rocks and through a narrow fissure, which led them to a grotto. The grotto of rocks grew narrower as they followed it to the end. At the end of the grotto, there was a small cavern. Eduardo's round face grew pinched. "I have never been down here before. I didn't know this was here."

"You have a flashlight on you, right?" Jeffrey asked.

"Sí, Señor. You may use it. I do not wish to go inside a cave. It's . . . it is just that I do not like small places. I get the confusion."

"Claustrophobia?" Laura asked.

Eduardo looked at her with an odd expression, as though he'd never head the term before. He offered Jeffrey the flashlight and then quickly shoved his hands back into the pockets of his green trousers. Jeffrey took the light, got down on his stomach and shimmied his way through the small opening. The dust gathered on his eyeglasses as he pushed his way in. As soon as he got the first half of his body through and could bring his arms up under him, he flipped on the flashlight, allowing his eyes to adjust to the contrast between light and dark. He reached forward with his elbows and continued to hoist his body weight forward, inch by inch, like a snake slithering into its hole, until his feet finally slid inside.

The cave widened significantly after the initial ingress. The room opened up into a second chamber. He turned the corner and crawled into a third cavity, which was even wider than the second. The stench inside the third cavity was almost overwhelming. Jeffrey pulled his shirt collar up over his nose and tried to breathe only through his mouth. He had kicked up a fair amount of dust while crawling around in the cave, and each breath he drew felt scratchy in his throat.

"Wait for me," he heard Laura's voice behind him. She could see the glow of Jeffrey's flashlight ahead, but that was all. It was pitch black in the second chamber. She shimmied her way next to him. "What do you see?"

Jeffrey did not respond. Laura waited another ten seconds before asking again. "What is it?"

"You are not going to believe this."

* * *

After Director Weiss received confirmation that the 9-1-1 call had been properly traced, she requested that a property profile be pulled for the GPS quadrants. She was informed that the property belonged to a single man by the name of Gilbert A. Bonita, a Columbian resident who had attained United States citizenship in 1997 in the State of California. Mr. Bonita's documents identified him as a businessman who worked in the pharmaceutical industry and who conducted business in Russia.

Chapter 48

Director Weiss gave the GPS quadrants for Gilbert Bonita's farmhouse to the new sheriff in Sheridan, Wyoming, and ordered him to surround the place and to contact her as soon as the house was secure. She specifically told him not to enter the premises until she was assured that the information she was receiving could be verified, and that she had sufficient measures in place to protect what could be a civilian hostage. She then turned her attention back to Vladimir Checovsky.

"Tell me, Mr. Checovsky, why do you think I should believe you? You've admitted that you deliberately created a strain of the avian flu so that you could infect millions of people just so that you could sell your antiviral drug. Now you want me to believe that Nicolai Petrescu, who you have already admitted is a partner in your scheme to obliterate millions of people, somehow double-crossed you and changed the genome of the virus? This makes no sense at all. Mr. Petrescu is not trying to sell a competing antiviral. What would be his motive to pull a change-up on you? You are friends. You claim to have saved his life. Why would he want to hurt you? I think that there is something you are not telling me."

"There is nothing else. I did save his life. He was a street urchin and I gave him a job and an education. And I exposed him to the world of luxury and travel–the finer things. This is how he repays me. He stabs me in the back."

"You set him up, Mr. Checovsky. You sent him out into the world to kill people so that you could make a fortune. What was in it for him?" Director Weiss asked.

"Money. He was entitled to half the profits."

"Why would you give this *street urchin* half of the profits? That doesn't wash. You gave this kid a chance at life. Why would you give him *half* of the profits? I could see you paying him a nice salary or a great bonus for doing what you are not willing to do here. But no good businessman doles out half of his profits to another man unless he is holding up half of the bargain. So what gives? What was Nicolai Petrescu bringing to the table?"

"He was my son."

"Your son?"

"I treated him like he was my own flesh and blood. I was grooming him to take over my business one day–like a father would do for his son."

Director Weiss paced the room for a few minutes, saying nothing. She re-read the emails that Henry Lewis had retrieved from the Tarirescu mainframe while she walked around the interrogation room. Finally, she stopped in front of Vladimir Checovsky's chair and leaned in so that she was about three inches from his face. "He was your lover, wasn't he, Mr. Checovsky?"

* * *

Mac was trying to edge her way around Gilbert's makeshift laboratory and make her way closer to the door. She didn't know how to play him. She needed Jeffrey there beside her, to talk her through it. She felt scared and alone, and realized, for the first time, that no one knew where she was. Mac had isolated herself this holiday, and she didn't call her family or her friends. Not one of them knew that she was cooking a meal for Gil. If something happened to her, her body would probably never be found. Her car was parked out front, but the keys to it were in her purse by the door. Surely, Gil would get rid of her car. He obviously was a premeditated man.

"You have had a very difficult childhood," Mac started out, as she slowly side-stepped toward the door. "Maybe if you and I talk about it, you will feel better. I know that when my dad died, I was too young to understand, and I really couldn't talk about it. But when I got older, and got into college, and started doing things that were not in my best interest, I realized that I was punishing myself for the loss of my dad. Maybe that's what you are doing. Maybe you feel guilty for the terrible things your mother did to you, and you are punishing people for your mother's misgivings. Maybe if you talk about them, you will feel more at peace."

"I am at peace. I don't care anymore about my mother. I killed her with my own bare hands." He smiled as he said this, as if the memory of his mother's suffering brought him a certain sense of joy.

"No one is at peace if they are killing people, Gil. You might think you are, but you are not. There are people who can help you."

Mac, still wearing black suede pants and a silver blouse, scooted another step toward the door with each plea. Gil followed her around the egg table, one step at a time.

"I don't need help. I am doing just fine, Ms. MacIntosh. All I need right now is for you to shut your mouth. And the way I like to make girls shut their mouths is by giving them a little duck liver cocktail. Problem right now is that I'm fresh out. I will have to take a moment and mix up some fresh concoction. I'm told that it is pretty tasty." Gil reached over to the freezer and opened the door. He pulled out an individual wrapping of duck liver and set it on the table. Mac took another step toward the door, but Gil jerked his head up. "You going somewhere, Ms. MacIntosh?" His eyes looked hollow and deranged, as if he was possessed by a demon.

Mac shook her head and tried to respond in a calm voice. "I-I-I'm cold. I'd like to get my jacket." Her excuse sounded fabricated and ridiculous. "And I am hungry. Why don't we go upstairs together, and I can heat up the meal that I made for us? What we need is some food."

Mac watched Gil's face, trying to gauge his reaction. She figured that the other women he killed had begged for their lives. Perhaps his mother did the same. She decided to try a different approach. Maybe if he felt like they needed each other—or that she understood him, perhaps he would spare her. She knew that she needed to keep him off track so that he wouldn't make more of the duck pudding. Obviously, he was capable of killing her without his concoction, but if, in his mind, the way he wanted to kill her was with the virus, she needed to stall him as long as possible. He seemed to be relaxing a bit with her statement. She reached out with her right hand toward him. He quickly recoiled.

"No one has ever loved me. My mother did not love me. She thought that I was a dirty little boy. She thought all men were despicable. I was beneath despicable. My little sister loved me when she was little. But my mother told her that I was naughty and dirty and sinful, and she stopped loving me. I am unworthy of love."

"What happened with your little sister?" Mac asked.

"Why? What do you know?"

"Is she still alive? Are you still in contact with her?"

"No."

"No–she is not still alive, or you are not in contact?"

"Neither."

"Did she die?"

"Yes."

Mac inched closer to the door. "How did she die?"

"I killed her."

Chapter 49

"There must be fifty dead bodies in there," Jeffrey said to the Peruvian police. Eduardo had immediately notified the officials as soon as Jeffrey and Laura emerged from the cave, and the authorities were quick to arrive on the scene. "The bones look small, like children. They have been there for awhile." Jeffrey and Laura described the horror of what they saw in the cave. "The skeletons were situated in a circle, and each had a tea cup either attached to a finger, or nearby. It was like a scary ride at a theme park, where dead people were set up to look like they were still alive."

The police asked a number of questions, mostly in Spanish and directed to Eduardo, about how the Americans knew to look into the cave. It was almost as if the Peruvian government was worried more about image and the fact that the bodies had never been discovered than they were about the victims. As Eduardo fielded questions, both Laura and Jeffrey were busy trying to get cell service. Jeffrey needed to talk with his YouSamRid team about the situation. He figured that there had to be a considerable amount of information about the Monster of the Andes on file, and he wanted his staff to get the data to him as soon as possible. He knew that he should go to Columbia and interview the prison officials where Pedro Perez had once served time, but what he wanted to do was help Mac. His stomach churned with fear that she was in danger.

When Jeffrey finally was paged through to Quantico, his YouSamRid team was already deep into information retrieval on Pedro Perez. As instructed, they'd analyzed fingerprint comparisons between two individuals: Nicolai Petrescu and Pedro Perez. Their prints were a perfect match. From her post in Russia, Director Weiss had asked them to enter the match into the CODIS database, employing specialized ridge comparisons to any other fingerprints within the system.

"Pedro Perez was freed from prison in Columbia in 1985. Apparently, he made his way back to Russia shortly after that," Director Weiss said to Jeffrey, as she flew from Russia back to the United States. "He changed his name to Nicolai Petrescu after he met Vladimir Checovsky. And guess what else? Nicolai Petrescu was Checovsky's lover."

"Petrescu, who was Pedro Perez at the time, was gang-raped in prison a number of times," Jeffrey said, repeating to Director Weiss the information he'd recently learned from his team. "He killed a few of the rapists with his bare hands. It surprises me that he would allow Checovsky to sodomize him based on his reaction to rape in prison."

"Maybe the situation was different with Checovsky," Director Weiss said. "From Checovsky's version, Petrescu was a desperate, starving unemployed young man. Maybe Checovsky treated him well, and the relationship developed slowly, after trust was established." "A serial killer is like a leopard. He doesn't change his spots. Maybe Petrescu tolerated the relationship long enough to get what he needed out of it."

"And when Petrecsu got what he needed, he retaliated against Checovsky by switching the genome in the virus," Director Weiss said.

"Can you hold the line for a minute?" Jeffrey asked. "My team is calling me." Jeffery took the call.

"We have another match," a YouSamRid team member said. "Pedro Perez matches Nicolai Petrescu who matches a man by the name of Gilbert Bonita."

* * *

After Jeffrey shared the information he'd learned from Director Weiss and his YouSamRid team, Dr. Laura Weckesser stood next to him staring at her cell phone.

"Are you listening to me?" Jeffrey asked, agitated.

Laura looked at Jeffrey with a furrowed brow. "No. I mean, yes, I'm listening. And thinking. I am comparing it to the information you told me from our team. Look," she said. "If you unscramble the letters on the message that Mary MacIntosh sent to your cell phone, she wrote that Nicolai Petrescu is Gilbert Bonita."

"That was what she was trying to tell us," Jeffrey said. "How would *she* know that?"

Laura's cell phone rang. She picked up the call. She listened intently and then hung up. "Oh shit," she said. "YouSamRid says that Gilbert Bonita closed escrow on a property outside Sheridan, Wyoming last month," Laura said. "According to the recorded documents, Mary MacIntosh was the bank's lawyer involved in the transaction."

"Oh my God! She knows who he is because he is trying to *kill* her!" Jeffrey's face lost color. He felt faint. Laura made him sit down and take deep breaths. She flipped open her cell and dialed.

"I'm calling Director Weiss right now. She needs to get the National Guard out there immediately!"

Chapter 50

Mac was inching her way toward the door of Gil's lab, but with every side step she took, he took a step closer to her. She wanted to keep the conversation going, but Gil's admission that he killed his sister made her feel tongue-tied. She had to force her words. "How did you kill your s-s-sister?

Gil pinched up his face, as if he tasted something sour. "You are nosey, aren't you?"

"I'm curious. I need to get to know you better. Maybe if I understand you more, than I will be able to–"

"Help me? Ha. You can't help me. That's not why you are asking. You are scared and you are tying to find out just how despicable I am."

Mac continued to inch her way toward the door. Gil inched along with her. "I am not trying to help you. I'm trying to understand you."

Gil contemplated this for a moment, smirking. "My mother and sister went back to Romania when I was still . . . still in South America. After I left South America, I found my way back to Romania. It was pretty easy to find my mom and sister–they were back living with my grandmother. I killed my mom first, with my bare hands. Then, I found my sister. By then, she'd had a baby of her own. I killed my sister next."

"What about the baby?" Mac asked, afraid of the answer.

"I dropped her off at an orphanage. I kept track of her, of course. And followed her to America, when the Bontierres adopted her." Mac sucked in a breath. Gil smirked at her shocked face. He had hunted Ana Bontierre, like prey. He had bought the farmhouse in Wyoming so that he could set up his science lab to develop the mutated formula for the avian flu virus. He squatted on the property before escrow closed so that he could stalk his niece. Ana Bontierre was his only living relative, and yet, he still had the capacity to kill her without remorse. Mac realized the gravity of his depraved heart. And she knew that she was in solemn danger.

Bzzzzz. "What was that noise?" he asked her, hearing her cell phone buzz with an incoming text message. Mac didn't respond. She was hoping that she could change the subject and distract him.

"What are these eggs for? Do you use them for your research?"

"The eggs are used to create antiviral medicine to fight against a certain strain of the avian flu virus. But you didn't answer my question. What are you holding behind your back?"

Mac knew that she had few options. She was close to the door by now, and if he found her cell phone, he would get very angry, very fast. Instead of answering, she bolted for the stairs. She dashed through the laboratory door, and tried to slam it behind her as she leaped up the basement steps, two at a time. She felt a hand grab her ankle and yank hard, pulling her feet out from under her, and causing her to land, chest first, on the steps. Her cell phone bounced out of her right hand and down to the step below her. She tried to scramble to her feet, but Gil was already on top of her, pushing his knee deep into her spine, forcing the air out of her lungs. He took his left hand and grabbed Mac by her long hair, yanking her head back hard. "You should not have done that, Ms. MacIntosh. I have been contemplating how best to deal with you, and I was leaning towards a painless death. But you seem to want to have a little fun dying—which is fine with me. I'm up for the challenge. It's just that I am pretty tired these days. Killing thousands of people is an exhausting task."

He reached down with his right hand and picked up Mac's cell phone, which had landed on the step near his right leg. He flipped the phone open and read the message out loud. "Get out of there. Gilbert Bonita is a serial killer." He was quiet for a moment. "You are a smart girl. I give you credit. I've been roaming the world for years now under aliases and no one has ever figured it out. That's the beauty of the train system. Didn't I tell you the first night we met how much I love trains? I do. They are terrific. No one asks for your identification—or if they do, they don't require authentic documents. I changed my name when I was just a kid and hired some guy in Columbia to prepare the documents. No one has ever questioned them. I changed my name again when I stayed in Russia. No one questioned those either. The biggest problem these days is the terrorists. Damn people made the governments so suspicious of airline travel. Slowed me down some. But the trains have always afforded me liberty to travel the world. And kill a few whores along the way."

Mac felt waves of nausea flow through her from the pain of Gil's knee in her spine. She struggled a bit, trying to edge sideways to get the fulcrum of his weight off her. He yanked back harder on her hair. "You're not going anywhere, smart girl. You may know who I am, but now we are going to find out who you are. What you are made of. What it feels like to be inside of you while you beg for your life."

"I won't beg you for anything," she said, hardly able to push the words out.

"They all say that, Ms. MacIntosh. All the feisty ones start out telling me to burn in hell. But in the end, when their blood is oozing out of their bodies and the pain is severe, they beg. My mother begged. My sister begged. Ana begged." Gil paused for a moment, and then leaned down closer to Mac's ear. "You knew Ana, didn't you? Well, let me tell you a little about her."

"I didn't know her well."

"I'd like for you to know her a little better." Gil forced his weight harder on Mac. The pain of the wooden steps against her chest was nearly as unbearable as the pain shooting down both of her legs from the pressure on her spine. "Ana Bontierre was a Romanian whore. Those Bontierre people rescued her from a Bucharest orphanage. And you know what they say? Once a whore, always a whore. She whored her way around Wyoming. When I saw her walking out of the college library one night, I approached her. She didn't rebuff. In fact, she was quite eager to have a drink with me. I took her to a run-down bar at the edge of town and gave her some beer. And what do you know? She made a pass at me while we were playing pool. I think she told me that I was handsome. Music to my ears. It was easy to get her in the car." Gil's tone of voice had a certain smirk to it. His inflections rose as he reminisced. "I'm sure that the sedative in her beer helped her sleep while I drove up the mountain. When she woke up, she was in the middle of the Medicine Wheel. She was bound and gagged. I'd already given her the duck pudding. It went down easy. She never knew about it. But, she put up quite a fight when she realized what was happening. It was one of the best struggles I've ever had. It was so thoroughly enjoyable that I just had to rape her. I love it when they fight."

Mac's cell phone beeped again with another text message from Jeffrey. Gil flipped up the silver phone and read the message out loud in a mocking tone. "We are on our way to help you." He threw the phone aside, breaking it into pieces.

"How endearing. Your lover is on his way. I didn't know that you were a two-timing whore, but that's okay. It excites me to know that I will be the last man to enter you alive, and the first man to enter you dead."

Chapter 51

Gil dragged Mac backwards down the steps. She tried to struggle to her feet once she hit the bottom step, but he kicked her feet out from under her. With his knee in her back again, he reached for a rope from the wall behind him and tied her hands behind her back. While lying on her stomach, Mac kicked her right leg back at him as hard as she could, connecting a blow to his right kidney with her wedged heel. He slapped her hard on the face, drawing blood to her lip. She kicked again, catching him again in the kidney. Gil fell to the left. Mac clambered to her feet and made a run for it back up the steps. She got to the top of the steps, but the door at the entrance to the basement was closed. With her hands tied behind her back, she had to turn around backwards try to unlatch the door. She could see Gil clambering up the stairs toward her, his bleached-blond hair glowing in the dark.

Mac wiggled the handle, trying to gain enough leverage to twist it. Her hands were tightly bound. He lunged for her at the top of the stairs. Mac pulled up her knee to her chest and drove a striking blow to Gil's forehead. He fell over backwards and tumbled back down the stairs, landing with a loud thud. She twisted the door handle again as far as she could, but the latch did not give way. She could see Gil coming up the stairs again, his bleached- blonde hair askew and his teeth tightly gritted. He was panting hard. Just as he was about to lunge at her, the door clicked. She burst through backwards, stumbling with her own momentum, and rushed down the hall toward the front door of the house. There was no way she was going to be able to drive with her hands tied. She knew that the only chance she had was to run for it.

* * *

Jeffrey rushed up the switchbacks of the Urubamba Valley to the airport in Cusco, where the reconnaissance plane was waiting. The high- powered jet would fly them directly back to the United States at a fast speed, but he didn't know it he would be able to make it in time to save Mac from the most despicable serial killer he'd ever known. Jeffrey realized that Gilbert Bonita had likely killed more people than any other serial killer in history.

He was anxious and nervous, constantly asking Eduardo how much longer it would take to reach the airport. Annoyed, Eduardo turned to him and asked him, point blank, "You are trying to make up for a mistake, no?"

Jeffrey realized that Eduardo was an intuitive man. "Yes, I have made a mistake. I found the most amazing woman, and I let her go. Now she is in danger and I don't know if I can save her."

"Why did you let her go?"

"Because I'm a fool."

"Yes, we men are fools, Dr. Plattenburg. My mother told me that from a very early age. She told me that I only had to do two things in life: live in balance and love deeply. The rest would fall into place. She was right. I try to work hard when it is necessary, and when I go home to my family, I try to forget about my work and focus only on loving them. My mother understood the importance of living a balanced life. I'm glad that she shared it with me."

"I could have used your mother's words of wisdom this week. I put my work in front of my love, and it was the wrong decision. After nearly fifty years of living, I've finally found the one woman that I know should be my partner in life–my soul mate–and I let her go so that I could work."

"You are right, Dr. Plattenburg. You are a fool. But even fools get a second chance."

Chapter 52

The front door to Gil's house was closed and latched, which was odd because the latch had been broken when she arrived. How long was he here before coming down into the basement? Had he been in the house the entire time? Her mind was whirling. She reached backwards and tried to unlatch the lock, but it was at shoulder blade height, and she couldn't get her bound hands high enough.

"You appear to be struggling, Ms. MacIntosh," Gil said as he sauntered down the dark hallway toward her. She looked left and ran into the dining room. Gil cut through the kitchen and trapped her on the other side. "You can run, my lawyer princess, but you can't hide," he chanted. "I am a very patient man, when I want to be. I stalked women for years before killing them. A little cat and mouse game in an old farmhouse is child's play. Don't take yourself too seriously. Your end is inevitable."

Gil's outspoken manner had attracted Mac to him when they first met. Now, it was annoying her beyond repair. She told herself not to pay attention to him and that his words meant nothing. She would have to be tough, mentally and physically, to survive. She would have to play the game her way. She needed to buy time. Help was on its way.

"I don't doubt your patience, Gil. I just doubt your charisma. Seems to me that you have some issues with your manhood. You need to kill a woman in order to have sex with her. You must suffer from one of those Freudian complexes. I studied about them when I attended the police academy before going to law school. I don't remember the name. Maybe it was the Oedipus complex? Is that the one where you lust after your mother? Is that your problem? You wanted to have sex with your mother, but she rejected you. So you tried to have sex with your baby sister. Is that what happened?"

"SHUT UP!!!!! Shut up shut up shut up."

"You were so ashamed of yourself that you had to kill them."

"SHUT UP, I SAID." Gil stammered towards her, his eyes flaring with rage.

"Your mother must have made you feel small. Insignificant. Worthless. So, you decided to take out your worthlessness out on the unlucky women in the world that resembled your mom. All that fury and resentment boiling in your veins for all those years. Tell me, Gil, why use the avian flu to kill the women? Is it too much for you to use your own hands? Remind you too much of killing your poor old mother and innocent baby sister?"

Gil was covering his ears and shouting "shut up" over and over. He appeared to be in a drunken trance, staggering toward her with one step, and backwards with another. He looked almost childlike for a few minutes. And then everything changed. Mac noticed his slumped shoulders stiffen and his somber face tighten. It was like he was changing gears—becoming someone else in his mind. Gil's anger became readily apparent again, as his face reddened and his eyes bore down on her.

Suddenly, outside the front windows of the house, headlights bounced up the gravel driveway. Seeing the reflection of the lights in the dining room mirror, Mac turned to look. At that moment, Gil seized her from behind and whacked her over the head.

Mac felt her body hit the ground and heard a voice in her head. "Don't let go. Don't pass out. He will pour the virus down your throat if you pass out." Her eyes fluttered a bit, as she tried to pull herself out of the daze, and she recognized that the voice she heard was her father's.

Chapter 53

Gil paced back and forth in his basement laboratory. He had decisions to make. It would take him hours to concoct the strain of H5N1 virus that he'd used to kill in Western Europe and the Americas. When he saw the headlights coming down his driveway, he knew that his time was running out. The car that had approached stopped in the driveway, backed up, and turned back onto the main road. It was a false alarm, but Gil knew that it was only a matter of time before the authorities came. He knew that he had no choice but to silence Mac and drag her down to his dungeon.

At the time he installed his basement laboratory he had the foresight to equip it with state-of-the-art security similar to what protected the Tarirescu lab. The laboratory security system was on when Mac came to the house to prepare the Thanksgiving meal. When he arrived at the house and found her listening to the radio in his living room, Gil quickly snuck downstairs, de-activated the alarm system, and deliberately left a light on in the basement to lure Mac down there. He wanted to catch her with a surprise attack. And now, he wanted to finish her off, but he needed time.

He knew that the security mechanisms would keep the police at bay for a while. But not forever. He thought about just killing Mac, with his bare hands, like he did with his mother, just to prove to her that he could do it. Because he could. But he was transfixed on keeping with his plan to use his formula. He was so proud of himself for his ingenuity in creating his own mutated strain of the avian flu. If he could hold off the police for a few hours, he could re-create another batch of the genome, force Mac to swallow it, and then take her on a ride up the mountain to Medicine Wheel. How befitting it would be to have her die in the same place that Ana died? Vladimir would have appreciated his cleverness. Gil's thought about Vladimir caused him to grow angry again. He did not need Vladimir's approval anymore.

Vladimir Checovsky had a wife and daughters. But his lust for young boys was well known among the upper crust of Russia. When a handsome, educated young man rolled into town on the Siberian Express looking for a job, Vladimir quickly took Gil under his wing.

While serving as Vladimir Checovsky's right hand man, which loosely translated into "sex toy," Gil, known then as Nicolai Petrescu, learned a lot about science. He was not a stupid boy–the Americans that had adopted him in Peru had seen to it that he had been properly educated. Science and math came naturally to Gil. When he worked at Tarirescu, he mastered lab sciences, and took great interest in learning his boss's trade. In all honesty, Gil didn't have a choice. So long as he was studying in the lab, Vladimir left him alone. But the minute that Gil grew weary, or disinterested, Vladimir took an interest in him, on an emotional level. Vladimir was very gentle with Gil and treated him with the utmost kindness and respect, both in the lab and in Vladimir's secret bedroom at the Tarirescu lab.

Not know the meaning of love, and knowing the ramifications of acting out from being sodomized like he was in the Columbian prison when he was a teenager, Gil dealt with Vladimir's indiscretions solemnly. He secretly hated Vladimir every time he took advantage of him, but all the while, Gil was gaining the knowledge he needed while planning his revenge against Vladimir.

As Vladimir's trust grew stronger, Gil's knowledge of the scientific community grew larger. Slowly, he learned the nature of cultivating viruses. He also made contact with Vladimir's satellite laboratories, and was able to establish relationships with people within the scientific community that could help him if he ever needed to branch out on his own.

That is how Gil got the blueprint for the H5N1 avian flu. And he used his resources to create a mutated version of the genome so that he could go on a killing spree across the world. He would go with Vladimir's plan at first–introducing his mutation that responded to Rescuflu. That way, Vladimir would make his millions. As would Gil. But after some time, it was Gil's turn to even the score with his father figure. If the police had found him, he knew that Vladimir had ratted him out. If Vladimir had come clean with authorities and told them about the genome mutation, that meant that Vladimir was also caught. The thought of Vladimir behind prison bars brought a wide smile to Gil's demonic face.

Chapter 54

Dr. Jocelyn Sharp gave a CNN-broadcasted interview about the capture of Vladimir Checovsky. "The FBI, CIA, WHO, CDC, and many world-based intelligence authorities and peace keepers have worked diligently over the last six weeks to track down and capture the Pandemic Predator. Although we respect the input of many scientists who believed that the avian flu was being spread by migratory fowl, we were convinced early on that the outbreaks were caused purposely. I want to make it clear that the CDC was in no way responsible for the outbreak and that our research regarding the 1918 Spanish flu pandemic did not give rise to the dissemination of the mutated genome. In simpler terms, my team's research was not stolen and the virus was not created based on our published findings. The virus was created in a Russian laboratory by two scientists who wanted to get rich by creating a viral strain that could only be treated by *their* antiviral medication. Tarirescu scientists caused this outbreak, which has killed several hundred thousand people by most recent estimates, and the CDC, and many other world authorities on disease have diligently worked together to contain and the horrific outbreak."

* * *

"How fast can you make this bird fly?" Jeffrey asked the reconnaissance pilot after they took off from Cusco, Peru. The pilot, Jeffrey, and the rest of the team wore special full pressure suits due to the high altitude and speed of the mission.

The pilot glanced down at his instruments, and then responded to Jeffrey through his microphone. "Technically, since you are a civilian, I am not at liberty to divulge the anticipated speed and estimated time of arrival of this mission. But, since you have YouSamRid clearance, I'll let you in on a military secret." He tapped on the instrument panel of the B-1B Lancer. "Seven hundred fifty-six miles per hour."

"Good. Not fast enough. But good."

"I'll get you there as fast as I can, Dr. Plattenburg. Once we clear the Andes, it is smooth sailing. Until we get to the Rockies, that is. I've been warned that there is a storm brewing in Montana, and it is making its way south. Hopefully, we can beat it, or they'll ground us in Denver."

Chapter 55

Mary MacIntosh slowly opened her eyes. The objects around her appeared blurry. She closed them again and squeezed her eyelids shut, trying to refocus. The back of her head was throbbing with pain. She tried to reach up to touch her wound, and then remembered that her hands were bound behind her back. Her memory flooded back to her, and she realized that she was in Gil's basement. Her legs were tied together also now, and her mouth was gagged. She could see Gil's large, black boots moving about his lab and she could hear glass clanging. How long had she been unconscious? An hour? A day? She had no idea.

Gil was working on something. She then realized what he must be up to. She pulled herself up into a sitting position and quietly got busy trying to loosen the knots around her wrists and ankles. It was cold in the lab, and she felt as though her hands had shrunk a bit. If she could wriggle through one of the loops in the rope, she could free herself. But she would have to work quickly and quietly, and without much motion.

While she was busy trying to escape, she looked around the room to see what she could use to defend herself against this monster. There were plenty of glass cylinders and instruments. She could break one and try to use it to cut him, she thought. There was also a heating unit.

She knew that Gil would use the virus as his weapon to kill her. If he created the virus, he must have created antiviral medication to counteract it, in case he was accidentally infected. Mac figured that he had already taken some, as a precautionary measure. Did he have a bag with him that he could have used to transport the virus and the antiviral medication? Mac scanned the room and saw a black bag in the corner near the door. She thought back on how the room looked before he caught her. She didn't recall seeing the black bag before. Also, there were the vials in the refrigerator full of a clear liquid. But how would she know what to use, and how much? The vials were labeled in Russian, or some other language. Panic rose in her veins and she could feel her face flush. She needed to stay calm.

She saw Gil's boots walk around the side of the table toward her. She quickly faked sleep and remained motionless for a time. When she heard his footsteps move away, she peeked out of her right eye, which was closest to the floor, hoping that he would not see her stir. Gil's boots were not within sight. It appeared that he had left the science lab. The house was quiet. Mac struggled for what seemed like hours in an attempt to free herself from the binding ropes.

* * *

"Just in time," Gil said out loud, after stomping down the basement steps. "Your friends will be here soon to get you, Miss MacIntosh, and I am pleased to report that my formula is now ready. It is time that our cocktail party gets under way, my dear. I hope you don't mind being the first to imbibe." Gil walked around the center table where the eggs were incubating and found her seated in the corner. He held a vial of brown liquid in his hand. He raised it into the air and proposed a toast. "To Mary MacIntosh. I was hoping that we could dine together in the Temple of the Condor. Some day, perhaps. Today, we will have to settle for this old farmhouse. I toast you, for you helped make this dream possible. We will soon depart for a nice moonlit ride up the mountains and you shall be laid to rest at Medicine Wheel, just like your friend Ana. See, I prefer to kill in spiritual places but sometimes it is not practical."

Gil set the vial on the table and leaned over to untie the gag around Mac's mouth. When he loosened the white cloth, Mac took a deep breath, filling her lungs with air. Gil forced a grin. "I can smell the sweet scent of revenge," he muttered while sniffing the air above him. "Somehow, in your willful little brain, you think that you can escape me. Let's talk numbers, since you are so smart." Gil motioned as if he were counting on his hands. "I don't have my log handy at the moment, but last I checked, I've killed seventy-three of my last seventy-three victims. I think the odds are in my favor."

Mac shuddered inwardly, but recovered fast. *Don't cry*, she told herself.

"And I am not counting the people who've contracted the virus from the whores. I'm just counting the whores themselves. I'm not boasting, Miss MacIntosh, because if I really wanted to take credit where credit is due, my success rate has been quite high. Don't you agree?"

Mac followed his movements with her eyes, but tried to show no emotion. Goosebumps formed on her arms as he reached for the vial, and the hair on the back of her neck stood straight up as she could smell his putrid scent wafting toward her. *Think of snowflakes kissing your cheeks. Think of home-cooking and the comfort of your grandmother's kitchen. Think of the protective armor of your father's love.*

He shoved the vial to her lips and grabbed her by the back of the hair. Mac pursed her lips together and shrugged her shoulders defensively. "Let's not make this difficult. See that girl up there named Silvia? She made it difficult. I had to slit her throat and pour the virus down her bleeding esophagus. That was unpleasant for both of us. If you cooperate, it will be better for you, and better for me."

"Go to hell!" Mac whispered, through her puckered lips.

"I'm already there, Miss MacIntosh. And I'm about to take you with me. Now drink this!" he yelled.

Mac struggled to get free from his grip, thrashing back and forth. Gil tightened his grip, his face growing flush. Beads of sweat formed at the edge of his hairline. And then, as if his persona completely changed, he softened his grip and his tone.

"It is a little bitter. My apologies." He shoved the vial back towards her mouth. She turned her head sideways and uttered under her breath.

"A hungry soul like yours wouldn't know the difference between bitter and sweet."

"Perhaps you are right. I was hoping you could teach me, but I'm afraid our lesson is going to be cut short. We will have company soon, darling," Gil said, looking up to the ceiling. "Our tête-à-tête must end."

Gil wrenched back Mac's head, forcing her lips to separate. She fought hard to keep her mouth closed. He got on top of her and pushed her over backwards so that her legs were caught beneath her back. She groaned in pain as he pinned his right knee into her chest. He shoved his thumb into the side of her mouth and jerked her mouth open, dumping the brown liquid into her throat. The vial fell to the floor, smashing into little pieces, as he clamped her mouth and nose shut, keeping her from spitting.

Mac tried to block the passage of the liquid by closing off her throat with the back of her tongue, but she couldn't breathe. She fought with her shoulders and tugged at her wrists until finally, when she could feel her lungs desperate for breath, her right hand broke free from the rope. Mac pulled her arm out from under her, and swung at Gil's hand, ramming it away from her mouth. She spit and coughed and sucked for air at the same time, allowing some of the liquid down her throat. Mac gagged and choked and thrust her arms at Gil, hitting him with all her force. Gil laughed at her in mock tone and then he hit her hard across the face, breaking open a gash near her mouth. Her blood tasted ashy.

Mac could see the picture of Ana Bontierre on the corkboard above her, and thought of how Ana might have tried to fight off this beast. She thought of the other poor women who must have been terrified of this monster. If hatred came in liquid form, it was what filled Mac's veins at that moment. No longer was she afraid of this soulless man. She was angry.

Mac flapped her hand on the cement floor, desperately trying to locate the broken vile. *This is for you, Ana*, Mac thought to herself, as she grabbed the broken shard of the glass vile from the floor beside her and thrust it deep into Gil's neck. Brown fluid dripped from the vile which protruded from under his chin.

Gil shrieked and fell backwards into the table, gurgling on his own blood. He ripped the jagged vile from his skin and threw it across the room.

Mac scrambled out of the ropes and dove toward the black bag in the corner, ripping it open. There was nothing inside.

"Looking for this?" Gil sputtered, standing over her with a vial full of clear liquid.

Chapter 56

Gil took the cap off the vial and swallowed it while towering over Mac. "The antiviral is very effective if taken within the first few hours. I'm sorry to inform you that I just swallowed the last dose." His white shirt was stained with blood which was squirting out of the wound in his neck. She must have hit his artery. His skin looked pale and waxen.

Mac crawled past his feet toward the refrigerator, yanking the door open and grabbing three vials. Gil kicked her hard in the back, sending her forwards against the freezer door. Two of the vials flew out of her hands and smashed on the floor. She reached down to take the cap off the last vile, but this time, Gil pinned her left hand against the cold shelf.

"I'm afraid that this antiviral isn't effective against the strain you just swallowed. This is Rescuflu. Won't do you any good."

Mac spun around and grabbed the vial with her right hand. He tried to knock it away from her. She quickly bit the top of the vial off with her teeth and swallowed it in one gulp.

Gil laughed at her in a mocking way. "Bottoms up! It won't help you. You'll be dead by morning. And when your friends find your rotting body, they will soon die. That's the beauty of this gift. It keeps on giving." His laugh rang hollow.

Mac grabbed another vial from the refrigerator door and drank it. And another. As she reached for the third vial, which was on a separate shelf, Gil smacked her hand away. She kicked him hard in the groin, sending him to his knees. She grabbed the third vial and drank it quickly, and when the clear liquid was rushing down her throat, she broke off the top to the vial and jammed the serrated edges into Gil's spine.

Gil roared back and yelled out in pain. Mac ran toward the door, unlatched the deadbolt and jerked the metal casing toward her. She could hear Gil gurgling and struggling behind her, but she did not look back. The door made a sucking sound as it released, and she bolted up the steps.

Chapter 57

Emerging from the basement, Mac could see headlights coming up the farmhouse road. She felt elated, knowing that this nightmare was about to end. She ran toward the front door, yelling "help" as loudly as she could. As she reached for the front door handle, she felt a sharp stabbing pain in her left shoulder, and within a few seconds, she felt her knees buckle beneath her and her body collapse onto the floor.

Gil dropped the syringe at her feet and grabbed Mac from under her arms. He dragged her out the back door of the farmhouse and loaded her limp body onto a sled that he had attached to his snowmobile. The wind had picked up, and the temperature had dropped significantly. Gil could see puffs of vapor coming out of Mac's mouth with her shallow breaths. He wanted her alive–at least until they got to Medicine Wheel.

Gil could hear the sound of car engines getting closer. He cranked the snowmobile and gunned the engine. The double track moved forward with a jolt, and soon, Gil was zooming through the four-foot powder with Mac tied to the trailing sled.

They bounced up the rough mountain road, quickly traversing the switchbacks. The beam of the snowmobile's headlight was the only source of light. The moon was hidden behind thick, winter-like clouds and the stars were hiding. The only other lights Gil could see were the flashing red ones heading up the farmhouse lane toward his house.

"You will be disappointed," he said out loud. "Miss MacIntosh will be dead by the time you find her." He laughed to himself, and then squeezed hard on the accelerator. The snowmobile rocketed forward up the steep mountain terrain.

* * *

The B-1B Lancer came skidding to a stop on the ice-slicked runway of Sheridan's tiny airport. Jeffrey burst out of the high-altitude reconnaissance aircraft and into the police cruiser. They raced south of town to the GPS coordinates where Mac's 9-1-1 call originated. When they arrived, they found the farmhouse surrounded by Army National Guard trucks.

"Is she in there?" Jeffrey yelled at the post guard. The uniformed man motioned for Jeffrey to remain quiet and signaled him to stay down.

"We have surrounded the premises and have barricaded all ingress and egress points. We are on stand-by for surveillance."

"But I think there is a hostage in there! What if she is still alive? We can't just stand here and wait for this madman to do something! He poisons his victims. He could be–"

"I am following orders, sir."

"Who is your commander?"

"Director Weiss."

Jeffrey grabbed his cell phone and dialed Diane Weiss's direct line. He was patched through to her air phone. "I am en route, Jeffrey. You need to calm down. I cannot send troops into a house that is likely contaminated with a lethal virus. I have spoken with Dr. Sharp and the CDC is also en route so that we can quarantine and secure at the same time."

"But I think Mary MacIntosh is in there. Her car is parked outside! I can't just stand here and wait for him to kill her. Please, Diane. Please order the troops in. I'm begging you."

"Jeffrey, I can't do that. You are making this matter personal, and I understand where you are coming from, but I have global issues to consider. The world is watching how we handle this crisis and it has to be done according to protocol. I am following strict–"

"PROTOCOL? Diane! There is a civilian's life at risk. Protocol calls for the protection of–"

"The greater mass. I must ensure that the majority of the population is protected. I'm sorry, but if I have to spare one life to save thousands, or millions, then I have no other plausible choice."

Jeffrey was pacing in the freezing pre-dawn air. Snow crunched under his feet as steam from his sweat rose off his back. "Then I have no choice. I'm going in."

"You can't do that and you know it. It would be in direct violation of YouSamRid protocol and I must forbid—"

"Fuck protocol. I'm going in."

Chapter 58

Mac felt her head bounce against something hard. She tried to pull her eyes open, but they were heavy. She felt as if she had been drugged. She had no idea where she was, but she knew that it was very, very cold. She could hear the buzz of an engine and could smell a diesel exhaust. With every bump, her body lifted up off the sled and then came crashing back down onto the hard wood. Her arms were tied to the front of the sled, while her legs were bound to the back. Her body was nearly frozen, covered with the powdery snow jettisoned off the trail of Gil's yellow, double-track snowmobile.

Mac looked to the heavens. There were no stars. There was no moon. No hope. Mac tried to pull her hands free, but they wouldn't budge. She could twist and turn them slightly, but the rope was too tight and her hands were too stiff from the cold. Mac tried to kick her feet free, but her ankles were bound so tightly that the circulation was nearly cut off. As the panic rose inside her, she rammed herself repeatedly against the wood siding of the sled. She could feel her bones smashing against the wood, but it was of no use.

Mac heard Gil's laugh over the roar of the snowmobile engine. He laughed harder as she jettisoned herself into the side of the sled. She felt her shoulder give way with a cracking blow, dislocating it from its socket. Mac screamed out in pain. The siding gave way with the blow. Mac slid her bound hands off the broken siding of the sled and then freed her feet. She rolled off the broken side of the sled and landed, spinning, in a pile of snow. She watched as the taillights of Gil's snowmobile continued into the darkness of the pre-dawn morning. She hoped that he would not notice that his passenger was missing.

The pain from her dislocated shoulder caused her to vomit. She was blanketed with snow, freezing to death, in pain, and all she could think about was Jeffrey. "JEFFREY," she screamed out into the stillness of the night. She heard no echo. At that point, she knew for certain that she was alone.

Hypothermia. Avian flu. She was certain that death was near. She prayed to her father to take her peacefully.

* * *

Moments later, she saw the white beam of light. She felt that her father had answered her prayers and had come to save her from an agonizing death. But then, she heard his crackling, arrogant voice, and she knew that the devil incarnate had returned.

"Death is not going to be *that* easy, Miss MacIntosh," Gil said, after shutting down his snowmobile. "Allowing you to freeze-dry in the snow would be too kind. And it would deprive me of the distinct pleasure of watching your body twist and turn, and the virus melt away at your heart, and liver, and lungs. You will feel like you can't breathe, I'm told. You will gasp for air, but then choke on your own blood. And while you are choking, I'm going to thrust myself deep inside you. You will rip and tear, just like I did when those bastards attacked me in prison. They laughed as my flesh tore apart. They laughed as my body bled. They laughed and I screamed in pain. Now it is my turn to laugh."

Gil started the engine again and turned the snowmobile around. He ruthlessly and carelessly picked up Mac and tossed her into the broken sled. She shrieked in pain as her dislocated left arm dangled at her side, and howled as her body crashed down onto the hard, wooden surface. He didn't bother to tie her up. He gunned the machine and took off like a bullet toward Medicine Wheel.

Chapter 59

Jeffrey scrambled to the front door and yanked it open. "DON'T SHOOT!" Jeffrey yelled.

"STAY BACK," one of the guards shouted to Jeffrey.

Just then, three Hummers came flying down the gravel driveway. Snow billowed behind them as they traversed the thick powder. Out jumped CDC personnel in protective suits. "Get back, Jeffrey," Dr. Sharp yelled. "We need to do this the right way. She's no good to you if she is infected."

Jeffrey buckled to his knees. "We have to save her," he shouted back to Dr. Sharp.

"We will save her, Jeffrey, but we can't help her if we are all contagious. Put on a biosafety suit at least, and let the professionals do what they are trained to do. Please," she urged, in a softer tone. "Please."

Jeffrey scooted away from the door, and backed down the porch steps. Director Weiss emerged from the third Hummer and gave orders for the National Guard to enter the farmhouse. "Shoot to kill," she said.

* * *

"The place is empty," a National Guardsman yelled from the porch. "We've searched everywhere. There's some kind of science lab in the basement and it looks like there was a struggle down there. There's fresh blood on the floor, and a trail of blood leading out the back door. There are fresh snowmachine tracks out back. We think that he made a run for it up the Red Grade."

"Into the mountains?" Director Weiss asked.

"Yes. The road up there is closed in the winter. The only way up is by a snowmobile."

"Can a Hummer make it?"

"Don't know. Snow is pretty deep, but we'll find out."

Jeffrey, Director Weiss, Dr. Sharp, and a troop of National Guardsmen piled into the three Hummers. They trail blazed through the back acres of Gil's farmland before joining the main road, leading up through the Bighorn National Forest.

* * *

The pain pulsed through Mac's body each time the sled bounced along the hard, snow packed trail. It seemed like Gil enjoyed the fact that Mac was in pain. Each time he hit a large bump on the trail, he looked back at her with a demonic smile. She could hardly feel her fingers or the tip of her nose. Frostbite was setting in. She tried to tuck herself into a ball to keep warm, but it was no use.

Dawn was breaking as they climbed the last hill to the top of Medicine Mountain. Above, Mac could see the crags in the rocks high on the cliff face and a few lone pine trees on the mountain top, glistening in the morning light. A light layer of fog surrounded the peak. She tried to focus on the beauty of nature. She was sure that she would never see another sunrise.

She felt her body sway to the right as Gil took a sharp turn and parked next to the wooded fence surrounding Medicine Wheel. He turned off the snowmobile and walked back to the sled. Puffs of air smoldered around his mouth as he approached her. "Today is your lucky day, Miss MacIntosh. I will take you where I took Ana." Mac was too tired and too cold to respond. She could feel her intestines cramping. She assumed that the virus was destroying her body and she felt alone and helpless and afraid. She closed her eyes and pictured her father. She tried to remember the last time she saw him. *Was she sitting on his lap in the living room?* Mac wasn't sure, but decided to make it her last memory of him, and focused on what he might have said to her. She needed him now. She prayed to him silently.

Gil grabbed Mac by her dislocated arm and dragged her over to the rocks of the Medicine Wheel. Mac vomited from the pain. She felt herself loosing consciousness for a moment, but then suddenly, she felt an overwhelming calm settle over her. The pain in her left arm subsided and she didn't feel as cold.

The white rocks of Medicine Wheel were covered in snow, and all that was visible were lumps where the rocks lay. As Gil hauled Mac's body over the rocks, she reached with her right hand and grabbed one of the snow- covered stones. She pulled it close to her side.

Gil dropped Mac in the center of the stones. He was winded and had difficulty catching his breath. Puffs of vapor formed each time he panted. Crusted blood was frozen to his neck in the shape of old tree roots. His skin was pale.

"This is what I've been waiting for," he said as he started to unzip his pants. A wave of nausea overtook him and he stumbled sideways and vomited in the snow. The waves of nausea did not relent. Soon he vomited blood. He stared at the blood splattered snow beneath him, curious at the dark red color. The blood looked almost black and speckled. He touched the blood with his gloved index finger. "Fuck," he said. He vomited again. This time, there were larger chunks of black splatter. "Wrong fucking antiviral," he muttered. He turned toward Mac, who was lying motionless in the snow. "That bitch must have switched them!" He coughed again and sputtered more blood. He wondered how he could have been infected. The virus would have taken affect long ago from the woman who bit him in Tucson. Perhaps when he was mixing the duck pudding for Mac, he inadvertently got some of the serum in his system. His neck was bleeding. Maybe he touched the wound with serum on his hand. It didn't matter now.

Gil figured that Mac was sure to die from hypothermia and the avian flu. He decided to leave without defiling her and rush back to the farmhouse, where he had extra antiviral medication stored in his refrigerator. If he took enough of the medicine, he would survive.

Chapter 60

"Can't we cut through there?" Jeffrey asked, looking at a map and pointing to a road they were passing. The Army National Guardsman who was driving the Hummer explained that the cut-off road to Medicine Wheel was closed in the winter. Jeffrey slammed his hand into his thigh. He was frustrated and nervous that they weren't making better time. Director Weiss's Hummer had been stuck in the snow twice and they had to stop and use a winch to pull it out. Jeffrey knew that every minute counted in saving Mac's life.

"It's only a few miles ahead. We're almost there," the Guardsman said.

"What's that?" Jeffrey asked, pointing to a billow of snow up ahead.

"Looks like a guy on a snowmobile crossing the meadow. He's pulling something behind him. A sled?"

"It's him!" Jeffrey yelled. "That's got to be him." The Guardsman radioed to the two other Hummers. They gunned their engines as fast as they could, barreling over a barbed-wire fence and into the deep snow. "The sled looks empty," Jeffrey said. The Guardsman radioed Director Weiss and she told him to continue on to Medicine Wheel, and that she would send the third Hummer after the snowmobile.

* * *

Mac lay motionless in the snow with her eyes almost closed. She could feel the snowflakes accumulate on her cheeks and stick to her eyelashes. She gripped the stone in her hand a little tighter. She could no longer hear the sound of Gil retching.

A minute later, she heard the roar of engines as the two Hummers arrived at Medicine Wheel. Jeffrey bolted from his truck and leaped over the wooden fence that surrounded the historic landmark. As he ran up the slope, he could see a motionless figure in the center of the stones, stiff and still, lying on the ground. Her body was blanketed with snow and her face appeared bluish.

* * *

The third Hummer plowed through the deep snow, bearing down on the snowmobile as it raced across the snow-blanketed field toward the thick forest of trees ahead.

"He's heading toward the Garden of the Gods," the Guardsman said.

"What's that?" Dr. Sharp asked.

"The Garden of the Gods is a group of huge boulders. Locals around here like to ride their snowmobiles down the steep hill beneath the boulders. There is no way we can take the Hummer down there."

"We have no choice," Dr. Sharp said. "We have to stay on him until aerial support arrives." As they blasted further into the deep snow, the Hummer bogged down.

"Radio the copter. Give them our quadrants. We can't risk getting stuck in here!" the Guardsman shouted.

"We have you on GPS. We're only a mile away," the pilot responded. "Turn back. We'll track him from here." With that, Dr. Sharp's Hummer turned around and started back toward Medicine Wheel. A few minutes later, the helicopter radioed again. "Wrong guy. The guy you were following on the snowmobile is a guest at Bear Lodge. His identification checks out. We've lost Gilbert Bonita."

* * *

Jeffrey sprinted toward Mac who remained motionless in the center of Medicine Wheel. As he grew closer, he saw another figure bent over on his hands and knees. He reached for the strap of the .357 Magnum strapped to his belt. "Freeze," he yelled, holding the gun in his right hand and pointing it straight ahead.

The man roared up on his knees and saw Jeffrey running toward him, gun drawn. Gil dove on top of Mac and wrapped his hands around her neck. "I'll kill her," Gil yelled.

Jeffrey stopped running but kept the gun pointed directly at Gil's forehead. He intended to steady his aim and fire. He held the gun with both hands and unlatched the safety. As he started to squeeze the trigger, Mac moved into the line of fire. Jeffrey pulled up on the gun, firing it into the air. Gil looked up for a moment.

Mac seized the opportunity and took the stone in her right hand and smashed it into Gil temple. He rocked backwards and landed sideways on the hub of stones in the center of the wheel. Mac heard a thud when his head struck granite but just to be sure, she reared back and threw the white rock at him as hard as she could. The rock hit Gil square in the forehead.

With his gun steady on Gil, Jeffrey rushed to Mac's side and held her close. She was frozen and silent. Tears were streaming down her face, yet she didn't let out as much as a whimper. "It's over, Mac. It's going to be okay."

She looked up into his eyes and shook her head side to side. "N-n-no, it's n-n-not. He infected me too. I'm going to die." With that, she fell unconscious.

Dr. Sharp, who had arrived on the scene and was wearing a biosafety helmet and gloves, hurried to Mac's side and grabbed her from Jeffrey's arms. Others were swiftly erecting a transparent quarantine tent to put her in. They hooked up a portable generator to heat the tent and quickly administered to Mac.

"You touched her blood," Dr. Sharp said, pointing to the blood on Jeffrey's face from holding Mac close to him. "You'll need to be quarantined as well." She finished putting on her biosafety suit and entered the tent to assist Mac, and motioned for him to enter.

As the doctor jerked Mac's arm back into its socket, she let out a deafening scream. Jeffrey was relieved to hear her voice. At least she was alive. He stood at her side, holding her right hand. He wiped the blood from her face and whispered to her over and over, "I love you." Like an echo, the words kept repeating themselves in her head.

* * *

Mac looked through the transparent tent and watched as Gilbert Bonita—the Monster of the Andes—was handcuffed and shackled to a gurney. His head was caked with blood and his skin appeared to be a deathly shade of gray. She'd seen enough. Mac turned her head so that she couldn't see him and silently allowed the tears to roll down her cheeks. Jeffrey wiped them away and kissed her forehead. "He will never hurt you again."

"What if it is too late?" Mac asked. Her lips were blue. Her hands burned from frostbite. Her intestines contracted in pain.

"It is not too late. You are going to be fine."

Diane Weiss entered the quarantine tent in full protective gear. Dr. Sharp held several vials with small, white pills in her hand. "Administer all of these," she ordered to the attending doctor.

"Is this all the antivirals we have?" Director Weiss asked.

"Yes. I can get more tomorrow, but I think we should dose them heavily today," Dr. Sharp said.

"What about Gilbert Bonita? Should we administer to him?" Dr. Sharp looked crossways at Director Weiss. Although Director Weiss remained silent, everyone understood the answer.

Epilogue

The worst of the worst of humankind don't make it to death row. That, Mac knows for sure. She supposes that she worries about this more than is reasonably healthy, but after meeting the Monster of the Andes, obsessing about this subject seems rational.

Nowadays, Mac sits and watches her neighbor melodically pushing his little girl on a swing, while sipping on what could be his sixth tumbler of whiskey and she wonders when he his temper is going to flare and whether the little girl or her loud-mouthed mother will bear the brunt of his beating.

Or Mac sees a man wheeling an elderly woman onto the Indian casino tour bus, cursing at her under his breath. Is this man her husband? Son? Is he biding his time, waiting impatiently for her to die? Will he do something to expedite the process, like add a splash of arsenic to her morning juice?

And she can't help but notice an old, balding man pacing the park, squinting and hollering at children as they run around after a day in school. Why is he there if he hates the noises that these rambunctious youngsters make?

Despite the fact that these souls appear unhappy with their place in life, they don't fit the profile of a killer.

The problem is that there is no profile for a killer. Especially a serial killer. The Behavioral Science Services division of the FBI may disagree, but truth be told, what makes a serial killer successful is his ability to blend into mainstream society. He needs to dodge the bullet of a profiler in order to keep on doing what he loves to do–kill. That is what Mac knows for sure.

Gilbert Bonita a/k/a Nicolai Petrescu a/k/a Pedro Perez was able to blend into mainstream society, again and again. He was a deliberate killer. In some cases, it took him fifteen years to attack his victims. He followed their whereabouts and tracked their moves. He was patient, yet keen and swift when need be.

Gil was a victim as well as a predator. His mother abused him. Vladimir Checovsky abused him. He sucked in the anger and resentment from his abuse, allowed it to simmer and boil over, and when the time was right, he unleashed it with fury on defenseless victims.

Gil was tolerant, calculating and thorough. Not all serial killers have these characteristics. Their motives are often perplexing. Gil's deep feelings of betrayal kept his burning desire to kill alive. He wanted every woman like his mother to pay her price of atonement.

Unfortunately, over five hundred thousand innocent people world wide died of the avian flu that year. The virus continued to spread untamed, as there was no antiviral left to address the particular strain that Gil had created in his lab. Scientists from many pharmaceutical companies joined forces and used samples of Gil's blood to create a replica of his antiviral, but it took time. And during this time, thousands more died, including several of the Army National Guardsmen who assisted in Gil's capture.

Mac was lucky. The antivirals worked. Her body healed, but her mind was taking its time. She decided to take a brief sabbatical from the practice of law and enjoy the splendor and beauty of Wyoming. This particular morning, she watched Jeffrey as he laced up his running shoes and pulled down his fleece cap. He was lucky too. He did not contract the virus, despite the fact that Mac's blood was on his face. Dr. Sharp was able to sterilize Jeffrey before the virus could take hold of him.

It is cold today on the banks of the Powder River, but not too cold for a brisk morning run. Mac sprinted out ahead of Jeffrey with a little head start. He yelled for her to wait. For the first time in her life, she does. He is worth waiting for.

Books by Maureen Anne Meehan

Dying to Ski, a Mary MacIntosh novel
Snake River Secret, a Mary MacIntosh novel
Powder River Poison, a Mary MacIntosh novel
Pandemic Predator, a Mary MacIntosh novel
Poisoned by Proxy, a Mary MacIntosh novel
The Five, a Mary MacIntosh novel
Rodeo, a Mary MacIntosh novel
60 Dates in Six Months (with a Broken Neck)
Push You Away
Let Me Be

ABOUT THE AUTHOR

Maureen Anne Meehan received her bachelor's and master's degrees in education before becoming a lawyer. She lives with her family in Southern California, where she is a mental health judge and crafts legal thrillers, as well as nonfiction dating satire.